SORDID

A DARK EROTIC ROMANCE

NIKKI SLOANE

Addison Edition

ISBN 978-0-692-73474-2

This book is dedicated to anyone with a black or twisted soul, or those who get turned on by something when they feel like they really shouldn't.

Chapter
ONE

YOU LOOK LIKE A SLUT. This was the thought repeating in my head.

I tugged at the knee-high white stockings and smoothed down my plaid skirt. It was much too short. The blouse of the sexed-up schoolgirl costume didn't have buttons to close above my bra. The white shirt gapped and showed cleavage. I felt . . . uncomfortable. Yes, I looked like a slut, but it was also the look I was going for.

Avery, my roommate, smeared on blood red lipstick, and although her gaze was on the mirror, I sensed she was watching me out of the sides of her eyes. She was waiting for me to chicken out.

"You're going out in that?" Her tone did nothing to disguise her disbelief.

"Yeah."

Perhaps I looked ridiculous, and perhaps my stomach had done a flip-flop when I looked at myself in the mirror, but I wasn't bluffing. Avery had been forced into inviting me to the party at her boyfriend's frat, but I was going. I hadn't been out to a party in ages, and Halloween was the one night I could reinvent myself.

A reinvention was needed.

I'd spent my whole life driving toward a medical degree, and everything else had been neglected, including a social life. It was my senior year at Randhurst University, and I'd never gotten close enough with another girl to find a roommate. Avery and I had been paired together randomly by a student housing computer.

She wasn't happy with the result. The spoiled sophomore was my opposite—she didn't study. She didn't care about her grades, her major, or have to worry about scholarship money. The International Bank of Mom and Dad was funding her pointless attempt at a college education, and it was likely she'd wash out by the end of the year. Perhaps even by the end of the semester. She wasn't focused, and I couldn't relate at all.

"You look different," Avery said. "Nice."

Her compliment threw me off-kilter. "Thanks. And thanks for letting me tag along."

"It shocked the hell out of me when you said yes. I thought you were a Mormon."

I blinked, confused. "Mormon?"

"Yeah." She fluffed her long brown hair. "They don't celebrate holidays and shit."

My brain played loud static, my defense mechanism against stupidity. "I think you mean Jehovah's Witness." Not once had I mentioned church to her. I wasn't even religious—unless you considered science a religion.

She continued to preen in the mirror and I was ignored, which was Avery's typical response. It could be worse, I told myself. She'd never outright been a bitch.

Her phone rang, singing an obnoxious song, but it cut off as she answered it. "Hi, are you downstairs?" Her gaze flicked my direction. "Yeah, Addison's ready, too. You remember she's coming." It wasn't said like it was a question.

I held down the hem of my skirt as I ducked into the back seat of Brent's car. He was my age, and hadn't been dating Avery all that long. The two-door Mustang's back seat was a joke. I had to position my knees to the side so I could sit, but the car was warm and clean, so I knew not to complain.

It was a short drive to the frat house. It'd be a hike back, but I could walk if needed. Although the campus was small, the city was a college town and relatively safe. Yet nerves fluttered in the pit of my stomach as the car parked behind the huge Tudor-style house adorned with the three Greek letters out front.

I'd never been to a frat party.

Would it be as wild as everyone made them out to be? I followed behind Avery and Brent, realizing now that their costumes matched. Batman and Catwoman. I tried not to stumble over the uneven walkway leading around the house and up to the front door.

Music thumped steadily, and loud conversation could be heard through the open door. I shivered in the October air. On Avery's suggestion, I'd left my coat back at the dorm. There'd be nowhere to put it, and she'd warned the place would get hot with that many bodies packed inside.

On the front porch, a guy stood and checked IDs. I dug mine out, but Brent shook his head. "You're good."

"It's fine, I'm twenty-one—" I started.

"Nah, you're with me, that's all my boy needs to know."

I jammed the plastic card back in the tiny pocket of my skirt as a shimmer of disappointment flowed through me. I'd only turned twenty-one in August and hadn't had many opportunities to use my new license. My birthday had been a sad affair. I'd spent the summer interning at the hospital, and a few of the other orderlies took me out. The evening had been over before ten p.m.

The entryway was dark and packed with people trying to

hold conversations over the loud music. Most were in costume and gripped a plastic cup. There were large rooms to the left and the right, a staircase ahead, and a hallway leading to the back of the house, lined with picture frames of past pledge classes.

"Let's get drinks," Avery yelled in my ear.

Relief washed through me. I'd expected her to ditch me the second we were inside. I wouldn't cling to her, but I was grateful not to be abandoned immediately. Brent led the way as we threaded through the crowd, down the hallway and into a kitchen where lines had formed at the two kegs.

I took my place, standing behind a guy dressed as an astronaut. He turned, gave me a glance, then his head swiveled forward with disinterest. It was a reaction I was used to. I wasn't homely, but I was incredibly average. Nothing . . . *special*. Normally, my dull brown hair hung listlessly to brush my shoulders, although tonight I had the front section pulled up into two high ponytails to complete my naughty schoolgirl look. My skin was pale. I'd forgone sports in high school because I wasn't coordinated, or fast, and that way I could focus on my advanced placement classes. My days were spent at a desk, rather than outside in the sun.

The line crept forward. The astronaut stepped up to the keg, but abruptly shifted to the side, slipping a hand behind my back. "Ladies first."

I went rigid under this stranger's hand. He gave me a friendly smile, but I got the feeling he expected me to be impressed. Like this was a grand, chivalrous gesture. A sacrifice, and not just polite courtesy. My gaze went from the astronaut to the empty red Solo cup extended out to me.

"Thanks," I said to both the astronaut and the guy

handing me the—

It was *him*.

My breath stalled in my lungs. He wore dark navy pants, a matching dress shirt, and a gold badge clipped to his chest. At his waist was a supply belt with a holster. The gun looked terrifyingly real, but it was also covered with the holster, and could just be part of the costume.

Or maybe Luka was a cop now. I hadn't seen him in two years. Although he had the perfect serious demeanor to match the uniform, I doubted my TA from Calculus 220 had gone into law enforcement. My gut said no, and a closer look at the badge proved it was fake.

I gripped the plastic cup so fiercely, it crinkled, drawing his focus.

His dark gaze swept over me and sharpened, cutting me bare. I felt naked under his assessing eyes. There was a flicker of recognition in him, which was surprising. We'd never spoken. I didn't know him and he didn't know me, but I'd spent countless hours of class studying him when it should have been the whiteboard.

Like me, Luka rarely smiled. He'd sat in the corner at the front of the room and faced the class while the professor demonstrated equations. Luka's head of espresso brown hair was always tipped downward, grading our worksheets. Every once in a while, he'd cock an eyebrow and circle aggressively with his red pen, as if the student's wrong answer had offended him.

I'd grown to love watching his subtle cues, so much so, I'd considered purposefully answering one of the questions wrong, just to get a rise. Yet, I wouldn't do a thing to screw up my scholarships. Luka's fun, displeased reaction would last a moment, but a bad grade could destroy everything.

With heels on tonight, I didn't have to tilt my head up as much to meet his gaze. His eyes were the color of onyx and framed with long, thick lashes. His nose was straight, his jaw defined. Tonight he was clean shaven with his hair styled casually. Two years ago he'd looked like an average grad student—well, better. Most looked like they'd just rolled out of bed and barely made it to class, but he'd seemed more pulled together. Always a coffee cup in hand for the early class.

So this version of Luka was downright intimidating. He'd been cute before, but this man was handsome. In fact, he was so attractive, my knees softened and my stomach trembled. He'd changed so much in the last two years. Perhaps it was the implied violence of the gun at his hip, but he seemed . . . dangerous now. It was a rush just to look at him.

The hand in the small of my back moved, causing me to jolt.

"He can't fill up your cup if you don't hold it out, sweetheart," the astronaut said.

Of course. I'd been standing frozen beside the keg, clutching the plastic cup tight to my stomach. It wasn't much of an invitation to pour me a drink, was it? I tried not to bristle at the *sweetheart* comment, and also not to stare at the man before me who had one hand on the tap.

Luka's gaze dropped down as I held out the cup and he filled it. His expression was total indifference.

"That's good, thanks," I said.

He rewarded me with a quirk of his eyebrow. I watched as it lifted into a perfect arrow, just like the mathematical symbol for a logical conjunction. How ridiculous was it I'd waited two years for this exact response? My knees grew weaker.

"You waited in line for a sip of beer?" The astronaut laughed and turned his focus to Luka. "Fill her up."

"No, thank you." I pulled my cup away. "I'm not much of a beer drinker."

"You want something different?" The astronaut said. It was unavoidable that my gaze connected with Luka's. *Yes,* I thought. I'd like something different than the stranger at my side who still had his hand on my waist like he'd laid his claim. I wouldn't mind something more like the quiet man before me. I shifted my weight to my opposite foot, easing myself away from the hand.

"They've got blackjack shots in the game room." Luka's voice was so deep it was startling, and froze me in place.

I tried to sound confident and unaffected. "What kind of alcohol is Blackjack?"

"No," Luka said. "They're playing blackjack. You do a shot of tequila if you lose."

"Oh?" It came out sounded eager, even when I didn't mean for it to.

He cocked his head to the side, as if noticing something interesting about me, although I couldn't fathom what. "You know how to play?"

I pressed my lips together. "I do."

"I got too fucked up on tequila last week," the astronaut interrupted. "If I smell it, I'll hurl."

A beast of a guy appeared beside Luka, grunted a *thanks,* and instantly Luka handed over the tap, abandoning his job of dispensing beer. It left the astronaut, Luka, and me standing awkwardly in a circle. His black-eyed gaze swept over me once more.

"I'm heading that way, Addison. You want to play?"

Oh my God. He knew my name? My throat closed up and I dry-swallowed. The question rang in my head. *You want to play?* Since I couldn't find words, I nodded quickly.

He jerked his head toward the doorway. "Come on."

I didn't even look back at the astronaut as I followed Luka. I watched his broad back while we wormed through the crowd into the darkened hallway where both the noise and the music grew louder. It was hot and humid from the bodies packed in the house, and the air in the game room was thick.

House parties were more intimate than the bars. You had to lean close and shout your conversations in the other person's ear to be heard over the pulsing, frenetic beats. It drew Luka up beside me and his lips hovered beside my neck.

"It's Addison, right?" he shouted. "Your name?"

He smelled like woodsy heaven as I leaned forward. "Yeah. You're Luka?"

I pulled back just in time to see the pleased look flash in his eyes. It only lasted a second, but it was exciting. He nodded as we continued toward the back of the room. When there wasn't a party going on, I assumed the couches that lined the walls were probably staggered in the room. The ping pong table in the corner was in use for beer pong, and opposite it was a green felt-covered poker table.

Luka didn't seem like the type to belong to a fraternity, but then again, what did I know? He'd always been aloof during class. Isolated from anyone else. Perhaps it was why I'd found him so attractive. We seemed a lot alike.

There was a deck of cards at the table, and beside it, two

bottles of cheap tequila with pourers capped in. A small crowd watched the guys playing a round, and when it was over, the loser picked up the bottle and poured a stream of tequila into his open mouth.

Well, I thought, *at least that's sanitary.*

"I need to watch for a minute," I said, when Luka motioned toward the table. The corner of his mouth curled upward. Was that a smile? It vanished instantly.

I loved card games in all of their forms. I'd spent many nights volunteering at the emergency room hospital, and played with the other orderlies and nurses during the quiet times. We'd gambled for money or snacks from the vending machine, and usually I cleaned up. Blackjack was my favorite. I'd learned from the internet how to count cards so I knew when my hand would be most favorable.

After a few more rounds, the two guys at the table cleared out and a new pair moved in. Luka's gaze drifted to me, but I took a sip of my beer to stall. I still didn't have a good read. I'd assigned a point value to each card I'd seen and kept the total running in my head.

"You keep drinking that," Luka's voice invaded my ear, "and you won't have anything to chase your shots with."

Tonight I was determined to be my opposite. *By God, Addison, you're going to attempt to flirt.* I peeled my lips back into a confident and unfamiliar smile. "Who says I'm going to lose?"

There was no change in Luka's expression, and yet the air seemed to shift around us. It closed in.

"You're right." His hand curled gently around my elbow and urged me forward. "You can't lose if we don't play."

We. I tripped over the word in my head. His hand was warm against my bare skin, and the hairs on my arm lifted in response to his touch. It wasn't cold in the humid game room, but I had to fight to hold back the shiver.

I'd never gotten flustered when it came to boys, but Luka wasn't a boy. He looked like he was in his mid-twenties, and his eyes . . . he seemed older. I wasn't surprised at my body's reaction, though. I certainly hadn't forgotten him in the last two years; in fact, I'd fantasized about him. I'd also compared the guys I dated to the fictitious Luka I'd created in my head, and always found them lacking.

The real-life Luka wouldn't be anything like the one I'd crafted, I was sure. The man with a hand on me was probably like every other guy. Too focused on sex. Average intelligence. *Boring.* I hoped I was wrong.

Luka pulled out the chair for me and I sat, and in my head I issued a sigh when he abandoned his hold and moved to the other side of the table. Had my sigh been audible? His dark eyes hinted at a smirk as he lowered to sit across from me.

His fingers were long and he moved with graceful precision as he picked up the deck of cards and dealt us each a card face down, and then one face up. I evaluated my cards quickly, pleased that I had an eighteen. His card up was a four, and there were a lot of high cards left in the deck.

"I'll stay," I said.

He pulled a third card off the deck, which was a queen. He flipped over his other card, exposing a ten, and wrapped a hand around the neck of the tequila. It was strangely erotic to watch him tip back his head and pour the alcohol into his mouth.

Luka's gaze was fixed on me as the bottle *thunked* back down on the table. He dealt a second hand, and his focus never wavered as I peeked at my down card. Was he gauging my reaction, hoping I'd give something away? I stared back at him, keeping my expression vacant.

My voice was quiet but firm. "Hit me."

My jaw tightened when he laid down a king. Maybe he'd think it was a grimace, but it was to hold back my smile. He flipped his card over, revealing a seventeen, and pushed the bottle of tequila at me.

Instead I smiled and revealed my ace. "Twenty-one." I shoved the bottle back his direction.

Beneath the table, my knees pushed together as his eyebrow arched. How was it I'd waited two years for that, and now he'd given it to me twice in ten minutes?

When I won the third round, something like malice flashed in Luka's eyes. He clearly did not like to lose.

"Why the hell did you stay with a fifteen?" After he'd finished his shot, his gaze narrowed. His head cocked to one side. Once again, his critical evaluation made me feel naked and vulnerable, but it was a feeling I didn't mind as much when it came from him.

"What are you doing?" It came out before I could hide the concern from my voice.

An evil smile dawned on the sharp angles of his face as he opened the table drawer and retrieved a new deck of cards. My heart skipped faster as he shuffled the two decks together, erasing all my hard work.

"Oh," Luka said. "Does that fuck up your count? Let's play for real now."

My face flamed red. The sound of the cards shifting couldn't be heard over the music, but I watched as Luka bridged the decks together. I fought to remain calm and collected. *What's the big deal? You came to have a few drinks and be someone else tonight.*

I busted on my first hand and satisfaction streaked through Luka's expression. I licked my lips, clenched the cold bottle in my hand, and took a deep breath. Just the smell of the tequila had my stomach turning, but I ignored it and leaned back. The burn of the liquor flooded my throat and I swallowed, forcing it down.

"You were counting the cards, yeah?" he asked. I nodded slowly, and he looked intrigued.

I lost the second hand and stared nervously at the bottle. I didn't drink much. If I lost too many hands, I'd be dangerously drunk. The second mouthful of tequila made me gag, and I chased it with my final sip of beer.

As he dealt out the next round, his fingers lingered on my card. "You look like you don't want to play anymore."

I pressed my lips together. "I'm kind of a lightweight."

Luka's dark eyes glittered and an invisible hand tightened around my lungs. His expression was seductive and sinister. Scary, and yet . . . enticing. It kept me rooted in my chair as he dealt the cards.

Thank God. I had a ten showing and an eight hidden. Across the table, Luka's up card was a three.

"I'll stay," I said.

He pulled one more card from the deck, and as a pleased smile teased his lips, a shiver rolled down my back. He turned his cards face up. Twenty.

My eyes pinched tightly shut as I gulped the mouthful down

and tried not to gag. The tequila seemed to scald more with each swallow, and tasted like gravel. I pushed back from the table to stand—

"One more." His voice was firm, like this wasn't a request.

I blinked. "I can't do another shot." Three was probably already too many.

"One more," Luka said. His gaze pinned me in place. "If you lose, you can do something else instead."

"Like what?"

He appeared to consider his options before speaking. "You let me give you a tour."

It was such a strange request. He thought this was a punishment? I drew in a breath and tried to find the downside to his offer. Since there wasn't one, I slid back into the seat. The room had grown crowded and louder in the short amount of time we'd been sitting at the table, and another pair was waiting to take our place, so Luka didn't waste any time.

I had mixed feelings when I won the hand. I watched my excuse to hang around him longer disappear as he poured the shot into his open mouth. When it was done, he looked . . . disappointed?

It came from me without thought. "I'll still go on that tour."

He paused.

A slight smile drew across his face and disappeared when he stood, gesturing toward the door. It was so loud he raised his voice over the roar of the party. "Let's get going, then."

I followed him out of the game room and into the entryway, jostling between people in various states of drunkenness. Costumes ranged from silly to slutty to almost non-existent. Luka stopped at the bottom of the stairs and I ran into the back of him. He was like a wall.

"Can't go upstairs," a guy dressed as a cowboy said. He stood beside Luka, his arms crossed over his chest.

Luka said nothing. He stood motionless, staring down the cowboy, who seemed to wilt under Luka's intense gaze.

"Wait a minute." The cowboy's arms uncrossed and his posture changed quickly. "You're Vas's brother?" He moved to the side to let Luka pass. "Sorry, my bad."

"If Vasilije starts looking for me," Luka said, "tell him to text. I'll be upstairs."

Luka's head turned and he peered over his shoulder, wordlessly commanding me to follow him up the steps. He didn't live here at the frat house, apparently, so why did he offer to give me a tour? I trailed behind him, confused, teetering on my heels as we climbed the steps.

Since noise traveled upward, it wasn't any quieter when we reached the landing at the top of the staircase. Luka's focus swung from one end of the empty hallway to the other, then turned to me.

"Do you know where you're going?" I asked, only half teasing.

Fingers rested gently in the hollow of my back and urged me to the right, down the darkened hallway which was lined with closed doors. He strode beside me, heading for the door at the end, and although the music grew quieter, my nerves grew louder. Being alone with Luka was exciting and terrifying.

He grabbed the doorknob and pushed the door open, revealing a room I hadn't expected.

Chapter
TWO

THERE WAS NO SIGN of this being a typical college kid's room. Luka waited for me to go inside, so I stepped hesitantly through the doorway. A queen-sized bed took up most of the far wall, a dresser occupied the left side, and on the right, a large, brown leather couch. The room was clean, nicely furnished, and the bed made.

"This is the resident advisor's room," Luka said. "And it concludes the tour."

"What?"

As I whirled around to face him, Luka shut the door, closing us in together. My heart leapt in my chest and raced. Oh shit, I'd been stupid. So, so stupid. I took a step back defensively, needing space.

"Whoa." Luka's deep voice was hushed and his arms held up in surrender. "This is the furthest place in the house from the party. We might actually be able the hear each other in here."

"Hear each other what?" Anxiety flooded my voice.

He took a breath. "I can open the door if you'd feel more comfortable, but it'll be louder, and I want to talk to you."

His words did nothing to calm me, but my anxiety shifted slowly from danger to my lack of experience with men. "What did you want to talk about?"

"You."

I'd swear he could sense the change in my nerves. The light

from the streetlamps outside flooded through the window, and shadows played across Luka's face, giving him an almost threatening cast. But it faded when a faint smile tugged across his lips.

"What's your major?"

My heart was lodged in my throat, making it difficult to breathe or speak. "Biology. Pre-med."

"Oh." Most people looked impressed when I told them that, but not Luka. His expression remained fixed.

"You?"

"I'm alumni now. I got my MBA last year."

A warning flashed through me. What was he doing at a frat party when he didn't go to Randhurst anymore? My unease must have been visible.

"My brother, Vasilije," Luka said quickly, like he wanted to explain. "He got in trouble, and part of the deal he made with my father was I *get* to keep an eye on him." His tone was sharp. "I have things I'd rather fucking do than hang out with a bunch of drunk, underage college kids."

The statement rankled. "I'm not drunk, underage, or a kid compared to you."

I wasn't prepared for Luka's smirk. It looked like sin when it washed through his expression. "No? If you're not underage, why aren't you at the bars?"

Crap. I shifted on my heels. "My roommate's not twenty-one." It wasn't a lie.

"So, Addison, we're both stuck here for other people." Luka took a step toward me, and even though there was still quite a bit of space left between us, his one small step felt enormous. Like he was now twice the size he'd been a second ago.

My chest was beginning to feel warm, no doubt from the tequila. "How is it you remember my name?"

"Probably for the same reason you remember mine."

That was incredibly doubtful, but I kept my face plain. "Calculus was that memorable for you?"

"Yeah, it was. You were there every class, staring at me."

I inhaled sharply, mortified, and tore my gaze away. "I did not."

"Look at me." His firm tone made it so there was no other option but to obey. When I did, his black eyes were focused and intense. "You stared when you didn't think I could tell, but you weren't very good at hiding it." I opened my mouth to deny further, but he cut me off. "I was better than you. I made sure you never noticed I was looking."

My brain disconnected and thought ceased. "Why?"

Luka's hands rested casually on his hips, just over the fake police belt and gun holster. "Because a girl like you . . ." He scrubbed a hand over his mouth. He seemed to search for the right word, but not find it, and every drawn-out second that passed made it worse. *Because a girl like you . . .* Isn't good enough. Rich enough. Smart enough. *A girl like you isn't experienced enough.*

"You shouldn't be interested in a guy like me."

"What?" I was intelligent and well spoken, and yet I couldn't choke out more than one word at a time.

"I'm not a nice guy."

I swallowed hard. "Well . . ." How was I supposed to respond to that? "I'm sure that's not true."

He said nothing. Luka remained like a statue with the light glinting off the shiny plastic badge clipped to his chest. He didn't argue or defend himself, and tension wound around us like ruthless vines.

My question was breathy. "Why did you stare at me if you weren't interested?"

"Did I say I wasn't interested?" He took another step, growing larger still, reaching a point where I couldn't see anything else. Just him. "Nobody looked at me the way you did, and I liked it. It's exactly how you're looking at me now."

All the air vanished from the room.

"And how's that?" I said. It was dizzying when he took the final step and brought us chest to chest, his mouth inches from mine. I stared up at him with wide eyes. Was any of this effect from the tequila, or was it all him? His gaze traced over each inch of my face, and I could feel it etching into my skin.

"Like you want me to do bad things to you."

Oh my God.

As he'd done, I stood motionless, neither confirming nor denying. I held my breath, waiting for him to make his move. I expected him to kiss me. Or maybe laugh in my face, although Luka didn't seem like the type to laugh easily. He was deadly serious.

"Do you?" His question was soft and indifferent, even as it carried the weight of an enormous challenge.

Did I want him to do bad things to me? "I don't know," I blurted out. "Maybe."

Luka looked just as I felt—surprised by my admission. What had I just sort of agreed to? A tremble began in the backs of my knees and moved upward when his head tipped down. His mouth lowered until his warm lips sealed over mine.

Everything was madness. My actions, the situation, and most importantly, his kiss. I spun out of control under his mouth, surrendering to it completely, even as the kiss was tame. Luka pressed his lips to mine tentatively, but when I parted my lips to gasp, he took advantage.

His tongue dipped into my mouth and was an electric jolt straight between my legs. Did I taste like tequila as he did to me, or could he also taste my lust? I had two years' worth, and this kiss broke the dam holding it back. It poured from me, and as I spun, I latched my hands onto his shoulders to keep myself steady.

What the hell was I doing? Making out with a stranger in a private room at a frat party . . . who was I? Luka's hands grasped my hips and pulled me closer to him, deepening the kiss and pressing me against his solid form. He wasn't really a stranger, though. I felt like I knew him.

My fingertips tangled in his hair. I hadn't realized my hands had wandered until Luka's mouth began to slide away from mine. It drifted across my cheek, down over my jawline, and onto my neck. I shivered from his hot breath beside my ear.

"What are you supposed to be?" His voice was low, verging on hypnotic. "Naughty schoolgirl, or Britney Spears, the early years?"

His mouth was drugging me, working in tandem with the tequila snaking in my system. His teeth skimmed the pulse racing in my neck, just below my ear. *Oh, that felt good.* My legs threatened to go boneless, and I clung tighter to him.

"Whichever one," I said between hurried breaths, "you like more."

I stood powerless beneath his kiss and his hands for a long time, trying to savor it. This wasn't my exact fantasy come to life, but it was pretty damn close. I'd let Luka do all sorts of bad things as long as he kept kissing me.

The thumping bass from downstairs abruptly cut off, followed by jeers and complaints from the partygoers. Luka's head snapped up and his eyes narrowed. Had the party been busted?

Just as quickly as it had cut off, the music began again. Perhaps they'd just had technical difficulties with the audio, but it had been enough of a surprise to pull Luka and me from the moment. The dazed look in his eyes melted away and he returned to his usual state. Serious and guarded.

As I reluctantly slid my hands down his chest and away from him, I tried to regain some sense.

"What about your roommate?" he asked. His hands remained on my waist, trapping me. "Is she going to come looking for you?"

No, not a chance. "It's doubtful."

"Maybe I should lock the door just to be safe."

His words brought a fresh wave of nerves to coil in my belly. Luka didn't want to be disturbed. What exactly did he think was going to happen?

"I . . ." It was impossible to organize my thoughts. "I don't even know your last name."

His hands released me and his posture went rigid, like I'd just asked something extremely personal. "You don't need to know it."

I scrunched my face into a scowl. "Then you definitely don't need to lock the door."

He took in a deep breath and let it out loudly, signaling frustration. "It's Markovic."

Markovic. Why was that name familiar? There was a hard edge to Luka's expression, watching me intently, as if waiting for me to recognize it.

"Markovic Motors?" I guessed. There was a chain of car

dealerships on the south side of the city whose jingle was annoyingly catchy. A universally recognizable melody to all of Chicago, but not terribly nostalgic.

His dark eyes blinked slowly. "Yeah. My father owns it."

I couldn't place the emotion on his face. Was he embarrassed about this, and if so, why? Was he one of those people who was uncomfortable with their own wealth? As a girl who'd grown up in a family that struggled to get by, I couldn't understand it at all.

Now that Luka had taken his hands off of me, I was cold. A large part of me wanted to go back to what we'd been doing moments ago. His mouth had been on fire, and I shivered in the absence of his warmth. I longed for his body to be pressed back against mine, but my head railed against it.

He didn't ask, so I offered. "I'm Addison Drake."

"I remember," he said. "Addison Drake with her perfect handwriting, except for her weird twos."

"What? My twos aren't weird."

"They're just loops. It took me a while to figure them out. I almost graded your homework wrong." His gaze drilled into me. "Would that have gotten you to talk to me? I can't imagine *perfect* Addison Drake would allow herself to get something less than an A."

My mouth dropped open. Was he playfully teasing me, or being a jerk? "I'm not perfect."

Luka softly brushed his knuckles over my cheekbone. When I shuddered from the contact, his eyes flashed with desire. "See, now, I disagree."

Jesus, where the hell was the air? Goosebumps lifted on the skin of my bare legs as his fingers cupped my chin and tilted my lips to meet his once more.

This time the kiss was dangerous. It flared wildly, consuming everything. I'd kissed boys before. I'd had boyfriends and fooled around, but it'd never been anything like this. Luka's grip on my chin gave way and his fingers dove into the hair at the nape of my neck, twining in the strands.

"Oh," I gasped as he yanked hard, tugging my head back. His grip was almost painful, but the shock of it was exciting. My one serious boyfriend had been timid and awkward, so this was unfamiliar.

Confidence rolled off of Luka like he knew with absolute certainty what he was doing. As if he understood just how much grip in my hair I could take. His teeth were less subtle this time on my neck. The sharp stubble dotting his jawline grazed against my skin and, when I instinctively tried to move away, his fist clenched tighter in my hair, holding me in place. Keeping me from escaping.

My breath raged through my parted lips as his other hand was on my hip, yanking me so our lower bodies collided, and I could feel something hard pressing against my stomach, something I was sure wasn't his fake gun.

"Am I hurting you?" His dark voice rang out between my gasps for breath.

I tried to shake my head, but his hold wouldn't allow it. I had no choice but to use words, so I said it in a shaky voice. "No."

"Good."

His hand glided down my hip, over the fabric of my skirt, all the way past the hem and onto the bare skin of my thigh. I bit down on my lip and closed my eyes as his hand crept inward, sliding toward my center. It inched up, raising my skirt with it. Up, and up . . .

I had to stop this before it went any further. My head was buzzing from the alcohol and his kiss, and I didn't want to make a decision I'd regret later, even though my body was eager for his hand to continue its journey north of my hemline.

Luka paused when I wrapped my fingers around his wrist, urging him to stop. "Wait," I whispered. I'd stopped him just a fraction of an inch from my panties, which was closer than any man had gotten in a long time.

His gaze locked on to mine, and then his fingers twitched. They reached up just enough to touch me through the damp cotton covering the most intimate part of myself. I bucked, but remained ensnared as Luka's captive.

He drew back and seemed pleased with my reaction. "I'm gonna lock the door," he said. His voice was so deep and quiet, it was almost a growl. "You'll go sit on the couch."

Chapter
THREE

Once again, his strict tone made it impossible to do anything but obey, and yet my anxiety leapt to a whole new level. *You can fool around a little bit,* the wicked, tequila-enhanced voice in my head whispered. *He didn't tell you to get on the bed.*

I went to the couch and sank down until the leather was cold against the backs of my legs. My hands tensed into fists around the hem of my skirt, holding it in place as Luka turned the small dial on the doorknob. I couldn't hear the click of the lock sliding in place, but I felt it. It snapped through my body like a bolt of electricity.

As he stalked toward me, he swayed. No, wait, was that me? The tequila was working fast. Luka's expression shuttered, and then he licked his lips. Was it intentional? Was I a meal he was about to devour? I crossed my legs beneath the skirt, feeling twitchy and weirdly achy.

My head ticked back with each step he took so I could keep looking up at him.

"What are you smiling about?" he asked in a light voice.

My hand flew to my face, confirming it was true. I was buzzing hard and had reached the first level of my drunkenness. Phase one, the uncontrollable smiling.

"Nothing," I answered quickly and tried to look sober.

Luka didn't seem to buy it as he sat beside me. *Right* beside me. As his weight came down on the couch, I fell into him, one hand bracing myself on his thigh. Beneath the fabric of his pants, the muscle was hard, and I stroked the length. Wait, what was I doing? Petting him? I ripped my hand back, embarrassed.

He leaned in so his lips were by my ear, and he gave one of my ponytails a small tug. "Are you getting shy on me?"

My cheeks burned hot. I was, but didn't want to admit it. Every breath I took was a struggle to sound normal and not rushed. I'd been metering it out, hoping he couldn't hear how nervous or excited he made me.

"No," I answered. "I'm fine." I commanded myself to touch him casually, and rested my hand on his thigh once again. "I haven't been thinking about this for the last two years or any—"

I snapped my mouth shut, horrified. *Shit!* I was never drinking tequila again. How in the world had I said that out loud?

"Have you?" he asked. His breath ruffled the wisps of hair over my ears, drawing more shivers. His hand found my knee and gently urged me to uncross my legs. "You've thought about touching me?" His fingertips skated along the inside of my thigh, and I watched in disbelief as my legs fell open. Encouraging him.

I was reeling and he took advantage. This time I didn't stop him when his fingers went all the way up my skirt. They settled right at the junction of my legs, and I flushed hot. Could he feel how badly I was turned on? It was so embarrassing, but I couldn't stop him. All I could do was stare, just as I'd done two years ago in that classroom.

Yet it wasn't only the environment and situation that were different, it was Luka as well. His face was hauntingly serious, like he'd aged ten years from that final day in December when I'd last seen him.

"What happened to you?" I asked in a whisper. The alcohol had disrupted my ability to filter anymore.

His eyebrow lifted. "What?"

"You look different."

His fingers stirred and applied pressure, pulling a gasp from me, but he didn't slow down. "Not as much as you." The pads of his fingers danced and manipulated, each stroke bringing foreign pleasure. So different than my own touch, and he shifted closer as if making himself comfortable. "I never got to see this *perfect* body you were hiding under all those clothes."

"Oh, God," I moaned, unable to contain it. "I'm not perfect."

"Tell me you weren't five minutes early to every class. Say you didn't care how you looked, or how neat your homework was," he said. "Even your scratch notes were clean. Go on and lie to me."

My body reveled in his touch even though my mind was chaos. I endured his teasing, unable to do anything but process. Holy crap, it felt so good. My head tipped up, thudding onto the back of the couch as he touched me. Blood rushed loudly in my ears, drowning out the sound of the music pounding from below us, and my eyes fell closed.

Was I that obvious to him? It was important to me that I looked my best. That I always *tried* my best.

"You like this?" Luka's voice seemed to invade my head.

There was no reason to lie, he could feel how terribly excited I was. "Yes."

Pleasure built in waves, each bringing more heat to the fire. His two fingers rubbed aggressively on my clit and I choked back a moan.

"Look at me," he ordered.

I lifted my head and found his gaze. Luka was turned, leaning into me, his face only a breath away. His forearm disappeared beneath the plaid fabric of my skirt, but the movement of his wicked hand was obvious.

I swallowed a breath as his fingers curled around the crotch of my panties and pulled them to the side. His deep eyes studied me like a hunter watching his trapped prey. His fingers stroked over my slick, heated flesh, which made my heart gallop and my hands clench into a death grip on my skirt.

His finger eased inside.

To the first knuckle, and then he pushed deeper. My mouth dropped open, rounding into a silent, "*Oh.*" The stretch of his intrusion was pleasurable, but the idea of it was infinitely hotter. The man I had lusted after for what felt like forever, was now between my legs, touching me. Possessing me.

Luka's thick finger retreated and slowly pressed inside me once more. I whimpered. It was quiet, but he certainly heard it. His gaze hooded, making him look intoxicated. I had the strange feeling he was drunk off of me, and not just the alcohol. At least, I hoped.

"Tell me," he said, "what you thought about me doing to you."

It was hard to do that. My brain was sluggish and foggy, swirling from the tequila. I felt reckless and stupid, and unable to think of a reason why I shouldn't tell him the truth.

"This," I whispered. "You touching me."

"Yeah?"

He kept his finger buried inside as he moved over me, kneeling between my legs. He smoothed his other hand down the front of his pants, massaging himself for a moment, but he didn't keep it there long. It slipped around the back of my neck, cupping at the nape. Something dark and dangerous flickered in his eyes. A second finger worked to join his other inside my body.

The warm hand on my neck yanked, hauling me up to him abruptly. His mouth crashed against mine, and it drove me down further on his fingers. It stung. I wasn't used to so much, and not so suddenly. My hands flattened on his shoulders to push him back, but then the fingers were moving, just as his tongue was moving in my mouth. It was too hot to stop him, and the sting gave way to pleasure.

"What else?" he asked between immobilizing kisses.

"What else, what?" Everything was spinning when I closed my eyes, so I had no choice but to leave them open. I'd moved onto phase two of drunkenness, the spins.

"What else do you want me to do, Addison?" He moved at a leisurely tempo while his gaze was fixated on my mouth.

I couldn't vocalize. I was far too shy to speak them out loud. Instead, I curled my grip into the meaty parts of his arms, digging my nails in. I couldn't say anything, but I no longer had shame or anxiety about how I was acting. His touch liberated the wildness I always kept tamped down. I wasn't worried he knew I fantasized about him, although I was certain regret would come later. Not now, though. All I could do was marvel at how good he made me feel.

Electricity roved over my skin as he increased the pace his fingers slid in and out. My knees trembled and locked around his hips, doing so without any authorization from me. Luka's palm inched down my neck with each deep thrust he gave. I both wanted and didn't want him to touch me where he was headed. My body ached for it, but my chest was heaving and he'd be able to feel how hard my heart was pounding.

His soft, damp lips were pressed to mine, swallowing my moan, and then he was lifting my breast. The weight of it filled his hand, and a thumb slid back and forth, teasing the nipple through my shirt and bra.

I could barely breathe. Luka's hands worked flawlessly, touching me just as I wanted them to, holding me on the cusp of something new and interesting. I'd never been with a confident partner before, and now I was sure I didn't want to go back.

His fingers captured my nipple between the layers of fabric and pinched. The tension built as he squeezed harder and harder, but his tongue filled my mouth and kept me quiet when he closed in on pain. It was a weird sensation as his pinch grew hot and achy. I . . . *liked* it. I wanted to know how much more I could take.

Yet it grew past the point of tolerable. I inhaled sharply when it became too much, and both his lips and his pinch were gone, making me sway in his absence. Luka's expression was deadly serious, as if deep in concentration.

"Oh!" I bucked when the pad of his thumb circled above where his fingers were driving. It was fireworks. Bliss sparked and flared, and made me crazy with need. It had to hurt, how I was digging my fingernails into his flesh, but he said nothing. There was no indication in his expression that I was hurting him.

His lips parted to draw in a single breath, and then he slowly blew it out, all while watching me squirm beneath him.

"Shit," I moaned under my breath.

The corner of his mouth curled up. Luka liked this reaction.

His fingers slowed to a stop but stayed inside, lingering. Was he judging me, and more importantly, did I pass whatever test he was putting me through? He withdrew his fingers and they trailed up through my slit. "Did you think about me putting my mouth here?"

I jolted. I had, but I was too nervous to say it.

His face hardened, like he was annoyed I hadn't answered him. "Open your mouth."

It was easy to do since my mouth fell open on his command. And then his wet fingers were there, smearing my own taste on my lips. He shoved them inside and I closed my mouth around them, causing Luka's nostrils to flare. He pulsed the fingers in and out, simulating how he most likely wanted me to use my mouth on him.

The salty, slightly sweet taste of myself wasn't unpleasant, but the action . . . It was so *dirty*, I shuddered. He leaned in and set his mouth against mine, tasting me in more than one way. When had I surrendered to him so completely? Was it that first moment he'd kissed me, or before, when I'd agreed to another round of blackjack downstairs? Maybe it had been from the very beginning. My crush on him had been intense, but that made sense to me. I didn't half-ass anything in my life, so why would my infatuation with him be any different?

"Answer me." It was quiet, but firm from him. "Did you think about me going down on you?"

"Sort of."

Confusion flooded his expression. This was not an answer he was anticipating. "What does that mean?"

I closed my eyes, not wanting to see judgment in the dark

eyes staring back at me, but the spinning was worse. So I set my gaze across the room, away from Luka. "I did, but I don't know what that feels like."

His broad shoulders tensed beneath my hands. "You don't . . . ?" He took a breath. "Holy shit, you're a virgin?"

He'd taken the small leap, but assumed correctly. I pressed my lips together and nodded quickly.

I'd had the opportunity to lose my V card once, on prom night, of all clichés. My timid boyfriend and I had parked at the marina, hidden behind the boats in dry-dock, and gotten into the back seat. Five minutes into the heavy makeout session, he'd blurted out the least romantic thing I'd expected.

"I've got a condom so we should fuck."

The ensuing conversation was so uncomfortable, it hadn't just ruined the evening, it had ruined our relationship. There'd been no prospects since that night. I'd gone on a few dates when I got to Randhurst, but there'd been no connection. No spark. Or we'd hit the roadblock of my inexperience and it weirded him out. Time only made me less confident in my ability to find a partner who'd be a good match. Someone intelligent, driven like me, and willing to deal with my social awkwardness.

My anxious gaze drifted back to Luka's. Was he as disappointed as the other boys had been when they learned I'd never given it up?

No, he wasn't disappointed.

He gave a wicked smile and looked *thrilled*. He straightened and his gaze slid down the length of my body. It came to rest exactly where his palms moved to, my knees. And then both began to work their way up my thighs.

"How?" he asked. "Why?"

"*Why*?" How was I going to explain? It didn't matter, the tequila made me mouthy and I spoke without thought. "The guy I was with . . . didn't deserve it."

Luka's pleased expression was even better than his displeased one. "Fuck, perfect," he said. "Let me show you what it feels like."

I snagged my bottom lip between my teeth as anxiety fluttered in my belly. His fingers were up my skirt, tugging at the waistband of my panties, urging them down.

"Wait, wait." My hands flew out to stop his, but it didn't work. He tugged one side down and then the other, working the panties toward my knees.

"Don't worry, good girl," he teased. "You can keep these on."

I trembled as the black cotton panties were bunched at my knees, and the tremble was more pronounced when Luka guided me to lift one leg free of the fabric. The panties dropped down my calf and hung at my ankle, where he gave them a tug.

"See? Still on." His expression was sinful.

I was aware I was in over my head, even as I reached the final stage of drunkenness—inability to organize thoughts. His warm palms pressed open my knees and he bent at the waist, lowering his face between my legs.

A trembling hand—my own—clamped over my lips to keep me quiet as he pushed my skirt out of his way. There was nowhere else to look but at the man licking his lips while he stared at my nakedness. It was indecent, and holy hell, he made me feel good. Desired like nothing else. He closed the last of the distance and claimed me with his mouth.

My moan was loud, but quieted against my palm, when

something warm and soft stroked me. I jolted. He did it again, and again, and each one wrung a new moan from my shaking body. It felt amazing. Better than amazing. I didn't want him to ever stop.

I was gulping down air through my nose, and slapped my other palm on top of my mouth for further protection from getting too loud. My knees tried to close, but his hands were on the tops of my thighs, forcing them apart. Holding me open for him as he feasted.

The swirling tongue did nothing to help my spinning issue, nor did his lips closing and sucking on the tight bud at the center of my pleasure. I bucked and groaned into my hands, my back arching from the couch, only for me to slump back down against it.

It was abruptly cold as he sat back, taking the heat of his mouth with him. He stared at me with lust-heavy eyes, and his hand ran between my legs. "You're so fucking wet." The hand slid through my folds and smeared the wetness all along the inside of my thighs. "Christ, feel how bad this virgin pussy wants me."

It was shocking, and although part of me was unhappy with the vulgarity, another part was terribly turned on. I'd thought Luka and I were the same, but in this room? We were polar opposites. All of my inexperience and shyness was a void he filled with his ultra-confidence, trapping me in his power.

He leaned back down and his warm breath spilled over me. That devious tongue slicked over my clit, fluttering with urgency, and heat built inside me at an exponential rate. Each stroke made me groan with choked pleasure. I peered into his eyes that were focused back on me intently, and my cheeks flushed red-hot. How could I watch him while he was doing something so intimate? Yet

I couldn't stop myself. My hands moved of their own accord, my nails gouging into his shoulders.

I closed in on the mounting release. It was . . . intense. It felt like an electrical surge as his relentless tongue cast me over the edge into a searing fire. When the shudders descended on my body, I let the waves carry me away. I should have cared about how he viewed me, but I didn't. The only thing I could think about was the pleasure coursing along my spine, pulling me into bliss.

Overwhelming sensations flooded along my nerve endings. Heat. Ecstasy. Desire. When my orgasm released me, my hands fell away from this shoulders and I went slack and boneless against the leather cushions.

For a moment, there was only the sound of my rapid breathing and the thumping bass from downstairs, and then Luka rose up, wiping his mouth. His lips bowed into the faintest smile, making him look seductive and dangerous. He undid the utility belt around his hips and the gun thudded to the floor. It sounded too heavy to be plastic.

"Unbutton your shirt."

He never *asked* me to do anything. It was always a command. Yet in the aftermath of the orgasm, I was euphoric, so I teased him. "You think you can tell me what to do?"

His serious expression didn't change. "Yes."

When he didn't move or say anything else, I sobered. He was waiting impatiently on me to follow his order, but I'd already done more and gone further with him than I'd meant to. It was insane how quickly I'd allowed him to get under my skirt. I barely knew him, and I wasn't a one-night fling kind of girl.

"I'm, uh . . . not sure—" I mumbled, letting my gaze

fall downward.

Strong hands seized mine and tugged me up until I was sitting on the edge of the couch. Luka set our hands together on his collarbones, his palms pressing against the backs of my hands. "Undo one."

I blinked away my confusion. He wanted me to undo one of his buttons? The chest beneath my fingers was hard and lean, and I wanted to see what was below the navy uniform. I'd only fantasized about it for two years, and he was telling me to take a peek . . . My fingers were clumsy as I undid the first button below the collar of his dress shirt.

Luka's fingers weren't clumsy. They were nimble as he unfastened my blouse button, which sat an inch above my cleavage. He could hold his liquor much better than I could. He seemed barely drunk, whereas I was getting worse. My brain moved sluggishly along, struggling to keep up.

"Now another." His voice was low, but firm.

My mouth went dry, but I could do this. It wasn't quite as real when he was the one undoing my shirt, versus myself. I popped open his next button, revealing tan, smooth skin below. I tensed as he tugged at my shirt, freeing another button so my black bra was exposed. His gaze drifted down, taking in my average-sized breasts encased in black satin.

"All of them," he said. This time his voice was tinged with something that sounded a lot like excitement.

I swallowed thickly as I undid the rest of the line of buttons, and sat back. He rewarded me by pulling the shirttails free from his waistband and left the unbuttoned shirt to hang open. Holy hell, there was faint definition of his abdominals. My gaze roved over his chest and I tried not to let it show how badly I wanted to touch him.

Things grew hazy when he hurried to undo and throw open my shirt. His mouth was on my neck, carving a path down my collarbone. I shivered when his whiskers scraped along my skin. Fingers were inside my bra, tugging the cups down, and then his mouth locked on a nipple. It snapped into a hardened point as his tongue swiped over it, and the dull ache between my legs grew hot and sharp.

I gasped as he nipped with teeth, hard enough it hurt, but instantly his kiss soothed the burn away. How did he do that? I shut my eyes and let him suck at me while I hung on, my fingers laced through his thick hair. To hell with the spinning, I thought.

A noise of surprise broke free from my throat when he abruptly grabbed my shoulders and flung me down on my back on the couch cushions. Everything moved so fast, and I didn't enjoy the sensation of being out of control. It was unfamiliar and scary. I had to concentrate and force myself to stay active, because the tequila made me slow and indifferent. *You cannot let this go any further.*

Luka's hands and mouth were still focused on my breasts as he settled on his knees between my legs. When I tried to scoot back and sit up, he lifted his head and shot me a surprised look. Did I appear as nervous as I felt?

He blinked slowly, and then returned to his task, running his lips over one of my peaked nipples. "We've still got all our clothes on." His words were soft and almost playful. "How much trouble can we really get in?"

The leather couch squealed as he shifted, sliding down along the length of my body. My stomach trembled beneath his scattered kisses. Was he going to . . .

Yes. The skirt was shoved up and his mouth was fire. This time I dug my fingers into my own skin, clutching at the tops of my thighs as he went down on me. The sight of Luka kneeling between my legs and licking me was unbelievable. Muscles low in my belly clenched, tensing to the point of pain.

That was exactly what he did to me. Made me want him so badly it hurt.

"I like that I'm the only one," he whispered, "who knows what you taste like."

I dragged air in and out of my body, watching him nuzzle my most sensitive part. He wasn't gentle. He attacked me like we were under an approaching deadline, rushing me along. Maybe we were. Perhaps the alcohol would wear off soon and I'd come to my senses about how irresponsible I was being.

But perhaps he'd realize any second how ridiculous this was, really. He would figure out that the quivering virgin spread beneath him was too shy and awkward to play in his world.

"Oh!" My back arched high off the cushions as he plunged a finger inside me. The action, combined with his tongue, was too much to stay quiet through. I moaned and writhed as he teased me mercilessly. The finger pulsed in and out, injecting me with pleasure. He made me feel so good . . .

Luka sat back on his heels and both hands hurried to undo his belt and zipper. The air in the room went arctic.

"Wait!" Panic gripped me, locking my muscles.

He leaned over and put one hand on the cushion beside my head. "Shh, relax." His voice was soothing, and followed immediately by his lips on mine. His kiss was slow and sweet. "We're just going to put skin on skin." His lips continued to assault and persuade, speaking and then kissing. "Did you like my mouth here?" His hand pressed to my damp body, touching my clit. "I'm going to put my cock on you, Addison. I'm going to tease you with it until you come."

I shuddered, alight with excitement and trepidation. His belt clinked as it tumbled open, and he pulled his pants off of his hips, one side, then the other. His statement was technically true. We still had our clothes on, but it was really a lie. I was completely exposed with my breasts spilling over the tops of the cups of my bra and the skirt corded around my waist. Basically naked, with nowhere to hide trapped beneath him.

Luka gripped himself with the hand he wasn't using for support, and slowly lowered onto me. The warm skin of his chest was our first connection, followed by his lips on mine, and then . . .

Holy hell!

Warning lights flashed in my head at how close I was to actual sex. His hard erection felt like it was wrapped in velvet when it pressed against my slit, only a fraction of an inch too high to gain entry. He groaned into my mouth and his lips were forceful and demanding. He kissed me as if I'd pissed him off and yet it turned him on.

Skin on skin, he'd said. I had no idea how amazing and torturous it was until he moved. His body slid over mine and I gasped as every point of contact between us came alive. The brush of his skin on my nipples was nice, but the ridge of his dick massaging my clit was something else entirely. A dark need roared to life and whispered terrible ideas, trying to bargain to get what it wanted.

Luka sawed his body back and forth on top of mine while he continued to control my mouth with his. His lips were incessant. They alternated between hard and soft, rough quickly followed by gentle and tender. It was impossible to match his ever-changing technique, especially when I was foggy with alcohol and lust.

The length of his glide seemed to increase with every pass, increasing the tension inside me, until I was certain I'd orgasm with the next rock of his hips. Yet it just kept feeling better. The coil of sexual release only wound tighter.

Holy hell, I could *hear* how wet I was, and my face heated with embarrassment. Was it normal to be this turned on? His dick was drenched in my arousal, and I was panting between his punishing kisses. He slid backward and readied to charge forward once more—

No.

His angle was too low, and the head of his hard dick was right at my entrance, pressing against my tight body.

I went rigid and once again panic filled my voice. "Luka."

He held perfectly still. He didn't advance, but he didn't retreat either. His dark eyes stared down with so much intensity, it stole my breath. What was he thinking about, and why hadn't he backed off? His expression slowly shifted into the seductive one from before.

"It's okay," he whispered. "You can still be a good girl." The tip of his cock dug into me, forcing its way toward entry. "It doesn't count if I'm barely inside you."

I inhaled sharply with discomfort and surprise, my mouth falling open. He was big and hard, and my body naturally resisted, but he continued to press forward. It didn't matter that I was trying to scoot backward—there was nowhere to go. My head hit the armrest of the couch, and his hand clamped down on my breast so tightly I couldn't retreat further.

"Wait a minute," I said, swallowing back the rising fear.

But he didn't.

Luka inched his way along, until I could feel the tip of his cock pushing past my entrance. It hurt. The stretch was a sharp pain followed immediately by a deep, uncomfortable ache. My eyes were as wide as they'd ever been in my life. *Holy God.* There was someone else inside me.

He ceased his movement, but then he was kissing me again. I turned my head to the side, away from him, and struggled to get my breathing under control. Things were spinning so badly now I couldn't focus on what I wanted to say. What I *needed* to say. Had I told him no?

"Stop," I choked out.

"I did." His voice was hypnotic when it was that close to my ear. His tongue traced a line down my neck and I shivered in response. "I'm hardly inside you, and fuck, you're so tight." He seized one of my hands with his and forced it down between our bodies. His fingers curled mine around his thick shaft that wasn't inside me. "See?" He nipped gently on the spot where my neck met my shoulder. "You're still okay, Addison."

He guided my hand to stroke him and groaned in pleasure. Was what he said true? Was I still a virgin even though an inch of him was lodged inside my body? There was a lot of him that wasn't buried between my legs.

His order was urgent and commanding. "Harder."

I clenched my fist tighter around him. He was thick. I stroked from the base all the way until he disappeared inside me, and then back down again. He was firm and warm. Did I like this feeling or should I be upset that he'd taken over and done this without permission? The only thing I knew for certain was I shouldn't have had the last shot of tequila. My inhibitions were too far gone. The dark voice in my head wanted to tell him to go further. *Deeper.* My head swung back to face him.

His expression was determination, but I didn't get much of a look. He slammed his mouth over mine, claiming me in a quick, but forceful kiss.

"Always doing what I tell you," he murmured against my lips. "So fucking perfect."

I whimpered as his hips moved and Luka slipped a little deeper inside. I squirmed like I could melt into the couch and evade the uncomfortable intrusion.

His lips parted and he blew out a loud sigh. "You want me all the way inside you?"

"No," I cried quickly.

"Then stop moving." Shear concentration was etched on his face, like he was in an enormous battle and losing the fight. "You feel way too goddamn good."

My thoughts splintered into two. It was empowering to hear he liked it, but logic screamed at me to stop this immediately. It had already gone too far. In my fantasies, yes, I had sex with him, but that was fantasy. It didn't carry consequences or cause regret.

I closed my eyes and tried to center myself, but it was impossible. Luka's teeth dragged over my breasts, followed by his hands, and I was on a merry-go-round spinning ninety miles an hour.

"*Fuck,*" he muttered. He pulled back just a fraction of an inch, then pushed forward. His shallow thrust hurt, and the ache flooded my lower body with heat. His breath filled my ear. "You can take a little more."

"No," I whined.

"Yes."

That single word tipped the scales, and I crossed from confusion into dread. It was clear now that we were going to go as far as Luka wanted, and I had no say in the matter. I slapped my hands on his bare chest and pushed up with all my might.

"You're not wearing anything." Like a condom.

"I'm clean, and you're a virgin. We're both okay."

Was he stupid? "No, Luka. Get off of me."

It flipped a switch in him. I saw the Luka I thought I knew disappear, and something else took over in his place. This version of him was all hard and cold, and utterly terrifying.

"Reach up and grab ahold of the armrest." His voice was detached and chilling.

"No—"

It died on my tongue as Luka glared at me. "Be a good girl and do what I say."

His threatening look made me reach up with shaky hands and clutch at the leather armrest. He grabbed my wrists, binding them together in one strong hold. The tight clamp on my wrists was too much to overcome or break free from.

"Please," I whispered, trembling so badly I was sure to vibrate off the couch.

"Shh." His lips brushed over mine. "Just relax."

It was an order I couldn't obey no matter how much I wanted to. I stayed perfectly still as he held me down and pulsed inside me, his dick sliding in and out in tiny strokes. My body was no longer protesting as badly as before, but it wasn't enjoyable. My heart beat so fast I became lightheaded and dizzy. And my heart stopped altogether when Luka's free hand slid over my mouth and covered it, silencing me.

"I'll go slow," he said. Warm lips trailed over my cheekbone. "But it's going to hurt at first."

I sucked in rapid gasps through my nose. *Oh my God.* I tried to speak, but my cries for him to stop were muffled against his rough palm.

No, no, no! Not like this.

I wriggled and tried to get him to release me, but he was unfazed. His singular focus was on my eyes, watching every rapid blink I made as I fought back, but my struggle was nothing to him.

Please, not like this! I silently pleaded with him. Couldn't he see how I was panicking? Didn't he care?

No, he didn't. His eyes were dark as black lava and his expression was complete dominance. I felt owned. Smothered under his power. He drew in a deep breath, preparing for something big. Then his hips sank further into me and I moaned in pain. There was a sharp stab of fire, which gave way to a burning, ripping feeling.

That was when Luka Markovic ruthlessly stole from me what was supposed to be mine to give.

Chapter
FOUR

HOT TEARS STUNG IN MY EYES, but I blinked them back. I used my anger to sink my teeth into Luka's hand. I bit as hard as I could until he swore and yanked the hand away.

Air poured in through my lips and I rasped, readying to scream—

He cupped my jaw and pressed his forehead against mine, his tone soothing and quiet. "Calm down. It's okay, it's over."

Nothing was okay. Was he insane? The air was too thin and I started to hyperventilate. I gasped and choked.

"Shh," he whispered softly. Did he honestly think I'd take comfort from him right now? The fiery pain radiated outward from my hips to the base of my spine, even though he wasn't moving. Once he'd forced himself all the way in, Luka hesitated.

"Addison." His thumb slid over my trembling lips and pressed down, stilling them. "*Fuck*, Addison. You feel so good."

I was trapped in a centrifuge, whirling in a blur, only instead of separating my emotions they were a jumbled mess. Lust. Hurt. Shock. The alcohol only added to the confusion. His voice was soaked with appreciation, and in spite of what he'd just done, it was hard to ignore the tiny tinge of warmth it gave me.

His mouth replaced his thumb, sealing his lips over mine. I went limp in his hold, not returning the kiss but not running from it either. The damage had been done, and what I wanted was irrelevant—Luka would take whether I gave or not, so I chose to lie motionless and give nothing.

My inaction seemed to drive him. His kiss was intense and his tongue pushed past my lips, slipping into my mouth. So soft and gentle, in total contrast to what he'd done.

What he was *still* doing.

A slight move of his hips brought on a new wave of discomfort, and I moaned my displeasure against his mouth. Probably because I wasn't responding to his kiss, he pulled back and examined my face . . . what the hell was his expression? Was it supposed to be worry?

"It'll get better," he said, his voice low.

I swung my gaze away from him and closed my eyes, desperate to shut him out. But how could I do that when he was deep inside me, making me ache and throb? Or with his hand clasping my wrists tightly together, his bare chest pressed to mine?

Inch by burning inch, Luka crept in and out of me. He was at least true to his word and went slow. The pain lessened to a point I could think over it. How had I been this stupid? I was almost as angry with myself as I was with him.

The leather couch squeaked to match his slow rhythm. I couldn't keep my eyes closed any longer. I stared blankly at the soft leather cushion back and tried to shut everything down. Like I could pretend he wasn't on top of me, his dick surging inside my aching body, or his mouth latched onto my ear. With all that was happening, it was his uneven breath that became too loud to ignore.

"Does it still hurt?"

I gave him nothing. Not even my attention.

He'd asked me softly, but this time he sounded annoyed.

"Answer me."

No, not in a million years. I was done taking orders from him—

His hand on my jaw clenched and tugged my face to meet his. His eyes were chaos. Desire flashed and anger smoldered. He was devastating like this. Aggressive and predatory.

"If I'm hurting you and you don't say anything, I'm going to keep hurting you and not know it."

"What difference does it make?" I snapped. I was weak. My self-imposed silent treatment lasted all of a minute.

His eyes narrowed. His hand let go of my jaw and reached down, finding my knee. He pushed it up and back at the same moment he thrust deeply, and I gasped in pain.

"Does that hurt, or should I keep doing it?" he demanded, knowing full well it caused me pain. He was pushing me to respond to him, or punishing me for not answering sooner.

"It hurts."

He looked strangely relieved as he released my knee and my wrists. I yanked my hands down and put them on his shoulders. I couldn't push him off of me, so instead I drove my fingers into his flesh. The muscles along his jaw flexed, telling me he'd clenched his teeth, hopefully in pain.

"Ease up on the nails, or I'll rethink letting go of your wrists."

He shifted, rising up on his straightened arms. We were still connected at our lower bodies, but he had slowed to a snail's pace. He glanced down, and issued a noise of surprise.

"Fuck, look at that."

I'd told myself I wasn't going to take orders from him, but it was unavoidable. My gaze went to where his was, and I swallowed hard.

There was dark blood smeared on his thick cock, which he pulsed in and out of me in long, languid strokes.

"So fucking sexy, seeing proof that you're mine."

This time when I dug my nails into him, it wasn't to cause harm, it was simply a reaction. He thought I was his? The thought detonated in my mind like a mushroom cloud. I *was*. He'd linked himself to me forever with one dark act.

I found myself staring up into his coal-colored eyes, unsure of anything. Luka would always be my first. He'd pushed and taken, but maybe he had done me a tiny favor as well? Everyone I'd talked to confided their first time had been terrible. The girls said it hurt and they were glad that it was over and done with. Sex apparently felt much better after you'd done it a few times.

Wait, no. That was the dumbest thing ever.

His mouth hung slack as he moved against me, breathing heavy. Satisfaction streaked his face. In the low light, it played up the sharp angles of his nose and jaw. Why did he do this? Why did he stare at me like I was the most interesting thing he'd ever seen?

My eyes fluttered closed. This wasn't a *favor*. Holy shit, I'd said no and he'd done it anyway. That was pretty clear-cut, wasn't it?

His hot skin was against my chest and his hands noisily slid beneath me, scraping over the leather. His fingers splayed on my backside, tilting my hips, so when he pushed down into me this time, there was new contact.

"Oh," I sighed, wishing instantly I could take it back. What the hell was wrong with me? Luka's body ground against my clit, sending warm shivers up my spine. I wasn't supposed to enjoy what he was doing.

His hands pushed and pulled, getting me to rock my hips against his. His tempo picked up until it was a steady pace, and the ache began to shift and give way to heat. My heart pounded furiously, but it matched his. I could feel his through my chest.

"That's it," he urged between short breaths. "Wrap your legs around me."

The conflict inside my head was widening with each moment that passed. It was starting to feel good, and I marveled a little in my drunken state. I was having sex with the guy I'd been dreaming about for forever. Logic's disapproving voice was rapidly dissipating into white noise.

Goosebumps exploded on my legs as I did what he said, and this time we both moaned together, although mine was more startled pleasure than his low, guttural moan. The slippery glide of his dick felt so different from what I'd expected. The fullness had started out uncomfortable, but it hadn't stayed that way for long.

"Goddamnit," he groaned, dragging out each syllable. His mouth was buried in the nook of my neck, licking and sucking. More goosebumps lifted on my skin.

When I began to pant, it kicked everything up a notch. I felt the effects of the alcohol stronger, and I felt deeper pleasure. Luka's thrusts increased until he was driving into me. It hurt, but felt good at the same time, and I clutched at his back, not sure if I was clawing him to push him away, or hold him closer.

"Does it feel good?" His lips wandered over my cheekbone, my jaw, my mouth.

I couldn't bring myself to say it. Something was obviously wrong with me, but I gave a quick, small nod. This time when he kissed me, I tentatively kissed him back. I'd pretend he was still the myth I'd believed he was until this night was over.

The muscles in his back corded and tensed. He crashed into me so hard the couch shook, and I gasped. Without prompting, I had to reach up and grab the armrest to brace myself. It was all that kept him from accidentally slamming my head into it.

"Fuck, shit," he growled.

The tension in him grew ten-fold, and I watched, fascinated. He shuddered and closed his eyes, letting a look of intense pleasure overtake him, then abruptly he was backing up. He pulled out and his hot, wet dick was set in the hollow where my leg joined my body. He rocked it back and forth as he came. Warm drops flicked on my belly, hip, and skirt. He was throbbing on my skin while he exhaled loudly, sounding like he was falling apart.

His rocking came to a stop, and his breathing began to slow. It was an odd sensation when he left my body. The ache was significantly reduced, but the warmth and fullness I liked were gone as well.

"That was," he whispered in my ear, "even better than I imagined it'd be."

I sucked in a breath. "You thought about . . .?"

His serious demeanor slowly blinked back into place. "Fucking you? Of course I did. What did you think I was doing the whole time during class?"

He brushed his mouth across mine, almost too fast for it to count as a kiss, and pulled back from me. His gaze swept down along my body, then returned to mine. "Stay right there."

It wasn't a request. He climbed off the couch, tugging his undone pants up around his hips and strolled to the dark room off to the side. The resident advisor's room came with a private bathroom. As the sink began to run, I tugged my bra back in place and pushed the hem of my skirt down to cover myself. I also attempted to button my blouse, but my fingers were shaking too badly. What had we just done?

The water shut off and rustling rang out, telling me he was doing up his pants, and it was followed by footsteps. I hurried to sit up, unsure what to do about the mess we'd made—

Luka had a handful of wet towels, and as he approached, his eyebrow arched. Was he mad I'd covered myself? He said nothing. He took a knee beside me on the couch and flung my skirt up, wiping the towel across my skin. I hissed at the touch—the towel was cold. But my face heated until it was on fire. He cleaned me up, his focused gaze between my legs, and then he moved on to the skirt. When he seemed satisfied, he ran the towel over the leather.

I was shaking in my core as he stood, disappeared once more into the bathroom, and returned. The utility belt was snatched off the floor and slung around his hips. Then, he crossed his arms and peered down at me. It was unnerving. Was he expecting me to say something? To do something? I grabbed the panties that clung to my ankle and stepped my other foot into the leg hole, and as I stood, I drew the panties upward.

My body ached, and I stood too fast.

Luka was there to catch me as I threatened to topple over, and I fell into his embrace. I felt sick with emotions, and didn't like the feeling of his arms around me. No, worse. It was that I liked his arms holding me; that was what I disliked. He'd . . . *oh, God.*

He'd *raped* me. Hadn't he?

"Are you okay?"

I stiffened and fought to appear sober. "Yeah."

I just needed to get away from him, and think about what my next step would be. Did I report this? Could I stomach going through all of that? Everyone would know how stupid I'd been to come up here alone with him. My mouth went dry. What if no one believed me?

His embrace closed in, pressing me against him. His thumb and forefinger grasped my chin and angled me up into his kiss. I was sure he could feel me trembling, and it was the reason his arms tightened around me. His mouth was gentle. Luka was trying to console me, yet it only made the word *no* swirl louder in my brain. I'd been captive under his power long enough.

I ended the kiss a little too soon for him, and his expression hardened a shade. His evaluating gaze was piercing, and I worried I'd fall apart beneath it. What was he thinking about? I didn't have a clue what was going on behind those dark eyes.

"Sit," he said. "I'll be right back. I'm going to check on my brother and grab us some drinks."

There wasn't time to answer, not that it was a question. Luka pressed his body into mine, forcing me backward and down to sit on the couch.

My voice was flustered. "That's okay, I should probably get back downstairs, too."

"Not a chance." He curled a hand behind my neck and tilted my head up to his as he lowered down into a kiss. "That was just the warm-up, Addison. When I get back, we'll do it for real."

I shuddered, even as my traitorous body responded to him. My nipples tightened at the idea.

But if I agreed to it, he'd leave, and I could use that opportunity to slip away. The party downstairs was loud and busy, and no one would notice me leaving. I'd probably be halfway back to my dorm before Luka realized what I'd done.

I attempted a timid smile. He gauged my expression, and looked satisfied when I didn't protest, indicating I'd stay.

"Okay, gimme a minute, I'll be right back."

I watched him go, air fisted tight in my lungs. How long did I need to wait to make sure he was safely downstairs and in the kitchen? I metered out my shaky breath, forcing myself to stay calm.

One breath.

Another.

What if I stayed on the couch? What would happen?

It was the tequila, I was sure. I'd never drink it again, as it clearly made me insane. I had to get up and out of this room before he came back.

I was sore and rose gingerly.

My legs moved like they were made of lead. The wicked voice inside me asked if I was sure I wanted to leave, but I squashed it. I put one foot slowly in front of the other, and teetered to the door.

The hallway was empty. I stumbled on the thick carpet and almost fell into the wall, but was able to pull upright just in time. Christ, the liquor had knocked me on my ass. I was a fool not to eat something before coming to the party, and an even bigger one for doing those shots.

People congregated at the foot of the stairs, clenching their cups and shouting conversations at each other, oblivious of the slutty schoolgirl at the top, looking down on them. I clutched the wooden banister for added support. My drunk legs and high heels were a deadly combination on the stairs, and I had to focus on my feet as I went down to ensure I didn't miss a step.

I was halfway to the bottom when the hairs on the back of my neck stood upright, making me hyperaware someone was watching me. I paused, and glanced up from my feet—

I'd waited two years to see his irritated expression directed at me, thinking it'd turn me on. Now Luka stood at the base of the steps waiting for me, a cup in each hand and a pissed off look splashed on his face. It didn't turn me on.

It filled me with fear.

Chapter
FIVE

Everyone standing around Luka was oblivious, but tension emanated from him and traveled upward in waves at me. I froze on the steps, caught in the act and not sure what to do. Did he want me to come down to him? Should I retreat?

He took the stairs two at a time and reached me swiftly, but managed not to spill the half-full cups of beer he carried. One was thrust at me and I took it, unable to meet Luka's searing gaze. His overpowering presence caused me to back up until I was against the wall and the banister dug into my side.

"Did you get bored?" His tone was flat and his lips right by my ear. I sensed he knew why I fled the room. Somehow he was completely aware of my deception.

"No, I . . ." I finally dragged my gaze up to match his, and found his eyes furious. "I think maybe I should head home."

"Yeah?" He moved in so there was no space left between us. "Having regrets about what we did?"

"You mean what *you* did?" I corrected, and tightened my hold on the railing. Logic told me to shut up and not push him, but I was stupid drunk.

Something dark flared in his expression and he shifted on the stairs, turning his back on the crowd below. It was so he could run his hand under my skirt, up between my thighs, and massage me through my underwear. Right out in the open, where anyone could see, although his broad back blocked most of it from view. I gasped and clutched my cup, making my beer slosh over my hand.

"Are you sore here?" His expression was predatory. "Answer me now."

I nodded, stunned beyond words.

"Good," he said. "Every time you feel that ache between your legs, you think of me."

"Holy shit, Luka," I whispered. As I pushed his hand away, I glanced around nervously, desperately checking to make sure no one was watching us. They weren't, but we were far too exposed.

"Go back upstairs. Now."

His forceful tone was too much. Rather than fall under his spell, it strengthened me. It cleared my head of the drunken fog, and I looked at him critically for the first time. Go back upstairs so he could date rape me again? "No. I'm going home."

Luka's shoulders lifted as he drew in a deep breath and appeared to consider my statement. Was he deciding whether he'd let me go or not? "Okay," he said. "Finish your beer and let's go."

"What?"

Oh, he did not like having to repeat himself. His nostrils flared and his eyebrow lifted in annoyance. So I took a long chug of the lukewarm beer to keep him placated. I hated the taste of beer. As a new twenty-one-year-old, I hadn't yet acquired the taste for it.

Before I'd finished my gulp, Luka was moving down the stairs, and I felt compelled to follow. I tried to buck against it, but how was it he had this power over me? Was it the fake police officer uniform that gave him false authority?

When I reached the bottom of the stairs, his hand grabbed

mine and he laced our fingers together. My heartbeat kicked in response. Not that this was romantic. It was pure dominance. Luka
not just staking his claim, but asserting his physical control.

"Find your roommate," he ordered.

"You don't have to walk me home," I said. His hand was a
vise on mine.

"I don't plan to. I'll text my driver."

His driver? Well . . . at least that was safe. It'd be warm in the
car, and better with an extra person around.

He'd asked me to find Avery, and it turned out to be no small
task. During the time Luka and I had been upstairs, it had grown
much more crowded. Luka's grip on my hand kept us connected even as he dragged me through the thick pack of people and
thumbed out a text on his phone.

We found Catwoman Avery on the back porch, shivering in
the cold while Batman smoked. I pointed her out to Luka and
he tugged me along, thrusting me out with him into the cold
October air.

"I'm taking Addison home," Luka announced before we'd
reached them.

"You're what?" Avery giggled incredulously. "Is she throwing
up already?" She grinned at Luka, then blinked, surprised. She
shot me a look that said she was impressed with the man connected at my side.

"Be quiet," her boyfriend snapped. "That's Vasilije's brother."

The color slowly drained from her face and left her pale as she
stared up at Luka. I'd never seen Avery serious, and her reaction
sent ice crawling along my spine. Nothing fazed her. So why had
the mere mention of Luka's family sent her into a tailspin? Her

gaze locked onto mine and spoke volumes. *Oh, shit.* She didn't usually care about anyone but herself, and yet she was *worried* about me. My knees went weak. What had I gotten myself into?

It'd been a night of bad decisions, so I made yet another. I slammed the rest of the beer in my cup, hoping it'd make me forget what I'd done.

"Addison, you okay?" she asked, her voice laced with concern.

"I'm fine." It came out less than convincing. I chucked the empty cup in the trash and shivered in the cold air. "He's not driving."

"Okay," Brent said quickly. "You guys have fun. Avery's hanging out over here tonight, if you guys want to be . . ."

Good lord, was that his way of telling Luka he didn't need to put a sock on my door?

"Thanks," Luka said. "Your name is?"

Brent looked nervous, like he wasn't sure he should hand the information out. "Brent Sherman."

Luka repeated it as if committing it to memory. Then his attention swung back to me. "Now we have to find Vasilije."

He headed back inside and pulled on my hand much like it was a leash. We squeezed our way through the people in the main room and went to the kitchen.

We were further away from the music, but the roar of conversation was much louder. Luka took a sip of his beer, and then tossed the cup into an overfull trashcan. The laminate floor was sticky with spilled beer, and the room was stiflingly hot.

His gaze scoured the area, and he scowled. Obviously Vasilije wasn't here. Luka pulled me to the giant guy who was still manning the keg. "Have you seen my brother?"

The guy shook his head. "You check the game room?"

It was our next stop, but again, Luka searched the sea of faces and scowled. "Where the fuck is he?"

I tried to extract my hand from his grip, but it only made him squeeze tighter. My head was buzzing again from the fresh wave of alcohol, and this one hit me fast. Luka was determined to find his brother, and I could use that to my advantage. "Why don't we split up and look for him?"

His jaw set and his expression turned icy. It made me feel like I was the dumbest person in the world, aided by his patronizing tone. "So you know what my brother looks like?"

Crap. No, I didn't have a clue.

"Or maybe you're just trying to leave without me again." He yanked me up against his chest, so I collided with his hard frame. "I'm taking you home, and that is not up for discussion. Got it?"

I pressed my free hand on his chest and pushed off of him, trying to put space between us. Why was I fighting him on this, anyway? The car would be faster, warmer, and safer than walking home drunk by myself. Nothing could happen once we got to the dorm. Luka could demand I invite him upstairs all he wanted, but male visitors after hours had to be signed in at the front desk. I'd simply refuse to do it, and he'd have no choice but to leave or face security.

Luka angrily tapped out another text message, but it must have gone unanswered, because he dragged me all over the house searching. After a while, his grip on mine became less about control and more about support. I stumbled on my heels, and he kept me from crashing to the ground.

Had I forgotten how to walk? It suddenly seemed so . . .

challenging. Not the act of it, but the physical exertion. I was so, so sleepy.

Luka pulled abruptly to a stop, and I slammed into him. As I ricocheted backward, he dropped his grip on my hand and his arm looped around my waist, holding me upright. He glared at the man in front of us. "Where the fuck have you been?"

This was Luka's brother? They looked nothing alike, not until Vasilije's eyebrow lifted in a perfect upside-down V, shooting the same look of disdain Luka was capable of.

"Dan got his drone out. We were at the soccer fields flying it around and shit."

Vasilije's costume was a fire-engine red suit and a black shirt, and a pair of horns rose out of his brown hair. He was the devil, and one look made me believe the costume was fitting. Luka's younger brother was the quintessential frat guy. Attractive. Probably my age or a year older. He looked big and toned beneath his suit, and gave off a cocky, entitled attitude.

"I texted you a bunch of times." Luka's face twisted with annoyance.

Vasilije shrugged. "My battery's dead."

"Whatever. I'm taking her home," Luka said, squeezing me tight against him.

Vasilije's gaze swept over me, like he hadn't noticed my existence until Luka prompted him to. Why did I feel the urge to stand up straight? Vasilije evaluated me as if I were cattle at an auction.

"Isn't she a little young for you?" He grinned, flashing a huge smile complete with dimples. Did Luka have dimples? He never smiled, so the world would never know.

"Don't get into any shit," Luka snapped, "and we'll both agree

I was here for another two hours."

"Sounds good to me." Vasilije waved us off. "You kids have fun, now. Make good choices."

I couldn't stop the giggle, and Luka's gaze snapped to me. His curious expression demanded I explain what was so funny. "*Make good choices*," I said. "I think it's a little late for that."

What on earth? A strange hint of emotion passed through Luka's eyes. Was that . . . hurt? It was fleeting and gone in a blink, but existed long enough for me to feel bad, which made no sense. He didn't care about my feelings; why should I care about his? But I couldn't stand the disapproval. I was a people pleaser down to the marrow of my bones.

"I meant I drank too much," I said, compelled to explain.

His expression had gone flat and it remained indifferent. "Come on," he said. "The car's waiting."

He threaded his fingers through mine and led me through the party, cutting a path to the front door. It was an enormous task, and halfway there, Luka's arm was once again around my waist, keeping me from collapsing. I had to fight to keep my eyelids open and stay on my feet.

"Why am I so tired?" I said, but Luka had no response.

The cold night air was only slightly sobering. Pulled up in the circle drive, a man in jeans and a button-up shirt waited beside a black town car. I was guided down the front porch and into the driveway, and when I blinked, I was sitting on leather covering the back seat.

"I'm in Deacon Hall," I murmured as Luka buckled me in. I couldn't be bothered to do it myself, and somehow he knew. I leaned my head back and closed my eyes, needing to take a minute. I didn't fight him when his hand rested possessively on my thigh, his fingers skimming right at my hemline. We'd be at my dorm soon, and Luka's spell over me would come to an end.

π

I blinked my blurry eyes and disorientation hit me, only to be crushed instantly by a wave of nausea and a horrifying pounding in my head. The pillow beneath me wasn't my own. There was green striped wallpaper on the walls, not bland cream paint and obnoxious white lights Avery insisted on hanging. Where was I?

"Are you going to be sick again?" a deep, male voice asked, and I jolted upright, only to moan in agony. My hand flew to the throbbing in my temple, trying in vain to massage it away. I had to process each piece of information slowly, one at a time.

I was in a strange bed, curled up under the sheets. All my clothes, except for my shoes, were still on, although one of my knee-high socks was bunched at an ankle. Daylight streamed from the large bay window. Holy crap, what time was it? And the voice . . .

Across the room, Luka sat on the edge of a gold colored love seat, wearing jeans and a T-shirt. He was leaning forward, his elbows resting on his knees. He appeared showered and shaved, not the least bit hungover. My pulse kicked, and I hated it. The sight of him still gave me a rush.

However, it was impossible to tell what he was thinking with his fixed expression. He pocketed his cellphone and gave me his full, intense attention.

"Where am I?" My throat was scratchy and my voice hoarse.

"One of the guest rooms." He stood and retrieved a red sports drink off of the floor, holding it out to me. I hadn't realized how parched I was until he unscrewed the top and handed it to me.

"Thank you," I whispered. I drank half the bottle before coming up for air. I tried to keep the nerves in check. I glanced around the room. "How did I . . ."

"Get here? You don't remember?"

I shook my head and drank the rest of the bottle. On top of the nausea, I felt shaky and weak.

Luka studied me intently. "You got sick in the car. I decided to bring you back here so I could keep an eye on you."

My ears burned with embarrassment. "Oh, God, I'm sorry."

"It happens," he said casually. "How are you feeling?"

I pressed my lips together. I felt like garbage. Things were still moving too fast and I was sluggish. Yet I had to answer, because he stood beside the bed, waiting on me. "Not great," I mustered. "I'm so sorry, I didn't think . . . I had that much to drink."

He took the empty bottle from my hands. "You'll feel better if you have something to eat. Can you stand up?"

Something was . . . off. It took me a second to recognize he'd just asked me a question, rather than give me a command. And that brought the whole of the previous night flooding back to me in a hurry.

I wasn't a virgin anymore. I'd slept with Luka Markovic. This was literally the morning after, and he was offering me breakfast. No, wait. He'd coaxed and persuaded me last night, maybe even manipulated. Things had spiraled out of control and gone too far, and then he'd forced himself on me.

I swallowed hard. I needed to get out of here before I let it happen again.

My legs were shaky but worked well enough as I tugged my socks up, climbed out of the bed, and smoothed my hands over my rumpled costume. I had to look like a hot mess. There was a doorway off to the side and I could see the darkened bathroom beyond.

The bedroom I'd awoken in was timeless and elegant. The greens and golds reeked of sophistication, not the style of a mid-twenty-year-old man. He'd said this was one of the guest rooms, indicating there were multiple ones. I assumed it was his family home. Luka still lived with his parents?

"Can I?" I motioned to the bathroom.

"Sure. I put a shirt in there, in case you want to change." His gaze drifted downward to the dried stain on my waist.

My face heated again with shame. I'd thrown up and gotten it on myself. It looked like it had been cleaned, but still. "Thank you," I choked out and darted into the bathroom.

The dark eyeliner and shadow I'd layered on last night was smeared beneath my eyes. I looked awful. I pulled quickly at the ponytails, freeing my hair, and raked a hand through my unkempt strands, forcing them to lay flat. There was a men's white dress shirt folded neatly on the marble counter top, and after I'd finished scrubbing my eyes, I contemplated what to do.

It was Luka's shirt.

I'd expected an old t-shirt, not something so nice and formal. The fabric looked expensive. Was this a test? He'd figured me out last night when he said I wanted to look my best, so this had to be deliberate. I shed the white blouse and put on the dress shirt that was too big on me. The shirttails hung as long as my short skirt did.

Oh.

It *was* a test. I was fairly certain he was waiting to see if I'd come out wearing just his shirt and nothing else. Seductive. I couldn't, not in a million years. Instead I made do by rolling up the sleeves and leaving the top few buttons undone.

He casually noted my skirt still in place but said nothing. It looked stupid, but I needed to send the message. I wasn't happy about the way last night had gone, and had to put distance between us, even though I was wearing his beautiful shirt that smelled like him.

"Come on, I've got breakfast ready. You want coffee?"

I wanted to leave, but I also didn't want to be rude. I was grateful he hadn't dumped me off at the dorms, and he'd been different this morning. A cup of coffee wouldn't change what had happened, but it wouldn't kill me either. It'd make it easier to politely ask for a ride home, so I nodded.

I followed behind him out into the hallway where the décor was sophisticated. Dark wood, crown molding, and beautiful paintings decorated the long hall of closed doors and stairs to the right. My footfalls were quiet on the plush carpet as we wound down the curved staircase.

The entryway to the house was impressive. Daylight from oversized windows glanced off of the tiered crystal chandelier, positioned over a gorgeous wooden inlay in the hardwood floor. Obviously the car dealership business was going well for the Markovic family.

Luka either ignored my gawking, or didn't notice. We traipsed past the dining room that had enough seating for twelve, and turned into a gourmet kitchen which was state-of-the-art.

There was a table tucked to one side, which held two place settings and a full breakfast waiting to be served. Fresh fruit, pastries, bacon, and eggs. How had he prepared all this?

I stood dumbfounded as he slipped into one of the chairs and set about pouring his coffee. He added cream and sugar, and when he realized I hadn't moved, his gaze turned up to mine. "You going to join me?"

There was an edge to his words, as if trying to walk a fine line between polite and commanding. I couldn't help but feel like he was restraining his true self, the version I'd seen last night. I took the chair across from him and watched him pour my cup. It was all so . . . adult-like.

"If you want something else, let me know. My chef keeps the kitchen stocked, so she can make almost anything."

My chef. Sweet Jesus. I stared down at my steaming cup, not wanting to say anything because I worried I'd sound like the poor, naïve girl I was. I added sugar and cream, stirring until the coffee turned a milk chocolate color.

"Tell me about your family," Luka said as I was mid-sip.

I swallowed and it seared down my throat. "My family?"

"Yes. I want to know everything about you. We'll start with your family." This he said in the tone I was more familiar with. An order, not a request.

I paused, my hand lingering on the handle to my mug as I considered his demand. He wanted to know everything about me? Why? A weird tickle crept up the back of my neck. "There's not much to say. They're pretty normal."

"Are your parents still together? Siblings?"

"Yeah," I said. "And yes. I've got a younger brother."

"Are you close?"

"In age, or relationship?"

"Both." Luka took a sip of his coffee, but his gaze was fixed on mine.

"No, not really. Jonathan is four years younger." My tone was clipped. We were night and day different.

Luka's focus sharpened. "Tell me about him."

My forehead wrinkled with skepticism. "You want to know about my brother?"

"You're an easy read, Addison. What's the deal with your brother?"

I scowled, not enjoying how good Luka was at cutting straight through my subtext. I was too hungover and off balance to muster much of a fight. "Jonathan's senior class elected him homecoming king last week."

"And?"

How was I going to explain it? My gaze wandered away to glance out the window. Beyond the large, pristinely maintained back yard, the house backed up to a golf course. Of course it did. I squinted against the sunlight, which made my headache throb.

"Tell me why that bothers you," Luka said. This time his tone was more forceful.

I sighed and swung my focus back to the man who kept me on edge. "Because things come easy for him. He doesn't struggle to make friends. He always knows the right thing to say and the right thing to do." I sounded jealous, because I was. "Everyone *loves* Jonathan."

"You struggle to make friends?" He asked it lightly, and I *had* said it, but it stung, regardless. I didn't want anyone pointing out what I didn't excel at.

So I didn't answer. Instead I grabbed a bagel from the tray of pastries and busied myself slathering it in cream cheese. No one was as driven or focused as I was, or had priorities as warped as mine. Therefore, I struggled terribly to make friends.

"Vasilije is the same as your brother. And that's . . ." His voice was surprisingly low and hesitant, but then his expression firmed up. "Friends are overrated."

I considered his statement critically. It sounded like a defensive response a person without friends would say. And although I told myself I didn't need friends, I also didn't believe it.

Luka hadn't touched the large spread of food. He crossed his arms over his chest. "Do you usually go home on the weekends?"

Randhurst wasn't a suitcase school, where the students went home on Fridays. It was private, and expensive, and had offered me the largest scholarship out of all my choices. It pulled from all over the country, was large and nice, and there was plenty to do with the campus being only an hour outside of Chicago. It was enough of a draw that students typically didn't want to leave.

Plus . . . "No. I don't have a car."

"Where are you from?"

I chewed a bite of my bagel and swallowed slowly. What was with the twenty questions? "Mokena. It's a suburb on the south side of the city."

"I know where it is." He took another sip of his coffee and set the mug down with a soft thud. "Why pre-med?"

"Why does it feel like you're interrogating me?"

He blinked slowly, and his eyes were so damn calculating, it made my heart race. "Maybe that's what this is now. You're the one who's defensive while I'm just trying to make conversation."

I didn't believe it for one second. There was an angle he was playing at, I was sure of it.

"Or maybe," he continued, "I'm working up to ask you a question I'm pretty sure will make you stop talking, so I'm trying to get what I can out of you before that happens."

I TENSED. "What? What question?"

Luka looked annoyed. "I just told you, we'll work up to it. First, I want to know why you want to be a doctor."

My appetite waned as I stared at him. Perhaps the morning had thrown him off. Maybe he was one of those people who couldn't get going until they had a cup of coffee, because now the Luka from last night was back in full force. The dark edge in his eyes and the commanding tone filled his voice, which was so good at pushing me.

"Do you already know what kind you want to be?"

"Yes," I said quietly. "A surgeon."

His face filled with surprise, and then the corner of his mouth lifted in half of a smile. "Oh, I see."

"What do you see?" My tone was laced with sarcasm.

"You don't want to go into the medical field to offer comfort and compassion. You're doing it for the challenge."

I swallowed a breath. How in the hell? I faked disdain. "What are you talking about?"

"My cousin's a nurse and she hates surgeons. Says they all have God complexes in the operating room." Luka put his elbows on the table and leaned forward. "They live to cut."

I sighed. "I understand what you're saying." I'd seen it with my own eyes at the hospital where I volunteered. "A lot of surgeons can be arrogant jackasses, but it's necessary. You want confidence from the person who's going to have to cut you to help you heal."

"So, they're, what? Excused from being assholes, because their position demands confidence?"

It felt like he was laying a trap for me, but I answered anyway. "Yes."

A shiver glanced down my back when Luka appeared pleased. "And what about you? Will your patients think you're an asshole?"

"No."

"Why not?"

Because I lacked the confidence needed, and . . . "Because I care way more than I should about what people think of me."

His half-smile was back, this time accompanied by a shake of his head, as if what I was saying was too good to be true.

"And to answer your original question," I continued, "I've always wanted to be a doctor. I loved my AP anatomy class in high school. I loved working in the ER on Friday nights when it was the busiest. And I've watched tons of different medical procedures, most of which I found fascinating."

There just wasn't any other career for me, and it made me realize I had no idea what career Luka was in. I'd allow this one question before pressing him again on whatever he was working up to.

"And you? What do you do?"

His eye color wasn't quite so dark in the sunlight, but he still looked intense. "I'm the controller at Markovic Motors." I wasn't sure what he meant exactly, and it must have been evident, because he continued. "I'm the head accountant."

"Oh." He seemed young to hold such a high position, but he'd gotten his MBA from Randhurst, which was an excellent school.

Nepotism may have played a role as well, although he seemed serious and older than his years. I forced myself to refocus. Breakfast conversation needed to move forward, and I needed to get back to my dorm. "Ask me the question, please."

He looked resigned as he rose to stand, took a final sip of his coffee, and pushed his chair in. "We'll go upstairs first."

It filled me with anxiety. "Why?"

"Because your shoes and shirt are up there?" His tone was pointed.

Tension released in my shoulders. We were getting ready to leave. I stood, pushed in my chair, and glanced up at him. "Thank you for breakfast."

My gratuity had no impact on him. I shuffled in my socks up the stairs and down the hallway to the room I'd slept in. I didn't remember coming in last night, and wondered if he'd had to carry me, but I wasn't going to ask.

Luka stood in the doorway watching as I gathered my costume shirt from the bathroom, and he pointed out my pair of black heels at the foot of the queen-sized bed. As I reached down to grab them—

"Tell me what you remember about last night." His voice was deadly serious and my lungs tightened in my chest.

I abandoned my goal of picking up my heels and turned to face him. He had one hand on either side of the doorframe. It was a casual stance that displayed the lean lines of his body, but it was threatening as well. His positioning made me feel trapped. Words were difficult.

"Do you remember going upstairs with me?" he asked.

"Yes." I hated how timid my voice sounded.

His expression was free of any emotion, but his eyes betrayed him. He looked nervous. "Do you remember kissing me on the couch?"

His nerves made mine worse, and my heart beat at a frantic tempo. "I remember a lot more than just kissing."

His grip tightened until his knuckles were white. "I'm going to ask you that question now, and I need you to think carefully about how you answer. You have to be completely honest." He took a deep breath. "Do you remember us fucking?"

Every muscle in me locked up at the memory of what we'd done last night. He'd stolen my virginity, hurt me, and now he was callously describing it as fucking. It made me so angry I could barely see straight. "No," I said, finding my voice, and it was powerful. "I remember you raping me."

"Shit," he groaned. "Addison, that's not how it happened."

I balled my fists into the shirt in my hands. "I said stop."

"And I did," he answered quickly. His chest was moving quicker now too, breathing rapidly.

"I said no." I clenched the shirt so tightly my hands began to ache. "I kept saying no, even when you put your hand over my mouth to keep me quiet."

"*Fuck.*" His hands came down off the doorframe and he took a step toward me. "Yeah, maybe I got a little carried away last night. I drank too, remember? But we both wanted it. Don't tell me you didn't." I backpedaled as he advanced on me. "We'd both been wanting it for years."

I shook my head as a tremble worked its way up my legs. "Not like that."

He paused where he was in the center of the room,

disappointment etching his face. "Tell me what I can do to make it right."

Make it right? There was no going back. He was smart, surely he knew that. "There's nothing, Luka. You can't undo it."

He held my gaze for so long, I wondered if he was broken. He didn't move an inch.

"No," he said finally, his voice grim. "I can't." His posture slumped as if crushed by an enormous weight, and he raked a hand through his dark hair, leaving it askew. "And I don't suppose there's anything I can say to change your mind?"

"About whether or not you raped me?" I choked on my words. Why was I calling him out like this, goading him? It was dangerous and stupid.

He snapped up straight and his eyes narrowed. "Don't use that word again."

I bit down on my tongue for reinforcement. He turned away from me and paced across the room, then back my direction. His forehead wrinkled as if he were deep in thought.

"Look," I said. "I'm hungover. I need a shower and a change of clothes. Drive me home and maybe I can move past what happened." It was a total lie, but I wanted to get the hell out of here.

His motion ceased, and his piercing gaze ensnared me, but it wasn't like before. There was a new emotion I hadn't seen. It looked very much like cold, hard fury.

Oh, shit! I stumbled back as he stormed forward, and I slammed into the wall so hard the picture hanging beside me bounced and rattled on its hook. Luka's hands were rough on my hips, pinning me to the wall, and he brought us nose to nose.

"You don't lie to me, ever. Understood?"

"You're hurting me," I gasped. His grip was uncomfortable on my waist. "Please. Just take me home."

I shook beneath his hands, but I stopped all movement as he leaned in, placing his cheek against mine, and whispered in my ear, his tone dark and full of malice. "You are home."

When he released his grip, I was in so much shock I almost slid to the floor. He went to the bedroom door and threw it shut with a loud crash. I pushed off the wall, crippled by panic.

I almost shrieked it. "What the hell are you talking about?"

"This is the situation now. My family can't afford for you to go to the cops, especially after the shit Vasilije got into."

"Okay, I won't—"

He held up his hand, cutting me off. "Maybe you wouldn't at first, but you could change your mind at any time, and I can't risk it. You were clear about what you *think* happened."

My panic made it hard to stay rational, and hearing him dismiss what he'd done was almost as bad as the act itself.

"You raped me."

He sneered, and his rage-filled expression was terrifying. "Did I not warn you about that word?"

He grabbed a handful of the shirt I was wearing, his expensive dress shirt, and hauled me up to him. I flattened my hands on the wall of his chest, bracing myself. And then his hands closed on the open collar, one on either side, and he ripped downward. A few of the buttons flew off, while others simply gave way.

I was too stunned to do anything but gasp at the sexual violence. My brain was paralyzed with fear. Instinctively, I tried to get away, but once the shirt had been torn open, he continued to pull it down my arms. It became a rope around my elbows, holding me in place.

"Stop!" My heart was pounding in my ears. My throat was a desert, and I trembled to the point I could barely stand. I fought him to pull the shirt back up and cover my bra. "What are you doing?"

"You've lost this privilege."

No, no! A panicked cry tore from my throat as he tugged the shirt the rest of the way down my arms. At least with them free I could fight back. I swung, slapping at his face and chest, but he quickly snatched up my wrists. He clenched them so hard I yelped and bent to try to alleviate the ache.

"Luka, no," I yelled. "Stop."

His face was an emotionless mask. "You don't have control over this situation. You can make it easier on yourself by accepting it." His grip pushed me toward his feet, forcing me downward. "Kneel."

"What? No!"

"Yes," he snapped. "I gave you an order."

My response was instantaneous. "Yeah? You and your order can go to hell."

He let go of my wrists and shoved my shoulders down, forcing me onto my knees. When I struggled to get up, his firm hands held me down. "When I tell you to do something, you do it."

"Are you out of your—"

"No more talking. Disobey, and you'll be punished."

His expression was serious, but . . . really? He expected me to just do as he said, after what he'd done? The words burned in my throat. "Let me go."

It happened so fast. His hands dipped behind me and undid

the bra clasp on my back. My palms flew up to hold the bra cups in place so I could cover myself, and his action effectively trapped me. I couldn't take my hands off without exposing my breasts. He gripped my shoulders once more, holding me on my knees as I stared up at him, shocked.

Why was he doing this? Words failed me, and when I was silent for a few long seconds, he let out a breath. "Good. I'm going to take my hands away, but you'll stay like this."

He obviously wasn't as smart as I thought, and I was grateful. As soon as his grip was gone, I slid my hands behind my back and hooked the bra closed, while attempting to climb to my feet. I moved as fast as I possibly could—

The result was I ended up face-down on the bed, the comforter smashed against my nose, and it was hard to breathe.

Shit, shit, *shit!* I scrambled up on my arms, but his strong body crushed against mine, pinning my hips to the edge of the bed. And he'd been ready for me to try it because his hands seized my wrists and wrenched my arms behind my back. Without support, I flopped down on the mattress, which muffled my startled cry.

I wasn't going to allow this to happen. *Goddamnnit, fight!* I slammed my heel down on the top of his foot. He grunted with displeasure, and suddenly red-hot, excruciating pain radiated up my arm. The agony of him twisting my wrist stole my breath and made me into a statue.

"Don't do that again," he ordered in his harsh, deep voice. "Fighting me is pointless." There was a loud smack as his palm connected with my backside, delivering a blow. "You're mine now."

Chapter
SEVEN

Luka's terrifying words twisted in my mind and a glacier crept in to surround me.

"This is how it is," he said, devoid of emotion. "It's going to be hard, but we'll get through it. You'll do what I say, whether you want to or not."

"I won't! Get your hands off of me!"

His grip twisted, sending more fire along my arms. "You will, or, as I already told you, you'll be punished." He used his foot to kick my feet further apart and pressed me down into the mattress. "Hold this position."

My brain emptied of coherent thought when the back of my skirt was lifted. When I tried to break free, his hand came down and slapped against my ass, stinging me through my panties. I choked on air and froze. He used my panic to position me again, pushing me into the mattress so my back was flat and straight.

"Perfect." His single word, uttered in a low voice, made me tremble. "In fact, prove to me how perfect you are, Addison." His tone mocked me. "Tell me pi to the eighth decimal place."

It was as if my brain hit a wall going sixty miles an hour. "*What*?"

He slapped his palm against my already flushed skin, and this one really, really hurt. "Pi to the eighth decimal place. Now."

I whimpered. Was he fucking serious? I swallowed a breath and forced my mind to cooperate. Maybe if I got through this bizarre exercise, he'd let me go. "Three," I said in a shaky, confused voice, "point one four . . . one five . . ." I didn't want to think about the number, I wanted to think about what was happening. I needed to think about escape, but it was like he was doing this to control every part of me. "Two—"

Even before I felt the lash of his hand, I knew I had screwed up, and it made it worse. I tensed for the blow and he didn't disappoint. I cried out right after the loud smack of skin hitting skin.

"Nine!" I said. "Three point one four one five *nine* two."

"That six places. You've got two more."

I bit down on my wavering lip and pinched my eyes shut. I had no idea what number came after two.

"I'm waiting."

"I . . . don't know," I admitted.

I expected him to deliver another strike, but instead he rattled off the full thing in a blur. In my confusion, I couldn't process what he'd said.

"Pi to the eighth decimal," he ordered.

Unexpected tears burned in my eyes. I still had no idea. "Can you repeat—"

His hand scooped beneath the band of my bra and he pulled so hard, I heard threads ripping. It forced me up and I arched my back to keep my arms from hurting more than they already did.

"Three point one four." He let go of the bra band and the elastic snapped against my back. "One five nine two." His arm curled around my body, shoving a hand inside my bra. "Six." His fingers circled my nipple and pinched. "Five."

Teeth latched onto my neck as his pinch on my nipple suddenly turned white-hot with pain. I cried out and went limp. Luka put his hand on the center of my back and shoved me on the bed, back into the position I'd been in before.

"Three point one four one five nine two six five." It spilled from my lips without thought. I just wanted it over. His hold on my wrists eased away, and I left them there, crossed behind my back. They'd gone too numb to move anyway.

As soon as he stepped back from me, I slid down the bed, collapsing into a puddle on the floor. I dug my fingertips into the thick carpet, trying to ground myself. To hold myself together.

Things went hazy.

"Shh," a voice whispered in my ear. "It's over. We won't have to do that again."

I was sitting on the bed, and Luka's arms were around me. Holding me in an embrace. Was I having traumatic delusions? I wondered what the hell his statement meant.

His lips feathered kisses over the curve of my neck, and he continued to whisper soft, reassuring words that only made my confusion worse. My hands clung to his forearm, holding him tight to me, which was in direct conflict of what I wanted. His fingertips brushed against my bare shoulder, and it made my skin crawl. I hated him touching me this way. Softly, as if I were something he cared about.

My mind screamed in protest, but my outer shell stayed hard and silent.

His expression had been unassuming, but layer by layer, his gaze went cold. The shift that went through him was obvious. Whatever game he was playing with me had just resumed. The bed we were on sat in the corner of the room so I was trapped. I couldn't get off without him stopping me, so I'd have to bide my time.

"What's your plan?" he asked lazily.

I stared at him. He didn't deserve anything from me, including the sound of my voice.

"For escape?" he continued. "You're smart, I'm sure you'll try. But let me fill you in on the reality." He brought his face level with mine. "Assuming you make it to an exit, the house has a security system and alerts are sent to my phone. You won't be able to get a door or window open without me knowing about it. And once you get outside, then what? Where will you go?" He scrubbed a hand over his jawline. "The house isn't close to anyone else."

He climbed off the bed and pointed to the bathroom.

"Come on, let's get you cleaned up."

When I didn't move, his shoulders lifted and fell in a sigh.

"Addison." His tone was harsh. "Do what I tell you, or I'll make you. I didn't really enjoy what just happened, but it was necessary, and I'll do it again if I have to."

I shuddered and tried not to think about it. My lower body was on fire from where he'd spanked me. I was too shell-shocked to go through it again, and forced my body to cooperate. So I moved like a zombie into the bathroom, and stood beside the sink with my arms crossed over my chest, as if it could shelter my bra-clad breasts from his eyes. He went to the large whirlpool tub and ran the tap, adjusting the water temperature. The rushing water was the only sound in the room as he filled the bath.

While he waited, he stood and rested his hands on his hips, his attention focused on me. I couldn't hold his gaze. I blinked rapidly, staring at the wall. It was so unfair. Yesterday I would have quivered over how good he looked. His strong arms and trim frame was accentuated beneath the fitted t-shirt, and jeans which hung perfectly on his hips. Now I cowered in fear, simply from his intense stare.

"Take off your clothes."

I clutched my arms tighter around myself, and my pulse began to climb.

His footsteps signaled his approach, and I sensed the shadow blocking out the light, but I refused to look at him. So I flinched when his warm fingertips lightly touched my shoulder. I stood motionless as those fingers curled over my bra strap and began to drag it down.

He's already seen you, I thought bitterly. *Let him think there are no more surprises from you, and use it to escape.*

My arms were pried slowly from my chest, and as the cup of my bra was pulled down, his mouth closed on my neck. What the fuck was he doing? He'd raped me last night, assaulted me moments ago, and his soft, gentle attitude now crossed the wires in my brain. I couldn't handle it.

He unhooked the bra and pulled it away from my shuddering chest. I was heaving my breath, struggling to remain indifferent. I'd pushed him earlier and he'd escalated, so maybe if I did nothing, he'd leave me alone.

It was a different kind of assault like this. His warm, needy mouth carved a line down my sensitive neck, and by the time he reached my breasts, my nipples had tightened. I'd turned away from him and stared at the counter, but his tongue on the bud of flesh forced my gaze up and into the mirror. I watched as he bent me back over his arm so he could better suck on my nipple.

The image was shocking. Even with his eyes closed, he

looked like he was in rapture. His pink tongue laved at my breast, then his mouth covered it. My eyes rimmed with red, threatening tears, and in his powerful arms I looked tiny. But my body . . . it responded to him, regardless. I hated it, and hated how I couldn't stop my response even more.

He found the button at the top of my skirt and undid it, and the fabric fluttered to a puddle at my feet. My teeth chattered as Luka eased me backward until my back was cold against the wall, and he sank to his knees.

I couldn't stop staring at the large mirror over the double sinks in disbelief. I barely recognized myself. My chestnut-colored hair was wild and streamed down past my shoulders, stopping just before the swell of my breasts. His broad back and dark head of hair blocked most of my lower body from view but it registered that he was tugging my panties down.

Somehow he'd stolen the fight from me.

There was barely any left once he had my underwear down around my ankles. I leaned against the wall as his palms slid over my legs, slowly working the knee-high socks off too, until I was completely naked. I flattened my hands against the wallpaper, pressing my clammy palms into the smooth paper.

"Look at me."

He said it just loud enough to be heard over the rushing water, and I wondered if the noise had thrown his voice off. It had almost sounded like a request. My gaze reluctantly left the mirror, where everything seemed like it wasn't quite happening to me, and found him.

Luka's jaw was set and his dark eyes were devastating. "Addison. You're so fucking beautiful."

What? I bit down on my lip to keep from
I closed my eyes and my head thudded bac
This was manipulation. Some sort of tactic t
off balance.

I moaned with shock as his warm face nuzzled between my
legs, and dug my fingers into his shoulders, trying to drive him
back. I didn't want his invasive kiss there, even if it had felt good
last night. Everything had changed since then.

He ignored my whimper, pressed further, and his wet tongue
caressed my sensitive, swollen flesh. I flinched and jolted, but his
hands were tight on my hips. Goosebumps pebbled on my skin,
not from the cold. The room was warm and humid from the running bath. My knees softened and I slid an inch down the wall,
trying not to let his bizarre seduction faze me.

He moaned, and the fluttering of his tongue picked up intensity. The quaking in my legs worked its way to my core and
threatened to collapse me. He'd brought me pain and fear, but I
wouldn't allow him to add pleasure to his list. I popped my eyes
open and search for something to distract.

The tub was getting full. If he stayed kneeling, it'd overflow
and could be a big enough distraction to use for escape. He could
be lying about there being no other place around. Or maybe I
didn't need to escape. Maybe it was as simple as finding a landline
to call for help, even though I had no clue where I was.

It wasn't an easy task, pretending to submit to him, but I
stepped my feet apart, giving him more room and encouraging
him to stay on his knees.

Luka stopped. He tilted his head and looked up at me with
curious surprise. The visual of him on his knees in front of my

d body stopped my breath. How the hell had we gotten here? This had been my fantasy before, and now it made me want to weep.

He pulled up to his feet so he was looming over me, and brought his mouth, wet with my taste, to mine. The kiss was passionate and desperate from him. What was I supposed to do? Did he expect me to kiss him back? Because it'd be a cold day in hell before that happened. I wanted to distract him, but this I couldn't play along with. His hands slid up to frame my face, but I broke the kiss. He blinked once and straightened, looking momentarily like he was coming down off of a high.

"Come on, get in." He left me there, naked and trembling on the wall. He went to the bath, turned the handles on the tub, and shut off the water.

I'd never felt more vulnerable or humiliated. My feet refused to work, so he put a hand under my elbow and forced me to step over the edge and put my feet in the water. He guided me down until I was sitting with my knees bent, and I hugged them to my chest. The water was pleasantly warm, but not hot, and I was grateful as I huddled in the bath. The sting against my abused skin would have been worse if it had been hot.

Luka sat on the edge of the tub, a hand resting casually on his jeans, and watched me with a face that was an emotionless mask. Less than a minute ago he'd kissed me as if he were hungry and wild, and now he looked bored. There was no point trying to figure him out. I hated him. That was all I needed to remember.

"I need to know your class schedule, and if there are group meetings you're participating in."

I stared blankly at the old scar on my knee from a fall at

summer camp when I was ten.

When he became aware I wasn't going to answer him, Luka issues an exasperated sigh. "You're upset, I understand."

Holy understatement of the century. But still, outwardly I stayed cold and robotic.

"But I don't think you get how this works." He put his palm on my cheek and forced my gaze onto him. "I can't let you leave. As long as you're in my house, it's my rules. If you don't do as told, there will be consequences."

Is that what had just gone down in the bedroom? *Consequences*? I shivered, and then steeled my body not to betray me again. I wanted him to believe his words had no effect. To pretend Luka Markovic had no control over me.

"How hard these next few days are, depends completely on you." His palm slid away, but I was snagged in his web, unable to drop his gaze. "The more you fight, the worse it will get. Just accept I am in control now. I own everything." He made a production of sweeping his gaze downward. "Your body. Your time. Even your choices. Those are all mine now, Addison."

My eyes burned "*No*" a thousand times over, and I clenched my teeth so hard I was about to crack my jaw.

"Your class schedule," he said again, this time with a demanding edge.

Instead of answering, I sank down in the tub, dipping my head beneath the surface of the water. It was nice to get away from him. He was saying something, but it was too muffled and distant underwater for me to understand. I stayed under as long as my lungs would allow, and finally reluctantly resurfaced.

"—of this, stop being so dramatic." Annoyance flared in his

eyes, and the eyebrow shot up into his dissatisfied arch.

I pushed the wet hair back from my face and listened to the water sloshing, rather than the rapist looming over me.

"You'll tell me your schedule, goddamnit, or I'm going to—"

I took a deep breath and ducked down under the water once more. I floated in the warm, weightless space and pretended none of what was happening was real.

A hand latched onto my throat, holding me down, and instantly I panicked. I shouted a stream of bubbles and kicked, flailing in the water, and I clawed at the forearm holding me down. My hands were slippery, and as soon as I got a hold, Luka's other hand peeled it off. *Oh my God!* My lungs begged for air and I thrashed wildly.

I'd just gotten my feet beneath me when Luka splashed into the tub, clothes and all, dropping his full weight on my hips, and locked me down. *Oh, fuck!* I was dangerously close to drowning. I choked in a mouthful of water the last second before he yanked me up. I gasped and sputtered, coughing out the water.

"Cut the shit, Addison. I'm not even asking you something hard!"

I blinked through the water running down my face. Luka looked furious, and his t-shirt was soaked in spots, no doubt from my wild thrashing. His grip stayed tight around my throat and I wrapped both of my hands on his forearm. His free hand grasped the edge of the tub, where his knuckles had gone white, and I had the terrible feeling he'd put me back under again if I didn't answer him.

We balanced dangerously on the edge.

Water rippled back and forth and settled while our gazes

were fixated on each other, wordlessly daring the other to keep pushing back. Would he do it? Did that kind of darkness exist in Luka? It wasn't that I had a death wish, but the adrenaline pumping in my system and what he'd put me through made me reckless.

I had to know exactly who I was dealing with.

Wet hair was plastered to my forehead, so I took one of my hands off of him and slowly, calmly, reached up to wipe the strands out of my eyes. Giving him a good, hard look at my defiant glare. *That's right. There's no answer coming from me.*

"Son of a bitch," he snarled.

A shallow breath was all I could suck in before he shoved my head down under the water.

Chapter
EIGHT

I SLAPPED AT LUKA'S FACE, scratched, and tore at his soaking shirt. It was in vain. Real terror exploded through me as the seconds crawled by and he didn't release his hold. The fingers around my neck were tight and choking. My stupid desire to see how far he'd go was going to come true.

He'd actually do it. Luka was fully capable of murder.

My legs kicked at the floor of the tub, desperate to find a hold, and my goal of hurting him shifted to trying to stay alive. I couldn't think over the roar of my heartbeat in my ears or the overpowering urge to find air.

This was it. All of my work was for nothing. I'd never get my doctorate, or pick up a scalpel in an operating room, because my life was going to end in a bathtub under his brutal hand.

Abruptly, I was lifted from the water, but nothing worked. My panicked belief I was going to drown had rendered me too paralyzed to remember how to breathe. He reared back, and the sharp slap of his palm across my cheek was what I needed. The sting forced me to gasp in air and brought me back to full consciousness.

"Fuck," he said with enormous relief. He dropped his hold, slid backward, and sat opposite me in the tub, his soaked jeans clinging to his legs as the water sloshed violently around us. His chest lifted and fell quickly, as if breathing hard.

I coughed, and coughed again, shaking the water from my lungs. My throat burned and my legs ached from thrashing against the marble. In fact, every inch of my body hurt. I curled up into the fetal position to make my body as small as possible. The bath was large but not really built for two, and I didn't want any part of him touching me.

There was a thump as he pushed and released the stopper, and water gurgled down the drain. I lay in the corner of the oval tub, shivering and trembling, with my eyes shut tight. Water, or possibly tears, streaked down my face, but I didn't dare move.

"Addison."

The soft sound of my name in his voice made me flinch. I clutched my arms tighter around my body, and tucked my head. I'd retreat as much as possible.

It was utterly silent.

I waited for him to lash out, but he climbed out of the tub. There were sopping noises as he took off his wet clothes and hurled them to the tile floor. A towel was pulled down off a rack, clothes were gathered up, and wet footsteps padded away.

I stayed in the tub until all the water was gone and my skin turned to ice. There were no sounds from the bedroom. Had he left me? Was this some new sort of game or test?

The towel I yanked down was thick and soft against my chilled skin, but it didn't offer comfort. I banded it tight around my shivering body and stared at the floor. He hadn't just taken his clothes when he'd gone—he'd taken everything of mine except for the plain black panties. I stepped into them and pulled them up.

Last night he'd cornered me on the stairs and demanded I think of him when I ached between my legs, and today it was impossible not to. I didn't want to give him the satisfaction, but how could I get rid of him in my mind, after the last twelve hours? I squeezed the towel through my hair, drying it as best I could, then draped the luxurious fabric under my arms to cover myself, took in a deep breath, and stepped out into the bedroom.

Luka sat on the same loveseat as he had this morning, only now he wore a new pair of jeans and simple evergreen colored t-shirt. He stood when I came into view, and his heavy, angry gaze was crushing.

I stared at his feet and watched them approach. I didn't fight him as he grasped the towel, pulled it away, and made a production of dropping it to the floor. My cheeks burned red. I wasn't comfortable being naked in front of Avery, and even though this was just my breasts, it was far worse being exposed in front of Luka. I continued to watch his bare feet as he went to and retrieved the wadded dress shirt he'd ripped off of me earlier.

"Put this on."

I took it in my trembling hands and hurried to slip my arms into the sleeves. When I went to do up one of the buttons that hadn't popped off, his hands closed on mine.

"It stays open."

And his hands remained clasping mine. When I tried to pull back, his grip went firm.

"Your schedule," he said.

I swallowed back the cry in my throat, which was a terrible, painful lump, and finally met his gaze. I'd expected more anger, but there wasn't any. His eyes were . . . vacant.

Wait, no. Not vacant. Curious, perhaps. It gave him a clinical look, like he was studying me with unsure, scientific eyes. He let go and immediately moved to cradle my face in his hands.

"All right. Let's try a different approach," he said softly.

His gentle kiss was the harshest blow he could deliver. His lips sealed over mine, and tried to coerce my participation, but I went rigid under the power of his mouth. He shifted my head, positioning me to a better angle, and attempted the kiss once more. The longer I endured it, the more frantic he became. As if I had issued a challenge and he was determined to meet it.

Why did it have to be like this? If I gave in, just a fraction of an inch, would I succumb to him as I did last night? With absolutely no effort on my part, the way he kissed me now was dangerous. The sick part of my mind, the one that I'd thought was only tequila-induced, whispered to me in my completely sober state. *Give in a little. At this point, what does it matter? He only pushes you when you say no.*

The decision wasn't made consciously; at least, I didn't think it was. My lips parted minutely, and Luka answered ten-fold. His tongue claimed my mouth, and his thumbs moved, sweeping over my cheekbones. The intensity of the kiss flared and burned wildly hot. There was a loud intake of breath from him. A sound announcing Luka was pleased I was allowing this to happen.

But it was all too much.

Too wrong.

"No," I whispered, and jerked back. A single word, which clearly meant nothing to him.

He paused, lingering close. "So I can get a response out of you after all." His voice was low and uneven, though, which meant I could draw one from him as well. Was there any comfort in that?

"I won't tell anyone," I said. "I promise."

His expression was resigned. "Even if I believed that, which I really don't, I already told you. I can't risk it." He released me and stepped back, and his cold veneer was installed back in place. "I'm going to explain to you how I see this working. Sit down."

He didn't tell me where, so I sat on the edge of the bed, clenching the dress shirt closed. Luka remained standing, and rested a hand on a hip while his other combed through his hair.

"I'm going to set benchmarks for you," he said. "Each one you pass earns you a new privilege. The first one is clothes. The next will be leaving this room." His logical tone was free of emotion. "Eventually, we'll have enough trust and you can leave the house."

Two thoughts stormed into my mind instantly. He'd let me leave? And...

"Trust?" Short, inappropriate laughter burst from me, but then my tone went flat. "You must have a short memory. You just tried to kill me in the bathtub."

His eyes narrowed a degree. "No, I knew what I was doing. In fact, I'm trying very hard to avoid your death."

I was more confused and disoriented than I'd ever been in my life, and anxiety constricted my vocal cords. "What the hell does that mean?"

His brow furrowed. "Focus. I've been up all night reading. Everything said training can take a long time, maybe even months, but I bet you can do it in under a week."

"Training?" My heart stumbled. "For what?"

"Your behavior. I'm going to modify it to suit our arrangement."

Like last night, all I could do was parrot back his keywords. "Arrangement?"

Before he could answer, his cellphone rang. Luka stared at

the screen as if considering whether or not to answer. He wasn't overly expressive, but it was clear he wasn't happy about who was calling. He put his finger to his lips and gave me a dark glare, warning me to stay quiet, before tapping the screen and pressing it to his ear.

"Hello?" he said, his tone gruff. He began to pace as the conversation began, and Luka looked visibly agitated. "It was . . . fine. I ran into a situation last night—" He finished a circuit of the room and his gaze froze on me. "No, actually, it had nothing to do with him."

It sounded like he was talking about Vasilije. Was this Luka's father, and was I the situation?

"It was just a miscommunication between me and a girl. It's nothing. I've handled it."

I stared down at the dress shirt wrapped on my body, which had become damp from the ends of my hair dripping on it. This was handled? Rape and water torture were *handled* for Luka Markovic?

"It's not necessary," he said quickly, and his expression flooded with exasperation. "Okay, fine."

He hung up, pocketed the phone, and I was struck by how much older he seemed. He was four, or maybe five years older than I was, physically. But mentally? I felt like we were far apart, and it was shocking. I wasn't arrogant. I tried to stay humble, but the fact of the matter was I was smart. I was accustomed to being more mature than my peers, even the ones older than I was.

Not Luka. The age gap for once felt like a real gap. As if his world was vastly different from mine.

"First benchmark," Luka said, his expression guarded. "I

know you won't like it, but understand it's a means to an end. We build trust and then this whole thing can work."

"What are you—" My throat closed up as he bent over and retrieved something from the other side of the loveseat. The thick, multicolored cord was in a large loop, waiting to be unfurled.

"There are two ways this can go," he said, unraveling the rope. "They both end with you tied to the bed. One is easy. You lie down and let me do this. The other is unpleasant."

The dark cast to his face told me he wasn't joking in the slightest. My gaze went to the wooden headboard. There were cutouts by the posts where it would be easy for him to tether me down, and I tensed. The thought activated my flight-or-fight response, and I glanced to the door. I'd never get past him.

So I turned, sought his black eyes, and silently begged him not to, but it was a lost cause. Luka wasn't going to be persuaded.

"You can do this," he urged. "You're so fucking perfect, I know you can."

He wasn't condescending, but sincere. His misplaced compliment knocked me sideways.

"It'll only be for a little while," he added.

I was exhausted, both mentally and physically, and my fatigue made me weak. Inside I issued a sob of self-pity and loathing, but on the outside I stayed numb. Oh, holy hell, I was actually considering it.

"Why?" I asked.

"Because I need to leave this room to get you new clothes."

He waited. If I obeyed, he promised there'd be no consequences. I moved hesitantly to lie down on the bed, resting my towel-dried hair on the pillow.

Luka blinked, visibly surprised by what he was seeing. He'd expected a fight, but I felt broken. I gave up a little. And although I was going to allow it, my muscles solidified as he came cautiously closer. We each watched the other with unease.

Could he feel my trembling as I surrendered my first wrist to him? I pressed my lips together and forced back the tears that threatened in my eyes. His face went serious with concentration as he corded the rope around my wrist and tied the first knot.

"Is it too tight?" he asked.

I hurried to wipe a disobedient tear away with my free hand and struggled to keep it together. "It's fine."

He hesitated for a sliver of a second, but then the moment was gone. The rope was threaded through the cutout by the post, and secured. A giant, invisible weight sat on my chest, making it hard to breathe.

Again, Luka waited. He could take my free wrist easily now since my other was bound, but it was obvious he thought it was my responsibility to offer it. I did, feeling even more broken inside. I was ashamed to submit to him.

The thick cord wasn't rough, and he didn't tie it too tightly, but being restrained was terrifying, and I stared up at him. He looked . . . fascinated. His gaze swept down along my body. As it slowly drifted back up again, his eyes were heated and he shifted on his feet. Was that excitement hiding in his expression?

"Are you scared?" he asked.

It was immediate from me. "Yes."

"Don't be. Nothing bad is going to happen to you like this."

The naïve girl in me wanted to believe him, but I told myself I knew better. He'd turn on me any second and make me regret this foolish decision. I picked a point on the ceiling and focused on it, rather than him, so I could think about the situation. The goal was to build trust, he'd said. I would fake it enough until Luka allowed me to leave, or gave me an opportunity to escape.

He'd told me he was going to get me new clothes, but he hovered at the side of the bed. "Christ, you're something to look at, tied to a bed, wearing nothing but my shirt to cover your gorgeous body." His appreciative tone was deep and rich. "We're going to reach a point where you want this."

My eyes widened and I turned to him. Was he crazy? "Being tied up? *Doubtful.*"

I couldn't get away when he leaned over and cased my head in his hands, holding me still. There was a bizarre electric charge in the air. Him in complete control, me at his mercy.

"I'm going to show you all sorts of things, like how much pleasure this body is capable of. But only," he dropped his lips to mine in a seductive kiss, "when you submit."

There was a soft, unspoken threat laced beneath his words. Would he show me how much pain I could take if I fought instead?

Luka stood up and stepped back from the bed, as if needing distance. "I'll be back in a little while." His mouth teased a half-smile. "Don't go running off like last time."

I swung my head away from him and stared at the wall until I heard the door close behind him.

I blew out an enormous breath, able to breathe now that he'd gone. The rope rubbed against my wrists. I struggled, checking to see if it would give, and when it didn't . . . I did. I allowed myself to break apart and weep for a minute, before refocusing. There was no way I was going to cast aside my dream of becoming a surgeon.

I'd overcome tough obstacles before. Hell, I flourished in the face of a challenge.

You can do this. I wiped my face against my arm and dried my tears.

It was Saturday afternoon, which meant I still had another day to figure this out before my Monday morning class. If I couldn't get away from him before then, what would happen? Would Avery tell someone I'd gone missing when I didn't come home tonight? Could I count on her to care, and not be thrilled her socially awkward roommate disappeared?

My professors would notice my absence eventually, but how long would it be before one of them followed up? I didn't check in much with my parents, either. They knew I was busy, and they were as well, so it was normal to go a week without talking. Emotion forced new tears, but this time it was disappointment in myself. I'd spent so much of my life being proud I was a self-sufficient island. Now I was filled with regret.

No one would miss me.

Chapter
NINE

LUKA WAS GONE a long time, much longer than I'd thought he'd be, and it put me in the awful position of hoping he'd come back. I was uncomfortable, thirsty, and I had an eyelash in my eye.

So I used the time to think about what homework I would start first when I got back to my dorm room, and I ran through the checklist of the other odds and ends I wanted to take care of before Thanksgiving break. I didn't want to think about what had happened in the last eighteen hours or my current situation. I had a secondary application for Michigan University's medical school I still needed to finish, and an essay to polish for my dream school, Johns Hopkins. I'd already been accepted into Duke, but it was my second choice.

Sounds of activity far off traveled down the hallway to me. Thumps, and heavy footsteps, and male voices. My pulse quickened. Did I scream for help, or would it incur Luka's wrath? Before I could make a decision, the noises ceased.

A little later, the door opened without a knock and Luka returned, carrying a black overnight bag and a bottle of water. He shut the door behind him, dropped the bag beside the loveseat, and set his gaze on me.

I was thankful I'd stayed relatively calm, which kept the dress shirt covering my breasts.

"That took longer than I thought it would," he said. "Your

roommate's annoying and dumber than a box of rocks."

My stomach did a flip-flop. "What? You talked to Avery?"

"Unfortunately, yes." He set down the bottle, unzipped the bag, and pulled out clothes. *What—?* He held up the tan A-line dress trimmed with black that I'd worn for my video interview with Duke's admissions department.

"How did you . . .?"

"Brent, one of Vasilije's frat brothers, is dating your roommate." Luka laid the dress out on the chair, retrieved the water bottle, and sauntered toward me. "She was helpful getting things from your room, but she doesn't know anything about your schedule." He sat beside me on the bed. "Because, as I mentioned, she's dumber than a box of fucking rocks. Why the hell are you friends with her?"

So many questions stormed into my mind, it was difficult to find an answer. "I'm not, really. You went through my things?"

He placed the pads of his fingertips on my collarbone and began to skate them down my bare skin where the shirt wasn't closed. "Yes. I had them brought here."

The goosebumps he gave me could have been from his words and not just his touch. What was he talking about? "What things?"

His expression was casual. "All of them. I had your dorm room packed up and moved the boxes into another guest room."

"*What?*" The invasion of privacy was overwhelming.

Luka blinked slowly and his expression was guarded. "I told you, this is your home now. When you've earned it, you can have your things back."

My mouth hung open, and as my fury built into a crescendo, his gaze hardened.

"Or you can throw a fit about it and I'll take my shirt back."

I closed my eyes and forced myself to take in a calming breath. I was smarter than this. I wouldn't succumb to an emotional reaction, not if I wanted to outplay him. When my eyes fluttered open, I found him scrutinizing me.

"Will you please," I said, each word deliberate, "untie me now?"

He paused. "Only if you let me tie you up again right after."

"After?" Dread coated my voice.

He waved a hand toward the bathroom. "I assume you need to use the restroom."

Luka was right, I did, but . . . "I thought you said I only needed to be tied up so you could get me clothes, which you did." He'd gotten *all* of my clothes.

"Do you want to use the bathroom or not?"

I exhaled loudly. "I do."

"Okay." He grabbed my wrist and began to undo the knots. "You'll come right back to the bed when you're done, and drink this."

He made me leave the door open as well, which was infuriating. After I finished, I rolled my aching shoulders and returned to him with trepidation. Our time apart had recharged Luka, and he appeared ready to go after me again at full force.

It would be so much harder the second time to lie down on the bed, and as I lingered in the doorway, I considered not doing it. He must have sensed it.

"Come here," he commanded.

I sat cautiously beside him on the side of the bed, leaving distance between us. He unscrewed the bottle, passed it to me, and I gulped it down until it was gone, taking my time. Stalling, really, but I couldn't put it off forever. I held the dress shirt closed as I willed my body to lie down on the bed, fidgeting to maximize coverage. Luka took one of my wrists in his hands, and rubbed the rope marks with his thumbs, mesmerized. A darkness flickered in his eyes.

He enjoyed seeing these marks of his control on my skin.

I shuddered.

He spoke as he wound the rope once again around my wrists, binding me to the bed. "Your roommate's an idiot, but she knows things about you I don't."

Normally, that would make sense. I lived with her, after all. But instead I wondered how it could be possible. Avery paid no attention to anyone but herself.

His voice was uncharacteristically soft. "You're going to Duke after you graduate?"

I opened my mouth to say something, then snapped it shut. Had Avery told him that? The realization came quickly. No, Avery probably hadn't. If he'd packed up my dorm room as he said, he'd found my acceptance package in the top drawer of my desk.

"I . . . haven't decided yet." Duke was expensive. Hell, all of the schools were. I'd be up to my eyeballs in student loans until I was forty.

"Why not?" His tone was almost angry. "That's a great school."

"I have others I'm waiting to hear from." I tried to organize my thoughts. Why were we talking about this? The restraint on me made me feel off-balance and knocked my filter askew. "I don't know if I can afford it."

"Your parents?"

A different level of discomfort grew, one which had nothing

to do with the situation. "They don't have a way to help."

What I really meant was we were struggling. My parents owned three hundred acres of farmland. Some seasons we came out ahead, but most years we merely survived, and it seemed like it had been year after year of bad luck recently.

"Not everyone lives in mansions on golf courses," I added under my breath.

His expression could almost pass for amusement. "You do . . . now."

"I don't *live* here, Luka." For effect, I jolted against the knots and the rope went taut. I was captive, surely he knew I would bolt the first opportunity I got.

"This is where you belong," he said. "I own you."

His fingertips crept beneath the collar of my shirt, nudging it over, threatening to expose my naked breast. The muscles low in my belly clenched, and I shifted subtly away, but I could only go so far. He could do whatever he wanted.

"You're going to tell me your schedule now," he said.

As I lay beneath him, anger swelled. "No. I held up my end of the deal, and you didn't." I glared into his deep black eyes. "You said you'd only tie me up for a little while."

His gaze followed his fingertips. They skimmed at the line of buttonholes on the shirt, down between the valley of my breasts, and over my quivering belly.

"Yeah, well . . ." His fingers stopped at the top of my panties. "I have something I want to use first, but it's taking longer to charge than I expected."

The way his voice was tinged with excitement made my heart thud and my pulse race.

"What are you talking about?" Again, I tried to scoot away from his fingers, but they continued to skim over me. They drew a line down my thigh, tracing patterns.

"I had my assistant pick something up for me this morning while you were sleeping. It's been charging for the last five hours." His hand froze. "Should I get it?"

I was fairly certain the answer was no, but he didn't wait for a response. Luka got up, exited the room, and shut the door behind him. In the quiet, my nerves swelled like an ocean during a storm. I imagined the worst possible scenarios. I fully expected him to return with a torture device. And . . . he had an assistant?

The door swung open abruptly, and he returned, carrying something small enough to fit in one hand. His expression was an enigma as he came closer. Was this interest? Desire? Lust? His eyes were magnetic.

He revealed it to me as he sat, and the bed shifted under his weight. It was black, U-shaped, and one side was larger than the other. I stared at it critically. The thing looked like it was made out of some kind of rubber, and I hadn't the faintest clue what it was.

I gasped when he set it down on the bed and put his hand right on top of my underwear without warning. I jolted against the straps to no avail. I couldn't stop him. My words wouldn't dissuade him. His thick fingers probed and circled, rubbing me on my clit, even as I pressed my knees together and tried to get him to stop.

Luka's voice was dark and sinful. "I want you to get off while we're fucking, but I know that's not going to happen just yet. So we can train for it."

"Don't," I whispered, filled with unease. My hips moved to

get away, but I worried all I was doing was making it easier for him, and then an even scarier thought took root. What if I was doing it on purpose? His touch felt weird. Almost, sort of . . . good.

I was sick. He'd raped me. How could I be responding to him, even a little? Shame stormed through me.

"You're so fucking sexy, Addison," he said. He dragged air in through parted lips as he watched me squirm. "So sexy, and all for me."

His hand moved faster, grinding the cotton of my panties to my flesh, teasing. I struggled against my bindings, but even that added to my enjoyment of the experience in a twisted way. I couldn't get free. And since I was his captive, the vilest part of myself whispered I might as well get something from it. Take pleasure from him the way he took it from me.

I clamped my teeth together, but it didn't silence my breathless moan. It slipped out quietly, but Luka definitely heard it. It kicked him into a new gear, and his fingers dove beneath my panties to touch me where I was hot and aching.

"Oh," I groaned. My eyes slammed shut and I turned my head away from him, trying to shut him out. It was the most bizarre thing ever. I'd spent countless nights envisioning him touching me like this when it was my own hand, and now that it was him actually doing it, I thought I should picture someone else.

I grew damp as my body rocked appallingly against his hand. The disgusting voice in my head wanted to beg him to put his fingers inside me, so I pressed my lips together to stay silent. I forced all thought from my mind, since any pleasure brought guilt, and I was feeling a lot of both of those.

"Open those perfect blue eyes and look at me," he ordered.

I blinked open and stared up at him, wishing for him to stop and wordlessly pleading with him to continue. Heat moved in waves from his touch. The pads of his fingers fumbled over my slippery skin, but never dipped inside as I was beginning to crave them to.

"I want to watch you come." Luka gripped the waistband of my panties and slowly worked it down until I was exposed.

I issued a nervous whine. Some of it was fear, and some of it was an emotion too scary to put a label to. He picked up the small, weird U-shaped object, stretched it open wide, and then eased the smaller end of it inside me.

I moaned with confusion. Pleasure and discomfort simultaneously, but then pleasure won out. The larger end fit tight up against my clit. Luka gave me half a smile, which I was beginning to recognize was his pleased look. My underwear was tugged back up in place, so I was effectively wearing the toy he'd halfway placed in my body.

It was surprising when he moved to the loveseat and sat down, digging his phone out of his back pocket. What was he doing? Hadn't he said he wanted to make me come? The distance between us felt enormous and weird, which made no fucking sense. Shouldn't I be relieved he was on the other side of the room, more interested in his phone than he was in—

"Oh!" I cried, arching up off the bed.

The toy inside me was vibrating. It started slow and the vibrations swelled, only to stop, then resume again. A relaxed rhythm of ebbing and flowing that brought my nerve endings to life. I stared at Luka, my mouth hanging slack.

"Are you," I said between cycles of vibration, "controlling it?"

He teased a smile. "It's an app on my phone."

I turned my gaze up to the ceiling, bashful. It was almost as bad as being naked, him watching me while the vibrations made my cheeks flush warm with color. The powerful waves were strange and addicting.

It was tortuous pleasure as well. Just as it began to feel *really* good, the tempo would crest and cease, leaving me on a cliff. I'd slide slowly away from the edge, only for the next wave to pick me back up, carry me to the top, and repeat the pattern.

"You don't own a vibrator?" he asked, like this was normal conversation. "I didn't find one in your room."

Oh my God. "No," I said quickly between the pulsing waves, "I don't."

"Why not?"

The pleasure radiating from between my legs was ... distracting. My mind wanted to focus on it, rather than Luka's question. "Because I'm a virgin?" I threw it at him with attitude, only to realize my mistake. "I was."

I didn't have to look at him, not that I could anyway, to sense the victorious look splashed on his face.

"You're saying virgins don't like orgasms?"

"No, I'm saying," I swallowed a breath and stifled a moan, "I didn't need battery-operated help." And, really. When was I supposed to use a vibrator? Besides being so busy I barely got seven hours of sleep, Avery never went to class. It meant she was always in the room, playing on the internet or watching TV.

"So you took care of yourself the old fashioned way?" he teased.

I ignored him as much as I possibly could, so I didn't see his finger move. The pattern on the vibrator changed to greater peaks and valleys, with more time between the swells. It was so good, and so horrible at the same time. My greedy body shifted subtly, wanting more whenever the vibrations went into a lull, diminishing to practically nothing.

"I want to hear you say," Luka continued, "you thought about me while you were sliding your fingers inside your pussy."

I gasped inward, and blinked rapidly, focusing on the spot on the ceiling. There was no way in a million years I'd admit it, even if it was true.

He was persistent. "You said last night you'd spent the past two years thinking about me." His deep, seductive voice invaded my head. "Did you, while you were touching yourself?"

My face flamed as hot as the sun, and even my ears burned. My mouth was a desert. I couldn't keep my composure like this while he had me bound to the bed with not just rope, but with his filthy questions and dark gaze.

"Eyes on me," he said. "Look at *me*, Addison."

It was scary and yet strangely erotic. Luka appeared to sit comfortably in the oversized chair, one elbow resting on the armrest, and his phone in his hand. Although his posture was relaxed, he still had presence. There was a gravity to him, and I could feel his control from clear across the room. Through the window, it was late afternoon and the sun was beginning to set, so it cast long shadows over his handsome face. He looked powerful and confident, but most of all, transfixed by me.

"No lies," he reminded. "Did you think about me when you touched yourself?"

His determined expression, coupled with the steady pulse

of pleasure, was too much to handle, and I cracked. "Yes," I whispered.

His smile began in one corner and spread across his lips like gasoline on a fire. I stopped breathing. Luka was smiling. Not a half-smile, but a bright, wide one where I could see his perfect teeth, and light in his eyes. It changed his whole face, morphing him into a man I barely recognized. Utterly gorgeous.

"Shit," he whispered appreciatively as his smile began to pass. "That's so fucking hot, picturing you like that. Did you get off to me? Did you imagine those were my fingers inside you as you were doing it?"

"Yes," I said on barely a breath. I hadn't fully recovered from his dazzling smile, which was now completely gone.

"You know what my fantasies were? I'd bend you over professor Kwon's desk and fuck you until you begged me to come on your perfect tits."

There were no words. Luka's statement unzipped my head and poured molten hot lava all over my brain, frying rational thought. It was vulgar and dirty, and yet the shocking image he painted turned me on. Because I was a good girl and would never think of saying such a thing, but Luka saw me like that. In his fantasies I wasn't shy, awkward, or inexperienced.

He tapped the screen of his phone.

"Oh," I moaned. Was he rewarding me, or increasing my torture? The pattern changed to a steady and deep vibrating pulse. I dug my heels into the bed and bowed upward. I needed . . . relief. He kept me dangling right at the edge and it was going to tear me apart.

"Looks like it's feeling good now, isn't it?" His tone was

indecent. "Are you thinking about what that would have been like? If I'd fucked you after class and made you go back to your dorm with my cum sticky on your chest?"

I whimpered and closed my eyes. The heat and need he'd created in me was a powerful drug and obliterated my inhibitions. I would have done it, in what had become our mutual fantasy. If he'd ordered me to in his authoritative voice, I would have followed just about any directive he gave me.

I strangled back a moan.

"Yeah, I bet you'd like to come now, wouldn't you?"

Without though, I struggled uselessly against the rope. If the toy lodged inside me had just a little more contact with my clit . . . A soft whine fell from my parted lips as I rasped in air. It wasn't a denial. If anything, it sounded like confirmation, and Luka gave a wicked chuckle.

And then everything stopped.

My lungs emptied in a burst, my skin cooled, and my heart thudded. *No!* I'd been so close.

"Your schedule, and then you can come."

I STAYED UTTERLY SILENT, not wanting to budge. This was where I'd foolishly chosen to make my stand. If I gave Luka this, I felt like I'd be giving in to him completely.

"No?" he asked, irritation edging his voice.

He stabbed a finger on his phone and the vibrations resumed. It took me hardly any time to pick up where I'd left off, and in two heartbeats I was panting and squirming, right at the edge—

The toy went still and the faint buzzing cut off, immediately followed by my groan.

His firm tone was almost scary. "Your schedule."

I stared into his black eyes, unable to find words. Couldn't he just give me this, after everything he'd done? I could get pleasure without it coming from him directly, and could absolve myself of most of the guilt. Not that I really wanted him to watch me at such an intimate moment, but since he'd led me to the edge so many times, I no longer cared. I was desperate for release. Each journey upward had wound me tighter and tighter.

"The vibrator has a battery that can last up to three hours," he said. "And if you don't give me your schedule before then, I'll find other ways to tease you. You liked when I went down on you last night. We could do more of that."

Tap.

Buzz.

Pleasure.

I was writing on the bed and out of my mind. I couldn't do three more hours of this. Hell, I couldn't do three more minutes of it.

"Monday," I said breathlessly, "I have molecular biology lecture at ten thirty." I started to blurt out more of my schedule—

"Stop." Luka thumbed at his phone, typing furiously. "Okay, keep going."

I rattled off the rest of the week as he put it in his phone, and although I had no idea why, I also didn't ask. All that mattered was the end goal. When I finished giving him my Friday itinerary, Luka climbed to his feet and moved swiftly toward the bed. He stabbed the phone with a finger and dropped it on the mattress between my knees, and the pulsing went into overdrive.

Giving him my schedule was surrender, but I was glad. The vibrator was pure ecstasy, and I gasped as Luka threw open my shirt, exposing my bare breasts to his hands. His fingers plucked and teased while he watched me squirm.

My moan was soaked with bliss. I should feel shame, but I didn't. I knew I shouldn't allow myself to come, but he'd tied me to the bed. I was powerless to stop him, and it was a kind of freedom. Luka took a knee beside the bed, and closed his mouth around my pert nipple just as his hand pressed the vibrator tight against me.

"Fuck," I gasped and tipped over the edge. I fell overboard into the sensations and cried out. I convulsed as the waves of pleasure rocked my body, each shockwave acute. Falling apart in front of him made me feel frayed and exposed, but sexy, too. He watched me as the climax rolled through my body, and his eyes were hooded.

Seeing me come apart appeared to please him a great deal. His expression was the perfect juxtaposition of hard and soft. The muscle along Luka's jawline flexed as he held his jaw tight, but his eyes were warm.

The phone was retrieved and the vibrating stopped, but this time I was grateful. It was too much now that I'd come. I swallowed a lump in my throat and peered up at him, unsure what to think or how to feel. The tingling of the orgasm was still floating in my body.

He was blur of activity.

Luka's fingers flew to the knot at my wrist, hurrying to undo it. First one, then the other, and when I was finally free, he scooped his hands beneath me and drew me up to a sitting position. I didn't get a moment to catch my breath. His lips followed the descent of the shirt collar, and his hot mouth on my neck gave me shivers.

Only, not with fear, but with enjoyment.

Too much was swirling in my head. His harsh, angry actions earlier. The bathtub. And now pleasure. I was adrift with nothing to cling to.

I sat still and let him taste me. His lips dropped kisses along my collarbone and up the side of my throat, and there he used a hint of teeth, which made me tremble. When he finally reached my lips, I sighed. With relief? I was needy and so fucked up.

"Goddamnit," he muttered against my lips. "Fucking kiss me."

I didn't argue, I followed his command. It wasn't a sacrifice since deep down it was what I wanted, too, but was too afraid to admit. His order allowed me to give in and pretend it was against my will.

The kiss exploded.

Our lips collided and the temperature in the room climbed a thousand degrees in an instant. His damp lips were urgent and fit perfectly to mine, insisting I match his intensity. I did, and then some. Two years of longing colored the kiss. Desire for the man he wasn't really, but it didn't change the tidal wave of emotion that swept through me.

I cradled his face in my hands and held on as I both delivered my kiss and endured his hot, dominating mouth. Luka would consume me until there was nothing left, I was sure of it. The fire between us burned too hot to last, but I'd do my best to hold my ground until the bitter end.

His hands clenched tight on my waist and pulled me up, off of the bed. As soon as I had my footing, he pushed me down, just as he had before. My knees thudded to the carpet, and I stared up at him, stunned. He'd been kissing me like I was the only thing keeping him alive a second ago. Now his expression was stern.

Had my response to him somehow pushed him too far? I'd done exactly as he'd asked, and yet he looked displeased. The hard look in his eyes grew, and I worried punishment was imminent. My blood went cold as he undid his belt and tugged it free of the belt loops in one swift action.

"No, no," I said, scrambling back on my knees. He was going to beat me with the belt, all because I had kissed him as he'd told me?

"Stop." The word was powerful, but not mean, and his voice made me freeze. "This is about trust, Addison."

Anxiety tightened my muscles painfully, making escape

almost impossible. I knelt with my knees buried on the carpet and watched him slide the end of the belt through the buckle, creating a loop. There was no air to breathe when he placed the loop over my head, positioned the buckle at the base of my neck, and tugged gently on the end. It cinched the belt tight, collaring me.

"No," I pleaded on a broken breath. Not that it mattered. He'd been clear my desires were irrelevant.

"I get pleasure," he said, firm, "or you get choked." The belt tightened just a fraction of a degree, making sure I was aware of his control. "Repeat it."

Oh, shit. How? I couldn't think once the leather had descended on me. "You . . . get pleasure," I whispered, struggling. "Or I get choked."

He jerked his hold and the belt became so tight I could feel it restricting my airflow. "Again," he said. "Louder."

It was uncomfortable as the leather strangled me, and humiliating kneeling before him, so I blurted it out quickly. "You get pleasure or I get choked."

The hand not holding the belt moved to undo his fly, and it was down a half-second later. "Hands behind your back. Open your perfect mouth."

It made more sense now. He was about to be vulnerable. I'd allowed him to put the belt on me, and he was trusting I wouldn't use teeth.

I'd touched him last night, but I hadn't been up close with Luka's anatomy before. He was already hard. Watching me come must have turned him on, or perhaps it was the image of me kneeling at his feet with his belt restraining me. The head of his dick was fat, and the shaft long and thick. A vein protruded, and in spite of how terrifying it was to have the makeshift leash on me, I stared, intrigued.

He *wanted* me to take him inside my mouth. I'd gone down on another guy before. It'd been sloppy and fumbling, and over in less than five minutes. I couldn't help but wonder what it would feel like with Luka. Maybe his directions would make the experience somewhat enjoyable, and I wouldn't spend the whole time wondering what the hell I was doing.

What would he taste like?

Would he let me trace the tip of my tongue along that vein?

I crossed my wrists behind my back, licked my lips, and parted them, hating myself for wanting this. I hated myself for wanting to please him after he'd fucked me until I was sore. He'd fucked me as I'd asked him to stop. What the hell was wrong with me?

His fingertips traced a line on my temple, pushing my hair out of the way, and they trailed down to curl under my chin. I welcomed him inside my greedy mouth, sucking on the fleshy head of his cock. It elicited a sigh from him, one which was coated in pleasure.

Unexpected heat blasted down my spine.

I inched further along on his hard dick, licking and sucking, and I reveled in the noises of satisfaction he made. How was it possible I felt power on my knees, with his belt wrapped tight on my neck? Was it his vulnerability? I could cause him extreme pain, but the belt was a strong deterrent, and . . . I sort of enjoyed it. I wasn't in control, but I wasn't powerless either. I felt more like a partner than a victim.

His skin was so soft, silk wrapped around stone. The deep, shuddering breaths he took fed into my satisfaction. Luka fisted his hand in my hair, tugging painfully at the strands as he guided me to take him deeper and faster.

I'd lost my virginity to Luka, and now I was blowing him with a belt wrapped around my throat. Somewhere along the way, I'd lost control of myself. He'd taken over, and part of me didn't care. I was even a little thrilled to shed the conformity of my good girl status. I could be a slut.

I could be *whatever* I wanted beneath him.

Fuck, I liked my lips on him. I swirled my tongue and he jerked, growing harder inside my mouth.

"Shit, yes," he moaned. "Suck that cock."

I did.

I kept my hands locked behind my back, but I increased my speed. He was too big to take completely in my mouth, but I skirted the edge of my gag reflex and pushed as deep as possible. The tip of him bumped the back of my throat.

What would happen if I used teeth? The belt around my neck was like a challenge, and since I no longer felt like myself, I wanted to push. He'd proven in the bathtub he had plenty of darkness, and he'd make good on his threat, I was sure.

But I wanted to know what his absolute domination felt like.

There was a sharp hiss from him as I gave him a hint of what I was about to do, dragging the edge of my teeth over his skin. Up to the tip, and then as he plunged back inside, I let my bite go razor sharp.

"*Fuck.*"

The belt constricted and made me a slave. I could barely breathe, and even though the control was exerted only where the leather looped on my neck, it blanketed every inch of my body.

My pulse roared beneath the belt, pounding against it.

And then it went so tight, it was no longer a corrective action. This was the Luka from last night when he'd held my hands over my head and forced his way inside. The Luka from this morning who'd pushed me under the water, my need to breathe be damned.

I slapped my hands on his thighs, trying to get him to ease up, but instead he shoved his hand on my head, forcing his dick deep into my mouth.

I gagged loudly, but he didn't relent. The belt was tight, so fucking tight. Behind closed eyelids, my eyes began to water. What did we look like? The dress shirt was down off my shoulders and bunched at my elbows. My hands were pressed against his knees, and my lips wrapped deep around his dick. Almost all the way to the base. Blood rushed loudly in my ears.

The harsh hand on the back of my head was gone. The belt loosened and I retreated all the way off, gasping for air.

"What the fuck was that?" His eyes were twin volcanoes of fury.

I wiped saliva from my bottom lip and stared up at him, not sure how to explain my actions, because they made no logical sense. My lips had lost some sensation so I mumbled it, my voice meek. "I wanted to know what it felt like."

"To cut my dick with your teeth?" He wound the end of the belt around his fist, pulling it taut.

I yelped and shook my head quickly. "No." I was so fucking stupid, I deserved his wrath. "I meant the belt."

A shock visibly went up his spine and his expression emptied of anger. It went blank. He bent at the waist, grasped my cheeks between his fingers, squeezing my mouth together, and brought his nose right to mine. "You wanted to know what my belt felt like choking you out?"

Coming up with an answer was the scariest thing I'd ever faced. He'd said no lies, but confirming was like telling Luka I was okay with . . . *anything.*

"Yes," I whispered.

He blinked, possibly evaluating me for deception. "Why?"

"I don't know." It was the most honest response I had.

When he released his grip on my face, he straightened and looked down his straight nose at me. The corner of his mouth lifted in his evil half-smile, and he shook his head, pleased surprise lighting his eyes. "You're so fucking perfect. It's like you exist only for me."

I couldn't wrap my head around the idea.

He let go of the belt and the end dropped down between my breasts, and it hung loosely around my neck. It was so he could grab the bottom hem of his t-shirt and peel it up, revealing his chest. I watch with awe as he cast the shirt aside, and then pushed down the sides of his jeans and underwear.

Now he was more naked than I was. My gaze slid over his hips, up the subtle notches of his abdominals, and to the smooth, perfectly-shaped pecs. Luka wasn't overinflated muscle. He was long and lean. Toned arms gave way to broad shoulders. He was in great physical shape, and the basic woman in me couldn't help but appreciate his look.

There wasn't time for appreciation. He snatched up the belt and yanked the loop closed, while his other hand fisted my hair and jerked my head back.

"I control every part of you. Repeat it."

I was trembling in my core. Instinctively I wanted to fight against him, but I also wanted to please. I wanted to succeed. I stumbled over the words. "You control every part of me."

He released my hair, wrapped his hand at the base of his dick, and yanked me forward with the belt. I barely had time to open my lips before he shoved himself deep inside. I opened my jaw wide to accommodate him, and allowed him to saw his dick in and out of my mouth in long, unhurried strokes.

Luka abruptly pulled out, holding himself less than an inch from my lips as if teasing me. Like he was keeping what I desperately wanted just out of my reach. "Again," he barked, ordering me to repeat it.

This time I had more confidence. "You control every part of me."

"Do you understand what you're saying? Let's make sure."

Again, the hard tip of his cock pushed past the seam of my lips and intruded. Only this time, he didn't stop when I began to back away, signaling I couldn't take him any deeper. The hand he used to hold himself steady moved. It went to the back of my head and pushed.

I gagged loudly, and my palms flew to his knees, trying to push off, but the belt and his large hand wouldn't allow it. My fingers spread out in discomfort as I fought the urge to gag again. The tip of his dick was down the back of my throat and I groaned against the unpleasant sensation. The belt was so tight, I could barely breathe, and my face felt hot and stiff.

I choked on him, fighting for air and fighting against him.

"I control everything," he said darkly, hunching over as he forced himself further in. "Even when you get to breathe."

The belt went slack as he let go, and then he pinched my nose shut with his thumb against the side of his hand, cutting off my air supply completely.

Chapter
ELEVEN

LUKA LEFT ME WITH NO CHOICE but try to take him all the way in. Logic was shoved aside by panic, which was willing to try anything to find air. My terrified sound was muffled under his flesh, and I dug my nails into the meaty parts of his thighs, scrambling to earn his release. My eyes teared up in a physical reaction.

There was certainly no doubt in my mind who was in control.

It lasted only a few seconds and a lifetime before Luka stepped back. I fell forward onto my hands, gasping and choking in air as I stared at the carpet. I shook with both fear and adrenaline, and everything was buzzing as oxygen poured into my lungs. I'd never felt more alive.

"Look at me," he ordered.

I snapped my head up and found him waiting for me with a strange emotion like concern edging his eyes. It was fleeting, and gone so fast I might have imagined it. We locked gazes in a wordless conversation, at least, it felt like it. He wanted to make sure I could handle what had just happened, which was so different than the aftermath of the bathtub. This was a check-in. A visual evaluation, and it looked like I'd passed.

"Get over here and suck my cock."

He controlled every part of me, so I followed him without hesitation. It was stunning how quickly I'd surrendered, and how exciting this new feeling was. Giving my trust and control over to this beautiful monster was so very wrong, but . . . shit, I liked it. He quirked his mouth in a smile as I crawled to him and sat back on my heels, readying to complete my task.

He undid the belt from my neck and dumped it to the floor, which announced there was some sort of trust between us. I told myself I was happy about it because it meant I was a step closer to escape, and for no other reason.

Luka's commands made it easy. I went faster when he ordered me to. I used my hands, and increased my grip as he instructed. I flicked my tongue on the sensitive underside where I knew there were the most nerve endings. When he groaned in satisfaction, pleasure washed over me as well.

"I tried to find you once," he whispered. "Right after finals, but I was looking in the wrong place." I paused as I considered his words, but his voice went severe. "Did I tell you to slow down?"

I resumed my steady pace. He'd looked for me? Why did that make me feel warm? He'd told me he wasn't a nice guy, I reminded myself, and had proven it more than once. I should have been glad he hadn't found me when I was younger. I'd grown up a lot in the last two years, and although I wasn't tough, I was stronger now.

"You were the smartest one in the class," he said. "So I assumed you were a math major, but no one knew you."

Of course they didn't. I didn't make many new friends my sophomore year, and definitely not in my math classes. I wanted to ask why he hadn't tried harder to find me. Luka's personality was all type A. He wouldn't give up easily if he wanted something. But he'd also changed since I'd seen him last, and I wondered if whatever had happened to him might have occurred at that time.

"I would have asked you out, and when I found out you were

a virgin, I'd have taken you back to your dorm and fucked your smart brains out."

My heart skipped at a hurried tempo. This was my fantasy, only in it he'd been patient and sweet. He'd been safe and comfortable and . . . maybe a little boring. I thought I wanted safe and comfortable, but what if I *needed* this aggressive, dominating version more?

His rapid, uneven breaths told me he was close, and I was anxious to see his release, this time with me being a willing participant. I tightened my grip, twisting it down his length as I slid my mouth up and down on him.

It rolled from his lips, loaded with sin. "You look so goddamn good like this. I'm gonna come in your innocent, little mouth. Would you like that? Huh?" He guided me to bob on him faster. "If I filled you up with my hot cum?"

His obscene words riled, but thrilled. I had no self-restraint. Like a kid who suddenly discovered a room full of toys, I wanted to play with everything, all at once. Now that I had dipped my toe into the dirty pond, I jumped in and was eager to get filthy.

Luka's chest was heaving. He'd stared at me last night as he'd gone down on me, so I forced myself to do the same in return. His expression was intense and primal. He looked like a man on the edge of madness.

The muscles along his frame hardened. A growl ripped from his chest and he burst on my tongue. Hot, thick liquid pooled in my mouth in spurts, and from above, he rained down filthy words that were moaned as compliments.

He was still pulsing as the movement of his hips slowed.

"Swallow," he said breathlessly, still recovering.

I did, and as I sat back, I wiped a finger over my damp lips. Did he notice my hand was trembling? I was sure he did. It felt like he saw everything. Yet he said nothing as he bent and tugged his pants and boxers up. He did the zipper, but not the button, and didn't reach for the belt or his shirt. Instead he reached for me.

I stared at his offered hand, spinning. Given what I'd just done, this was nothing. So why did it feel like it was everything? As if I were crossing a threshold with him? Taking his hand was another huge step as we tried to forge trust. I slipped my hand into his, and although he didn't smile, I knew he was pleased.

He didn't speak as he helped me to my feet. When I was beside him, his hand on mine shifted. His long fingers curled around my wrist so he could lead me along toward the bathroom. He could have easily held my hand with our fingers linked together, but no. This wasn't a partnership, and we weren't equal. This was just another way for Luka to exert his control.

He scooped up the duffel bag, and once we were in the bathroom with the door shut, he set it on the counter and unloaded the contents. I shouldn't have been surprised, but it was surreal to see my things in his hands. My makeup bag. My shower caddy. My birth control pills.

I gripped the edges of my shirt and wrapped them around myself, crossing my arms over my chest. I was still shaky from the intense scene that had played out, and now I was cold and awkward. He turned the dial on my birth control pack and punched out the pill for today, then handed it to me. My fingers trembled as I took it from him, popped it in my mouth, and dry-swallowed.

Satisfied, he put a hand on my arm and guided me deeper into the room, herding me to the glass door of the shower.

He opened it, turned on the water, and then set his dark gaze on me. It was clear what he wanted. I let out a shuddering breath and peeled the shirt down my arms, dropping it to the tile. The silence from him was stifling, and I ached for him to say something.

But he said nothing.

Instead he turned me and pressed my back to the cold glass, which made me inhale sharply. He leaned over, setting his forearm on the glass over my head, and his other hand slipped down the front of my panties.

My lips parted so I could pull in air. His touch had purpose. His fingers closed around the vibrator still lodged in me, and slowly pulled it out. It was tossed into the nearby sink.

The glass at my back was beginning to warm with the heat of the shower, and I felt feverish as Luka set a hand delicately on my cheek. At first I thought he was going to kiss me, but his gaze wasn't on mine, or on my mouth. His thumb brushed my cheekbone. It took me a second to place what he was doing. He was evaluating me for injury from the belt. Broken capillaries, or bloodshot eyes, or signs of ligature.

My voice was quiet. "Did you leave any marks?"

"No." His gaze clicked with mine and my knees wanted to buckle under the weight of it. "Did you want me to?"

I pressed my lips together and shook my head.

Stubble darkened Luka's jaw and I studied it up close. He looked sculpted. Flawless skin covering high cheekbones and a strong jawline. And, God, his mouth was sexy with its cruel, wicked lips. He must have noticed what I was looking at, because he gave me a hint of a closed mouth smile.

His fingers dipped below the waistband of my panties again,

and his kiss swallowed my gasp. My skin seared from his touch, and burned as his hard body pressed against mine. I didn't know if I was allowed to touch him without permission. He'd always had me pinned down, or had ordered me to put my hands behind my back. So I risked it. I set my palm flat on his chest, over his heart, and noticed its steady beat. Even his heartbeat was controlled.

But his skin was on fire like mine. Luka's tongue filled my mouth as the pads of his fingers swept and stirred, and I moaned softly.

Had I cracked an invisible whip? Luka sank to his knees and tugged my underwear down my legs, pulling one foot free and then the other.

"Wider," he ordered, pushing on my knee and getting me to stand with my feet wide on the bathmat.

"Mmmm," I whimpered, strangling back the full moan. He'd planted a kiss right on my most sensitive spot. His forceful hands trapped my hips and held me still, and then he got to work.

Holy shit. I slid six inches down on the door, my skin squealing on the glass, as heat blasted up my legs. His soft, wet tongue made me squirm and left me dizzy with confusion. Once again, I wasn't supposed to want pleasure from him. I should be clawing his eyes out, not holding back moans and running my fingers through his soft, thick hair.

"I like that I'm not tasting anyone else's cock right now. This pussy is all for me. *Only* for me."

My eyes slammed shut and I tipped my head back, panting though my open lips. Emotions and sensations battled for attention. Luka's hands were braced on my waist, and they were the only thing keeping me upright. My trembling legs were made of jelly.

He paused only for a moment. "Repeat it."

"This . . ." The word was dirty, and I faltered for a moment. "This pussy is only for you."

Saying it out loud catapulted me right to the edge. Everything was tingling and my heart raced. Need clawed inside, threatening to tear me to shreds.

"Oh, God. Oh, God . . ." I pulled at his hair, overwhelmed as the orgasm bore down.

Luka sucked at my clit, and his fingers dug in, denting the skin on my hips, which triggered my release. The climax was intense. I opened my mouth to cry out, but the pleasure stole the sound from my voice. I arched my back, my body possessed, and then I slammed back into the glass with a loud bang.

I groaned as the last wave passed, and reality came back into focus.

He wasn't kneeling anymore. Luka stood over me, watching every breath I took intently. There was no outward reaction. His eyebrow didn't hint at displeasure, and his mouth didn't lift into a soft smile, but I sensed his satisfaction. He'd enjoyed making me come.

It wasn't a reward for what we'd done in the bedroom, I was fairly sure. This had been about power. He was ensuring I was still under his spell.

"If I let go of you," he said, "will you fall? Your legs are shaking pretty bad." He didn't use a patronizing tone, but the edge lingered and was further proof of how much he liked having the upper hand.

"I'm fine," I said, pushing off of the glass to stand. It took an enormous effort not to sway, but I did it.

He released me, yanked open the shower door, and gestured. "Get in."

I hesitantly stepped in and was relieved when he shut the now-fogged door behind me. Both the shower and the bathroom were well lit, and I was horribly uncomfortable being naked in front of him. It was something I was going to need to get over. As a doctor, nudity would be necessary, but that was different. It wasn't sexual nudity.

I couldn't put myself in that mindset here. Everything about Luka was sexual.

The shower was tiled with pretty green and blue glass accents, and there was a low ledge on the wall opposite the shower head. It was just big enough to consider it a seat. The water was hot as I stepped under the steady stream and closed my eyes.

How long would he give me to shower? Long enough to make sense of all the shit that just happened?

No. Cold air wafted as the door swung out and my eyes fluttered open to see a fully naked Luka step into the shower. I scrambled backward and turned away to stare at the wall. "What are you doing?"

"Saving time. We're having dinner with my father in an hour."

My gaze burned a hole in the tile. "What?"

Of course he didn't say anything. I pictured him with an annoyed look plastered on, not wanting to repeat himself when I'd obviously heard him. Which I had, but it didn't mean I understood. He wanted to hold me prisoner here, and meet his parents?

There was a quiet thud, and I glanced over my shoulder to see him set my shower caddy on the ledge.

"You won't talk during dinner," Luka said. "Answer questions if he asks, but that's it."

Since he couldn't see me, I made a face.

Stupid. I should have guessed he'd know. Maybe my body language had given me away. I found myself spun around and my back flattened against the wall. He loomed above and his face was deadly serious.

"This is fucking important, you understand?" He looked . . . different. Holy hell, he looked concerned. It was such a strange fit on him. "My father's an asshole. He's mean, and cruel, and decisive, so you won't say a goddamn word, or he'll make you regret it."

I blinked against the water misting in my face. It was coming off of Luka as the shower beat against him, but he didn't pay any attention. It ran in rivulets over his shoulders and down his chest, and I wanted to watch the path it carved, but didn't dare take my gaze off of his onyx-colored eyes.

"Not a word," he repeated, every syllable weighted.

"Okay," I whispered. His intense stare made me uncomfortable, and my awkwardness couldn't be contained. "How does you being in my way in the shower save time?"

The muscle along his jaw flexed.

Since it was his only response, I pushed further. "Or did you mean we didn't have time to play 'Let's drown Addison in the bathtub' again?"

Uh oh. The eyebrow arrowed upward and a scowl threatened. "I wasn't going to drown you. That was a lesson so you'd understand who's in charge."

"Oh. Not me," I said, my words bitter. "Got it."

His cold façade snapped back into place. "I told you, these first few days will be hard. You can make it easier on yourself by

SORDID

not fighting. It just wastes energy. I'm going to win every time."

I swallowed down the rising anger. *Let him believe that*, I thought. The faster he got comfortable in his position on top, the sooner he'd make a mistake. Plus, he couldn't be around me twenty-four seven. He had a job.

I took a page from his book and let my face go blank. I didn't say anything. I grabbed my shampoo bottle, turned away from him, and lathered my hair as quickly as possible. But Luka was standing under the water. To rinse off, he'd have to move out of the way. Why did he have to make everything so difficult?

It must have been clear I was waiting to get under the shower. He pulled me to him until my back was pressed against his hard chest and we shared the water cascading from the huge, fancy-looking showerhead. This wasn't saving time at all. Was he . . . using this as an excuse to put his arms around me? I rinsed the last of the suds from my hair, and stayed in his unexpected embrace. What the hell was wrong with me? Why did I keep having to remind myself that I hated him?

While I refused to admit I liked his strong arms around me, I could *not* get myself to step away.

"What about your mother?" I asked.

His tone was guarded. "What about her?"

He'd only mentioned his father, so I assumed his parents were divorced. "Where is she?"

"She died when I was nine."

There was a stab of pain in my heart. "Oh." Good lord, what was I supposed to say? Something sympathetic? I was ill-equipped to offer him any words of comfort.

Luka's arms eased away, and painful awkwardness descended

130

on us. I stepped into the corner out of the water and stared blank-ly at the pattern in the tile while he showered. It was cold, and I crossed my arms over my chest to hold in my shiver.

"Okay," he said dryly, "the shy girl routine has got to go. Turn around."

I frowned. "I can't just shut that off."

"You will, because I like looking at you. You're fucking gorgeous."

His words were a sucker punch to my center. Gorgeous? I was average at best. No one noticed mousy, proper Addison.

No one but Luka, apparently. I closed my eyes and turned in a slow circle until I faced him.

"Eyes open," he said. "Stop hiding from me."

I opened my eyes to glare at him, but he wasn't looking at my face. His gaze swept appreciatively over my body, lingering on my breasts, before it finally settling on my eyes. There wasn't a hint of a lie in his expression. Only desire. I had no idea how to feel about it.

Bottles and other shower accessories were shoved to one side of the ledge, and when Luka stood back up, he pointed to the bench. "Sit."

I had to remind myself of the end goal. I would play my part as the obedient captive until the time was right. I lowered to sit and cringed at the cold tile against my bare skin.

"Good," he said softly.

His all-seeing gaze was fixed on me, so I focused on the wa-ter swirling down the drain at his feet. The direction of the shower shifted away from us. He must have moved the showerhead. He sank down onto his knees before me, setting his dripping hands on my knees that were pinched together. His palms pried my legs apart, shoving me wide even as I began to resist. "Open."

He was so much stronger than I was, and it forced my full attention on him. His hair was black when wet, and it only made him look more dangerous. More sinister and seductive. He edged closer between my legs so I couldn't shut them, and his palms pressed me wide until I was entirely exposed.

"When I give you your signal, this is how wide you spread for me."

What? I gaped at him. "Signal?"

He snapped his fingers in my face.

I lost the tenuous control on my emotions. "Are you fucking serious?"

Oh, it was the wrong thing to say. I was unaware his eyebrow could arch all the way up his forehead, like a barometer of displeasure. His fingers curled inward and he raked his nails over my thighs, leaving tracks that stung.

"Yeah, I'm fucking serious," he growled. "If I want access to you, you'll give it to me at the *goddamn snap of my fingers.*"

Chapter
TWELVE

LUKA LAUNCHED TO HIS FEET, blocking most of the overhead light, and backlit like that . . . he looked menacing and scary. I sat upright, my back straight as a board and my knees pulled together. I didn't like being talked down to or scolded.

It happened in slow motion. His hand extended out to me until it was an inch from the tip of my nose, and his fingers moved, producing a crack that reverberated like thunder. *Play your part, Addison.* It was humiliating and I wasn't sure if I could do it. Spreading my legs for him on command made me feel sick and inferior.

But if I didn't, what would happen? Would he retrieve his belt from the bedroom and find a different way to use it on me? Or would his powerful hands wrap around my throat and leave marks this time? I was too terrified to find out.

I peeled my legs apart and looked away, not wanting him to see I was blinking back tears.

"Jesus, you look so good." He was back on his knees again, only this time his hands smoothed gently up my thighs, captured my waist, and pulled me tight to him. His mouth dropped kisses from the base of my neck to the shell of my ear.

He'd said he controlled every part of me, so I put myself on autopilot and found a way to retreat inward. He wasn't kissing me anymore, it was a husk. A shell who simply looked like me.

When he ordered me to kiss him back, my body performed the task, but the connection he'd been able to forge before didn't work this time. He was sending lust and passion, but receiving none in return.

Abruptly he pulled back, mumbled something about needing to hurry, and tugged us both to our feet. When the shower was over and he handed me a towel, I flung it quickly around myself, relieved. He had no problem being naked, and I was annoyed at how comfortable he was without a stitch of clothing on.

"What else do you need to get ready?" he asked.

My face heated. "New underwear?" He'd brought me the dress and a clean bra, but forgotten that.

His expression was plain. "No. You won't wear anything under your dress."

It was crushing, and went against everything I knew. I was meeting his father and he wanted me bare and exposed? This was another instance of Luka flexing his power over me, and I wasn't sure how much more I could take.

We both dressed quickly, not saying a word, and when it was done, he crossed his arms and casually leaned against the bathroom counter, watching me expectantly.

"If you had full control over my closet, why the dress?" I asked, towel drying my hair.

"Because it's important you make a good impression."

I slowed my movements, considering his statement. He'd told me his dad was an asshole. That didn't sound like Luka cared much for his father. Why was he concerned with what the asshole thought of me? And wasn't Luka an adult?

"I also assume," Luka continued, "you'll want to look your

best. You'll feel more comfortable like this."

"I'd feel more comfortable with underwear."

Amusement flashed and then vanished from him. "No. I like you like this, knowing I can touch you anytime I want." To prove his point, his hand darted between my knees and traveled up swiftly, brushing through my cleft.

I gasped and stepped away.

"So shy again. Where's the girl who likes my belt wrapped around her delicate, little throat?"

He was saying it to get a reaction from me, and I unfortunately delivered. My gaze swung to the floor in confusion. My bravery seemed to be directly proportional to the amount of control he held over me. Now that I was dressed, I felt like I had some power back, but my courage had evaporated.

"That was . . ." I started, but had no idea how to finish the sentence. "That wasn't who I am."

He made a noise which was almost like a chuckle, but it was dark and wicked. "You're wrong." Luka had his hands on me in an instant, creeping around my waist and sliding up my back. "I'm gonna rattle the monster's cage." He brushed his lips over mine. "And then I'm gonna let her out."

As his mouth claimed mine, I wondered if he was implying what I thought he was. Would he really release me? He kissed me now like a man who craved ownership and I was his prized possession.

The kiss ended abruptly, and he pulled back. "I'm distracting you."

I was so far past using the word *distracting* to describe Luka, his statement was almost funny. He returned to his post leaning against the counter and pulled his phone out. We didn't speak again as I dried my hair with a hairdryer and then set about putting on makeup. He was right, after all. I hated not looking put together, and if Luka said I needed to make a good impression, I was going to do it. I'd become obsessive about succeeding.

I snuck glances through the mirror at him while I put on mascara. He was reading something, scrolling through the phone, and a serious look etched his face. He was a dark shadow of the man I thought I'd loved in secret.

Talk about ridiculous. I hadn't spoken to him once the whole semester. I'd studied him relentlessly, and inferred what I could, but love? I was so hopelessly naïve. I didn't know the real him. I'd only had surface data, like how he took his coffee and that he preferred a messenger bag over a standard backpack.

The memory stormed in and the words came before I could stop them. "I almost bought you a cup of coffee once."

His attention lifted from the screen. "What?"

"You usually had a Starbucks cup in class. I thought about buying one and bringing it to class for you." I despised not only how shaky my voice was, but that I was telling him the story at all.

He blinked, visibly intrigued. "How did you know what kind I drink?"

"It was always marked on the side of your cups." I finished capping my mascara and dropped it into my makeup bag. "I was determined to be outgoing and talk to you. So one day I ordered your tall, dark roast, got to class early, and . . . I couldn't go through with it."

He pushed off the counter and stood. His expression was focused. "I would have liked that. Sounds like you wasted an opportunity and a cup of coffee."

"No, I drank it."

His lips pulled up into the half smile. "Fuck," he said, brushing his hand over my arm. "I would have eaten you for breakfast. And you would have enjoyed every goddamn minute of—"

There was a short knock at the bedroom door, followed by a male voice. "Sir, your father's waiting in the dining room."

The half smile faded. A black storm of disgust crawled over his expression and Luka turned cold. "Are you ready?"

Was I? His angry expression left me feeling unprepared.

Luka's hand was tight on my wrist as he led me down the stairs, and my pulse roared beneath his fingertips. It wasn't until I smelled the food that I realized I was famished. I'd only eaten the bagel this morning. Yet that was standard fare for me these days. I didn't put on the freshman fifteen, mostly because I skipped meals. Studying for the MCAT last year on top of everything else had me down to eating once a day.

We turned the corner and I fought not to dig in my heels and skid to a stop. Luka had presence and gravity, but Mr. Markovic was a black hole.

He was seated at the head of the long dining table and looked to be in his early fifties. His patterned dress shirt appeared tailored and expensive. His face was rugged, his eyebrows thick and dark, and his hair had a few streaks of silver near the temples. If this was an indication of what Luka would look like in twenty years, he'd be handsome and distinguished when he was older.

But there was a dark, frenetic energy radiating from the elder Markovic man, and I could sense it clear across the dining room. A quiet rage boiled just below the surface of his skin.

My mouth went totally dry and my throat closed up as Mr. Markovic's discerning gaze discovered me alongside his son. Luka had warned me not to speak, and it was not going to be a problem. I'd held out the tiniest shred of hope that Mr. Markovic could help me, but no. I suddenly had no desire to say a word. His eyes were as black as Luka's, but far scarier.

"Who's this?" His voice was loud and accusing. I wanted to shirk behind Luka's broad shoulders, but Luka's insistent hand pulled me forward toward the table.

"This is Addison Drake. We met at Vasilije's frat party last night."

Mr. Markovic's face twisted into a scowl, and he peered at me like I was dirt. "You brought the situation home with you?"

"I didn't have any other options." Luka squared his shoulders to me. "Addison, this is my father, Dimitrije Markovic."

Was I supposed to espouse some sort of pleasantry after he'd just referred to me as a *situation*? My mouth wouldn't cooperate, so I stared at Luka's father and nodded my acknowledgement.

Luka put his hand on the back of one of the dining chairs and his tone was flat. "I see you brought the whore."

Dimitrije Markovic was so dominating, I hadn't even noticed the blonde woman sitting to his left until then, and my mouth fell open at Luka's insult. It was impossible to guess her age. Her casual dress was tight and low-cut. She had flawless makeup, perfectly colored blonde hair, and a wide, bright smile. The ageless woman could have been thirty or fifty, and I suspected she was closer to the latter, maybe with an excellent plastic surgeon at her disposal.

Her laugh was shrill and she grinned, waving away the comment like it was hilarious, her wedding ring glinting in the chandelier light. "Oh, Luka."

Only there was nothing in Luka's demeanor that said his statement had been a joke. He looked like he'd meant it exactly as it sounded. He pulled out the chair and pointed to it, wordlessly demanding I sit. I collapsed into the seat, and as he sat, I was thankful Luka was a buffer between me and his father. It put the blonde woman directly across from us, and my gaze naturally went to her.

"I'm Tori," she said, when it was apparent neither of the Markovic men was going to introduce her. "You're the first girl Luka's brought to meet Dimitrije." Her sharp blue eyes shifted Luka's direction. "I was beginning to wonder if he wasn't into girls." She'd said it with a light tone and a smile on her lips like she was teasing, but I could hear the burn beneath.

There was no love lost between these two.

Beneath the table, I balled my hands into fists. The tension in the room was stifling.

"You met at a party?" Tori asked me.

"We know each other," Luka answered. "She was a student in the calculus class I was a TA for."

I stared at the plate in front of me. The china was simple but elegant. White with a silver rim, and I wondered if a single plate cost more than my mother's entire set of good china.

"Why is she here?" Dimitrije demanded.

There was an excellent question.

Luka drew in a long breath. It was the same as he'd done on the couch at the party, right before he'd forced himself on me. "I drank last night," he said, "and so did she. We went upstairs and things got out of control."

Oh my God. I had to breathe through my nose to try to keep myself calm.

"How out of control?" Dimitrije's voice sliced through the tension-filled silence.

"We fucked. She said I moved too fast."

I gasped and glared at Luka, my eyes burning with furious rage and my face flushed hot.

There was a terrible crash as Dimitrije brought his fist down on the edge of the table, making the silverware rattle and both Tori and me jump. Then a slew of words burst from Mr. Markovic, but I couldn't understand a word of it except for *Vasilije.* Was he speaking nonsense? No. My stunned mind was slow. It was a foreign language, and one I didn't recognize.

Luka did. His posture snapped straight and his eyes narrowed, and then he was responding in the language with the same vitriol his father had used. From Tori's blank expression, it seemed doubtful she understood any better than I.

"You don't think I tried?" Luka said, abruptly switching back to English. "It didn't work. All it did was make her sick. She remembered everything, and it didn't matter. She was a virgin."

I stood up so quickly the chair almost tipped backward. I had no plan, only that I needed to get the hell away from the table before I lost it completely. I couldn't listen to Luka tell his father all the sordid details of last night.

"Where the fuck do you think you're going?" Dimitrije bellowed. "Sit back down."

The voice stopped me cold, but I couldn't get my muscles to comply. I stood as a statue halfway to the front door, facing the illusion of freedom. I was in a sleeveless dress, it was November, and I was barefoot. Plus, it was dark outside and I hadn't a clue where I was. The cards were stacked against me, and yet every cell in my body was still screaming to run.

"Luka," Dimitrije said. "There's a simple solution to this problem."

A chair squealed as it moved back. "No," Luka said quickly. "I'm handling it." Footsteps approached, but I still flinched when Luka grasped my shoulders. "Come back to the table." His voice dropped low so only I would hear. "*Please.*"

I would have been less surprised if he'd stabbed me. The single word was a request, and I got the feeling Luka didn't make requests, not unless it was something extremely important. His strained tone was unsettling, and I allowed him to turn me to face the table, but I kept my focus on him.

"Please," he whispered again, his face desperate.

It was the most emotion I'd seen from him, and it was heartbreaking. Did he realize he was more powerful than he'd ever been when he was like this? In spite of everything, I wanted to do whatever I could to take his worry away. The desire to please was absolute. I found myself back in my seat, staring at the plate once more.

His father's voice was deep and booming. "How exactly are you handling it?"

"She'll stay here."

There was a pregnant pause. "Until when?"

"Until she changes how she feels about me." Luka corrected himself quickly. "How she feels about the situation."

It was achingly silent for a long moment.

Tori laughed softly. "Your plan is to make her fall in love with you?" Her grating laughter swelled until it was a cackle. "Jesus, Luka. You can't be as smart as your father says you are, because that's the dumbest fucking idea I've ever heard."

"Be quiet," Dimitrije snapped, and the laughter ceased instantly. "Although she has a point."

"It'll be fine," Luka said. "Addison understands who's in control, and I'm confident I can do this."

The blasé tone dug under my skin like a splinter, and grew more uncomfortable with each breath, until the words spilled out. "I'm not a puppet you can manipulate."

Luka's head snapped my direction and his whole body seemed stressed. "I told you to keep your mouth shut."

His father's eyebrow lifted in the same arch all the Markovic men had. "This is under control?"

"Yes." Luka's tone was strict and harsh. It commanded me to obey. "It won't be difficult. Addison's halfway in love with me already."

Fire erupted from deep inside me like a volcano. "The fuck I am! You *raped* me."

My words pulled the trigger in the already tense room, detonating like a bomb. Dimitrije sneered at my profanity and his face had a violent cast, while Luka launched to his feet.

"I warned you," he said. He fisted my hair and yanked upward so hard he pulled strands from my scalp. I cried out in pain as I scrambled to stand, only for Luka to slam me down on my stomach, face turned to the side on the flat surface of the dining table. The place settings jumped from the impact.

I stared at Mr. Markovic in shock, my cheek pressed against the polished, smooth wood. Luka grabbed the back of my skirt, flung it to my waist, and the air was cold on my thighs. He exposed my naked lower body for everyone to see, and my heart screeched to a stop.

Chapter
THIRTEEN

THE ROOM BECAME A VACUUM, lacking oxygen or sound.

Luka's hand pressed firmly against my spine, pinning my hips to the edge of the table. I was saying something, but my level of panic had crossed into hysteria, and my brain would only operate on a lower level. Its focus was solely on getting up and decent again.

I slammed my palms on the wood and pushed up, but a sharp crack rang out, followed instantly by acute, stinging pain. The force knocked me into the table and my arms gave out. I flopped down in pure shock. Luka had slapped his hand so hard against my bare skin, I expected it to burst into flames. I locked my teeth and tried to breathe through the burn.

He'd spanked me right in front of his father.

Dimitrije watched the scene with surprise painting his expression. His gaze was on Luka, evaluating and curious.

"You want to behave like a child," Luka said, his voice verging on a snarl, "I'll treat you like one."

His father's mannerisms were no different than Luka's. The subtle curl at the corner of Dimitrije's mouth hinted he was pleased with his son's actions.

The hand came down again. I heard the slap of skin against skin before the agony thundered up my body.

"Luka," I cried. Angry, shocked tears sprung into my eyes. I could take the pain, but the humiliation was too much.

A hand latched on my shoulder, yanked me to my feet, and shoved me down. He flung me back into my seat so hard, the chair squealed in protest across the floor. I gripped the sides until my knuckles were white and ached, but I needed something to hold on to. I'd shatter into a million pieces if I didn't. I sat dumbfounded, staring at Luka.

What had he just done?

"Are you sure," Dimitrije said, his gaze lingering on Luka, "you want to go to all this trouble? If you're looking for a girl to have fun with, it can be arranged." His focus snaked over to me. "This one is messy."

Luka shook his head as he marched behind my chair and shoved me back up to the table. "I can handle her."

As he dropped down into his seat beside me, my hands clenched into fists on the armrests and my fingernails dug into my palms. The pain kept me centered and my vision from going red. I'd never been so embarrassed or humiliated in my life.

"Fine. I'll help you make your point with her," Dimitrije said. He turned and called out through the arched doorway which lead to the kitchen. "Michael."

Luka's voice was tight. "It's not necessary."

But it was too late. A brawny-looking man appeared, who seemed to have a permanent scowl on his face and ears too large for his head. He wore slacks, a black polo shirt, and a gray sport coat. When Dimitrije summoned him, he stood right beside his boss's chair, looking alert and wary.

"Take out your gun," Dimitrije said, "and set it on the table."

Michael didn't hesitate. He reached inside his coat and

produced a very black and very scary looking gun. It had heft to it, because it made a deep thud when it was set down with the barrel pointed toward me.

"Do you have a family—" Dimitrije glanced at his son. "What did you say her name was again?"

Luka stared blankly at the weapon. "Addison."

His father resumed his focus on me. "Do you have a family, Addison?"

My vocal cords pulled as tight as piano wire. "Yes."

"Good," he said. "That's good. Family is important." I didn't miss his thinly veiled threat. He set his elbows on the table and leaned forward. "I don't know what you think happened, and I don't really give a shit, but you should know I'm not going to let you put my family in jeopardy."

His face was menacing and almost as scary as the gun that rested between him and Luka. Dimitrije's gaze was consuming, and the walls of the dining room closed in.

"If you try to destroy my family," his voice was a low growl, "be assured I'll return the favor. My family owns Chicago. There's no escaping. You can't hide from us." His head cocked to the side as he scrutinized his son. "And you should keep in mind, *Addison*," the long, drawn-out way he said my name was chilling, "Luka is particular. Do what he says, or I'll make him put a bullet in you."

The emotional impact was so strong, so overpowering, my shoulders collapsed under the weight. I couldn't look at anyone, and although my eyes filled with tears, I tipped my head up to the chandelier and blinked them back. I willed the tears back into my body by shear force. Crying wouldn't help my situation. It would only waste time, and give both of the Markovic men more power over me.

I was smarter. I would survive them.

The final word was a sneering challenge from Luka's father. "Understood?"

My teeth locked tight together as I pinned my gaze on Luka. I said nothing with words, but hoped my determined look was enough for Dimitrije to receive my confirmation. Luka wouldn't meet my unforgiving gaze. He sat motionless with a blank expression, not even blinking.

"Fine," his father snapped. "Michael." He gestured for the gun to be removed, and then asked for dinner to be served.

I had no appetite, but a meal was placed before me, and Luka ordered me to eat. I did, only so I could keep my strength, but my brain refused to acknowledge the taste. The men spent most of the dinner speaking in the foreign language. Tori drank three glasses of wine and picked at her nails that were painted a garish orange-red.

The gun was gone, but I still felt its looming presence.

My skin had hardened into a shell and I retreated inside until the horrible dinner was over. I didn't fight Luka's hand on me as he grasped my wrist and dragged me up the stairs. My feet shuffled over the carpet in the hallway and into the room he'd been keeping me in. It wasn't until the door was shut that I came back to life, and Luka seemed to fall apart.

His hand remained on the doorknob, his head turned away from me. "Jesus fucking Christ, Addison. I told you not to say anything." His face was a mystery to me. He looked both angry and relieved at the same time. "Are you all right?"

Was he serious? And . . . when did he start caring about that?

He'd hit me so hard, I still felt the dull heat on my skin.

When I had no response, he let go of the door and encased me in his arms. "You don't know how dangerous that was. I'm sorry if I upset you, but you didn't leave me a lot of options."

I pushed his arms away, but they came back, stronger and persistent. They kept me captive in his embrace and pressed the length of my body against his.

"I told you," he said, his voice like steel, "I'm trying to avoid your death. I had to show him how far I was willing to go to keep you in line. He would have had you killed otherwise, and I . . . don't want that."

He admitted it like it was embarrassing, and the idea that not wanting me to die was shameful left me reeling. My eyes had to be impossibly wide as I stared at him.

Luka frowned. He moved, forcing me to backpedal until I hit the bed and fell to sit. His hands braced on my shoulders, steadying me or possibly himself. "Fuck, let's just do this. We're going to have an honest conversation."

He straightened and pulled his shoulders back, making him look confident and comfortable, although I was certain he wasn't. He began to pace a tight, controlled circuit as if even his unease was metered out carefully.

"Are we?" I said, my voice choked with rage. "What language was that?"

"Serbian."

"Explain what you meant when you said you 'tried that with me, but all it did was make me sick.'"

He halted his pacing. "When you started to freak out about the sex, I roofied the beer I brought you." His dark gaze swung to me. There wasn't an apology in his eyes, and the chill made me shiver. Part of me had already figured it out. Three shots and half a beer didn't account for the massive blackout I'd experienced.

"I'd hoped," he returned to his pacing, "you'd forget last night. I'd seduce you in the morning and you'd think it was your first time."

I sucked down a deep breath. It explained why he'd been different when I'd woken up. He'd been trying to be sweet, disguising the monster who waited beneath.

His hand coursed through his hair and unsettled it. "It was pretty obvious you remembered, though." He exhaled loudly, resigned. "If you decided to go to the police and say I forced you, they'd be crawling all over the house in a heartbeat. The FBI has been up our ass ever since my cousin's trial, and this is the excuse they're looking for to exploit. They tried to get a warrant after Vasilije got busted with weed, but he'd been living at the frat."

His cousin's trial? The FBI?

I closed my eyes as I mentally kicked myself. There was another reason why the Markovic name had a familiar ring to it. It was why Luka hadn't been keen on sharing his last name. This house said Luka's family was dirty rich. I just hadn't realized how much of the emphasis was on the *dirty*.

I couldn't recall all the details. It'd been the spring of my hectic sophomore year, I thought, when I'd heard about it. A federal judge presiding over a high profile case had been assassinated, which was noteworthy enough, but the defendant in the case had the last name of Markovic. The local news had sensationalized it because he'd been related to the popular chain of car dealerships in the Chicago area.

Luka's cousin.

The Markovics were mob.

"I can't make you forget," Luka said. He squared his shoulders to me and set his hands on his hips. "But this arrangement will work."

"What are you talking about?" I bit out through clenched teeth.

His expression was intense and serious. "I said I control everything, including your choices, but that's not true until you make this final one." His feet carried him to me, and he cupped my face in his hands. "You live under my rules. You might even learn to like them." His long fingers caressed my face. My skin wanted to crawl away, yet also enjoyed the sensation. How could any part of me like this? Was there a darkness inside me that responded to his darkness, like our connection was magnetic?

"Or you can fight." His eyes were hard. "That doesn't end well, and I don't want that."

"Why?" I whispered.

"Because," he said, annoyed, although it seemed self-directed. "Because I fucking *like* you, all right? I have for a while." The muscles in his fingers tensed, clamping on my jaw. "You're perfect."

"I'm not."

"Shut the fuck up. You're perfect *for me*." He slammed his lips over mine in a harsh kiss. "So choose."

My choice was to live under Luka's thumb, or not at all? What kind of choice was that? And I couldn't run, could I? Luka's father had threatened my family. He'd said he'd find me, and even if he didn't, I'd have to throw my whole life away. Everything I'd worked for would be *gone*.

Luka's whisper wasn't a request. It was spoken softly, but

filled with so much command, it rang loud in my ears. "Pick me."

"Over death?" I closed my eyes in a long blink, and a rogue tear slipped out. I moved quickly to brush it off, horrified, but he beat me to it. His thumb swept over my cheekbone, smearing it away. He'd changed the course of my entire life with one thoughtless act. Did he realize? "You took *everything* from me last night."

"I know." His eyes were honest. "I had to have you, and I wasn't thinking about anything else."

I noticed it wasn't an apology. If he could do it all over again, he still would. He lowered to kneel by the edge of the bed, bringing our gazes level. There was nowhere else I could look but at those intense, deep eyes. Maybe I could take some comfort in the fact that his life had changed, too. He was saddled with me now, at least until his father ordered him to kill me. Then he'd have to carry the weight of my death forever.

"I'm not going to be easy for you," he said. "As much as I try not to be, I'm like my father. Most of the time I don't give a fuck about feelings, and I expect you'll hate me like I hate him." His voice was weirdly hypnotic. "But your hate will fade until you can learn to live with it. You won't even notice it after a while."

I gave him a wary look, conveying how unpersuasive his sales pitch was.

"Maybe," he continued undeterred, "one day it'll change from hate into something . . . different. We got a hint earlier of what you and I could be like together." His lips met mine, brushing in the briefest of kisses. "Just a taste." His teasing mouth lingered a breath away. "I want more. You can tell me you don't, but I said no lies." His eyes darkened from a flat black to a rich, layered one. "I can give you anything you want, including your freedom."

The familiar tremble he caused in me was back, shaking my foundation. I needed to know who I was surrendering to, and my voice was a ghost. "Have you ever killed someone?"

"No."

I blew out a long breath.

His emotionless mask cracked and darkness seeped out at the edges. "I came very, very close once."

It was clear he wasn't talking about our episode in the bathtub. The temperature in the room plummeted and goosebumps pebbled on my bare arms. "I'm going to be a doctor. I want to save lives, not take them. I can't be with someone who could do that."

The air swirled around us and thickened as he considered my statement. His voice was sharp. "I haven't, but the world's not all black and white."

"And I'm not halfway in love with you," I blurted out. "You raped and drugged me. What you did at dinner—"

"Was to save your fucking life. One word from my father and Michael would've been standing behind you with his gun. You'd have been dead before your head hit the table."

It was surely true, but I couldn't deal with the reality this was my life now. Yesterday my biggest worry was if I'd secured enough scholarships. Today it was whether or not I'd survive the night.

He didn't appear to be lying to me. His pupils weren't large and his breathing was steady. Had his actions really been to prevent my death as he claimed?

"I'll never love you," I said.

A tiny voice whispered in my head, telling me I'd just given Luka a challenge, and I'd done it on purpose. The sick part of me wanted him to rise to meet it. And when his eyes flared with interest and the side of his mouth tugged up, I knew I'd made a terrible mistake.

"Yeah? We'll see."

Chapter
FOURTEEN

LUKA WAS SUMMONED back downstairs, and left me alone in the room, stating he'd be back in a minute. Obviously this was a test. If I ran, I'd made my choice. A bullet from his father's bodyguard would end it, and no one would know what happened to the smart, yet abrasive Addison Drake.

If I stayed in the room, he'd return and assume I'd also made my choice, picking him.

Not that there was a choice to be had, but I struggled against it. I needed time and space. I was angry. So goddamn angry, I wanted to pull my teeth out. He deserved to feel that same anger. I needed him to understand.

What I'd said to him was true. I wanted to save lives. I'd spoken candidly with Dr. Gupta once, and he'd talked about the kick after leaving the OR, knowing he'd just completed a successful surgery. It was powerful holding someone's fate in your hands, and the feeling was addictive. Was that how I was to Luka? Was he high off of controlling my life?

Like a tumor that was slowly killing a patient, I want to excise the bad part of him. I needed a weapon. Something small he wouldn't see coming until it was too late. Something small, and sharp.

There was nothing under the bathroom sinks except for paper products. My razor was suspiciously missing from my shower supplies. The only artwork on the wall was a canvas, so there was no glass to break. I stared at the huge mirror in the bathroom. He'd hear me break it, and could be on me before I could get a shard free to wield.

There was a table lamp on one of the dressers. I unplugged it and hurried to the bathroom, grabbing a towel. I then set it over the lightbulb and unscrewed, twisting quickly and trying not to burn my fingertips on the hot glass.

I had to hurry. He could be back any second. I wrapped the lightbulb up in the towel, rolled it in the rug in the bathroom, and wacked it against the tile. Just hard enough to hear the glass break, but not loud enough to draw suspicion.

My heart fell when I unrolled the rug and discovered most pieces weren't useable. They were too small or rounded. There was only one that had a point on it, and it was the size of a postage stamp. It'd have to do. I cleaned up the mess quietly and efficiently, grasped the fragile piece of glass between my fingers, then went into the bedroom to wait.

The glass wouldn't cut deep. It wouldn't do much of anything but piss him off, and logic told me it was a bad idea, but my emotions overruled it. Luka needed to feel at least a fraction of what I felt. I wanted to see him bleed.

Heavy footsteps approached the door, and my heart pounded. I urged my hand to stay steady. If I tensed too much, I could crack the glass further and have nothing. The door swung open. Luka stepped in, shut it behind him, and looked satisfied I seemingly hadn't moved from my spot sitting on the bed.

His hand darted behind his back, and when it reappeared, it gripped a gun. I held my breath. Well, if that wasn't us perfectly.

Me, a tiny piece of fragile glass, compared to him, an experienced, strong weapon. I could only maim, whereas he could do so much more damage.

He dropped the gun on the dresser and for a single moment looked relieved the weight of it was gone from his hand.

"My father," he said, gesturing to it. "He wants you to pick this." Luka's gaze sharpened on me. "But you're still here."

"Yes," I whispered. I'd have to lure him away from the gun.

"Stand up."

I climbed to my feet, concealing the scrap of glass in the folds of my skirt. Oh, Luka looked thrilled. His half smile reached all the way to his eyes. He strode rapidly to me, each footstep exponentially increasing my anxiety. What if he discovered the glass before I got to use it? What if he picked up the gun after?

"I've made my choice, Luka," I said as his hands slid into my hair, forcing my eyes up. "But I won't be easy on you, either."

The half-smile spread wide and engulfed his face with a beautiful evil. "I'm counting on it."

His reaction only strengthened my desire to show him pain. "I'll hurt you."

"Yeah?" He licked his lips, either preparing to kiss me or devour me like the big bad wolf. "You can't hurt me."

He brought my face to his and when his tongue shoved past my lips, I made my move. I set the pointed edge against his forearm and slashed down the length of it.

"The fuck?" He shoved me away as he hissed in pain, staring in surprise at the angry red streak on his skin. It wasn't even a cut. It was more of a scratch, although I had drawn a little blood. Red began to blossom and seep from the center of the scrape.

Only I'd pressed too hard, and the glass splintered, cutting into my fingertips.

He snatched my hand up, painfully bending my palm back until I released the tiny bits of glass. "Where'd that come from?"

I whimpered in pain. Blood streaked down my finger and the cut throbbed. "The lamp. I broke a lightbulb."

He looked, of all things, confused. "You could have used that to go for the gun. Why didn't you?"

"Because I made my choice and there's no point in running. Even if I knew how to get it to fire," because I assumed it had some sort of safety lock, "I wouldn't use it." I glared at him with defiance. "I don't want to kill you, but I do want to see you bleed."

He stared at me with disbelief, and then something scary flickered in his eyes. "Yeah, well, we're both bleeding now." His grip increased pressure, and I yelped. "Happy?"

The ache spiraled up my arm, but I shoved the pain away. "Yeah, I'm *fucking* thrilled."

He could move so fast. His hand lashed out and gripped my throat, shoving me along. He backed me up until the dresser dug into my spine, and I wrapped my bloodied hand around his forearm. It smeared our blood together, which seemed fitting. A deal forged in blood, started when he'd made me bleed last night.

He pressed me so hard into the dresser, I knew the fancy drawer pulls were going to leave bruises on my body. I needed relief and unleashed a slap across his face. It probably hurt me more than him, since his cheekbone was hard as a rock, but his eyebrow rose up and his skin flushed pink.

Fury burned in his eyes.

He released me so he could pick up the gun. I was thrown

157

across the room and hurtled into the wall, getting a face full of green wallpaper. I stopped moving, or breathing, or thinking, when Luka pinned my hand to the smooth paper with the barrel of his gun. It was the same hand I'd slapped him with.

"How successful of a surgeon can you be with one hand?" he snarled. "Do that again and you'll find out."

The gun drew away, and was probably tucked back in the waistband of his pants where it had been when he'd come into the room. I stood stock still as his fingers found the pull on the zipper at the back of my dress. He tugged it down, and as soon the dress was open, his hand dove inside and undid the clasp of my bra.

"You've lost the privilege of clothes." He clenched a handful of the dress by my shoulder and jerked down aggressively. "Off."

I complied immediately. I'd known there'd be retaliation, and had already accepted it. The dress and bra fell away from my body and I stepped backward out of them.

"Go into the bathroom and wash your hand."

I didn't look at him or myself in the mirror. I performed the task and ran the cold tap over my sliced fingers. They'd stopped bleeding, at least.

"Is there any glass in the cut?" He asked it, but then checked for himself. He held my wounded hand up in the light and examined. I stared at his arm. The scratch had barely bled at all. Luka seemed satisfied and marched me back into the bedroom.

His command made me go boneless. "Get on your knees."

He wouldn't kill me, I reminded myself. He'd have done it already. He also wouldn't have examined my cut for glass if he was about to perform an execution. I knelt on the carpet, sat back on my heels, and wrapped my arms around myself.

Luka carefully picked up the bits of glass and tossed them into the wastebasket with a soft clink. Then he lifted the black duffel bag up and set it on the loveseat, searching through it.

He found whatever it was he was looking for. It was a thick, black leather circle, and the thin metal chain attached gleamed in the soft light. There was a leather loop at the end, signifying what this was, and my stomach turned.

A collar and leash.

"I expected you to try something," Luka said, as he worked to undo the buckle. "I'm not angry, but your behavior is not acceptable."

I dug my fingers into my arms, strengthening myself to stay still. The only part of me that moved as the collar descended around my throat was my rapidly heaving chest. The leather was thick and cold, covering two inches of my neck.

"Lift your hair."

I scooped it up and held it out of his way as Luka buckled the oppressive collar. It wasn't too tight, but it wasn't physically comfortable either. When it was done, the long metal chain hung down my bare back, swinging slightly and the cold metal kissed my skin.

Luka dangled something in front of me. A small combination lock.

"This has four dials on it," he said. "Each with ten numbers including the zero. How many possible combinations does it have?"

My heart sank. "Ten thousand."

It clicked into place at the base of my neck, locking the collar on me. His firm hand dipped under my arm and hauled me to my feet, then shoved me toward the bed. "Lie down."

Once again, I followed his orders. I'd drawn blood from him, albeit less than I wanted to, so I'd achieved my goal. Now the adrenaline was fading and I was exhausted both physically and emotionally. I lay down on the sheets, staring blankly at the ceiling and expecting him to climb on top of me.

He didn't.

Another combination lock was held in front of my eyes, showing me ten thousand more numbers I wouldn't guess. The leash was run through the headboard cutout, and the top of the lock threaded through the leather loop and a link of chain. That left me with five feet of slack. I could get off the bed, but that was the limit of my range.

I peered up at him, fearful, but his expression was blank. He glanced down my body and back up again, giving me no hint of what he was thinking.

"Good night, Addison."

Then he went to the door, turned off the lights, and left.

π

I woke with a start. It was morning, and the smell of coffee lingered in the room. I turned my head to find Luka sitting on the same loveseat as yesterday. He wore jeans and a navy blue v-neck, his fingers casually wrapped around the handle of a mug while he stared at his phone.

My movement drew his attention.

"Morning. I thought you were going to waste the whole day."

I'd pulled the covers over me last night after he'd left, and I held them to me as I sat up. "I had a hard time falling asleep last night without your drugs."

He set his coffee down on the floor, stood, and strolled casually toward the bed. His relaxed posture set me on edge. He'd clearly regrouped last night, whereas I'd fought to hold it together. I'd tried different combinations in a futile attempt to get free, starting of course with pi, but nothing worked on either lock. So after that, I'd shifted into seeing if I could break the bed frame to get free, which had also been futile. There was nothing within reach of the bed that would help me escape.

There wasn't a clock in the room, but it was probably the middle of the night when I'd come to the realization that my best hope for freedom was to do exactly as Luka said. I'd quietly cried myself to sleep.

His hand covered the lock around the end of the leash and freed me. "Use the restroom and come right back."

I did. I told myself I no longer cared about being naked. He'd seen me plenty by now. When I came back into the bedroom, he pointed to the bed. I lay down and said nothing. At least the choker last night gave me use of my hands and allowed me to sleep on my side if I wanted. He took the leash in a hand. It was slack and he was simply holding it, but I was incredibly aware of the control.

There was a loud ticking I picked up on then. A large, round alarm clock with hands on the face sat on the nightstand. Luka must have put it there when I was in the bathroom.

"This clock," he said, "is going to help teach you." He sat beside me and the mattress sank with his weight, causing me to roll into him. "When the second hand hits zero, you'll watch it and count each second in your head."

The thin hand ticked up the clock, heading toward the twelve. I studied it attentively as the new minute began. *One. Two. Three.*

I blinked and forced my mind not to wander as it ticked along. By fifty seconds it was a struggle. As it climbed back to one, Luka's single word shattered my focus. "Again."

One. Two. Three.

The exercise went on, three more rounds of it. Somewhere in minute five, he spoke. "Count out loud."

"Thirty-six," I said. "Thirty-seven. Thirty-eight."

"Stop and look at me." His face was stoic. "What is this lesson?"

I inhaled. "That my time is your time."

He teased a smile. "So fucking smart."

There was a sharp click as he snapped his fingers and I swallowed thickly. I hesitantly spread my legs open, ignoring the unease channeling through me. First, his gaze scored down my bare flesh. Over the tops of my breast, along my belly, and down to my hips where I was totally exposed. Then, his hands, even the one holding the end of the leash, followed the path of his gaze.

His hands were warm as he caressed me. His touch was gentle and almost loving, but I told myself I didn't like this. I flinched when his fingers traced a line at the hollow where my leg met my body. It both tickled, and made the muscles low in my belly clench. I knew where this was going and a dark hunger growled in me.

Luka climbed onto the bed and settled his knees between my legs. He put his hands on the mattress on either side of my arms, and his mouth repeated the path. Warm, wet lips trailed over my breasts. One, then the other, and back again. I bit down on my bottom lip. *I'm not enjoying this,* I repeated in my head as a mantra, although my nipples tightened under the command of his mouth.

It became difficult to remain indifferent as he dropped a trail of kisses lower. And lower. His hot breath rolled over my skin, and I grew shamefully wet between my legs. I cursed my betraying body, and the indecent desire I had for him to finish his journey. Hell, I wanted his mouth on me. His hold on the leash was symbolic of his hold over me.

The clock continued to tick away over the sounds of Luka's quiet kisses, and the occasional noise of him shifting over me, working lower. My pulse had quickened, speeding much faster than the slow ticks of the second hand.

When he was nestled between my thighs, he halted, teasing his lips just above my slit. His focus wasn't on me. It was on the clock. "You're going to come at exactly nine twenty-two. Not fifteen seconds before, and not ten seconds late. *Perfectly* at nine twenty-two."

I swallowed a breath. It was about to be nine seventeen. He waited until the clock struck the new minute, and descended on me.

Five minutes. At first I thought it wasn't enough time to allow myself to enjoy it enough to get off. I'd had to throw out my mantra and start over, telling myself how much I *did* like his touch. But as his tongue glided over me, massaging the nub that held most of my pleasure, I began to worry five minutes was *too much* time.

Could I fake my orgasm? Would he be able to tell if I did? And what if I came too early, could I stay silent as the sensations gripped me?

He started slow, licking me gently in one long stroke. It made my legs shudder. He repeated it, this time with more pressure, and I bit back a soft moan. I didn't need to persuade myself this felt good. His mouth was very convincing.

As he increased his pace, my hands balled into fists on the sheets beneath me.

His gaze was on me, watching how I fought my body. I forced my back not to arch, and refused to shift to a position to make his mouth line up where it would feel even better than it did already. But his gaze, like mine, would occasionally drift to the clock, checking to see how much longer.

"I could eat this pussy all day long," Luka mumbled. He sucked my clit into his mouth. Teeth were involved, and I bowed off the bed with a cry. It hurt, but in a good, surprising way. The sensation had me sweating.

When I had less than two minutes left, fear whispered at me. *You won't make it, and he's going to punish you.* My eyebrows tugged together in concentration. I couldn't think like that. I focused on the heat his tongue generated, and didn't restrain my moan. It was long and sounded like a plea, and . . . it turned me on. The sound of my own voice filled with pleasure carried me upward, causing another moan.

"Fuck, yes," he urged. He glanced at the clock and back to me, writhing beneath him. His faint smile was sinister. "You seem to like it too much. Maybe I should stop."

My muscles tensed. "No!" I said, far too desperate sounding. "No." The second one was calm, but filled with worry. If he stopped, I'd never meet his ridiculous goal.

Desire, mixed with victory, painted his face. "You want me to fuck you with my mouth?"

Oh, how quickly he'd turned the tables on me. He'd left me with no choice. "Yes. Please."

His hands curled around my thighs and held me tight as his mouth closed over my clit. His tongue slid around and fluttered, occasionally slipping down to dip all the way inside. I groaned and burrowed my hands in my hair, then hurried to check the clock.

Forty seconds left. I was getting close. In fact, if he stayed right where he was, I'd just need to hold back the orgasm until it was time. My breath had gone ragged and I was still squirming, but his hands held me open to his invasive, seductive tongue.

Then, it was gone.

Luka hovered above, his lips wet and breathing hard. His face was faintly flushed, and his expression wild. He looked gorgeous.

"*Please,*" I whimpered. There was twenty seconds left, and he'd ceased all action, leaving me right at the precipice. I put my hand on his head and pressed downward, signaling what I needed. "Luka, please."

But he ignored me and held fast, his powerful eyes staring at me in a challenge.

Chapter
FIFTEEN

THERE WERE ONLY TEN SECONDS LEFT, but forget it. I wasn't going to fail this test, not when Luka had gotten me ninety-five percent of the way there. He hadn't said how I was going to come, or who was responsible for getting me off, so he'd forced my hand. Literally. My face burned with humiliation as I set my fingertips on my clit and began to rub in tight circles.

I couldn't believe I was doing this in front of him. It was so intimate and private, and it was as if he'd stripped me bare of my decency, forcing the raw, carnal version of myself out onto a stage. Luka's eyes flooded with desire, turning into dark pools of lust. He seemed fascinated and excited to watch the show.

I was panting as I glanced at the clock a final time. Three seconds. I squeezed my interior muscles, and lifted up on my feet as the orgasm approached like a sudden hurricane. My hand moved furiously to encourage the swell.

"Fuck, yes." It came as a gasp from him.

The orgasm tore through me, splitting me apart. I collapsed on the bed, gasping and shuddering as I pulled my hand away. My center was quaking in the aftermath of the explosion. The pleasure had been fast, but strong, and it took me several breaths before I could think again and the tingling faded.

Luka was a blur as he crawled off the bed and tore at his clothes. The t-shirt was yanked off and tossed away, followed by the descent of his jeans and boxers. He moved with precision, like he didn't want to waste another second. Ironic when we'd spent five silent minutes staring at a ticking clock.

He was a clever bastard. If he'd demanded I touch myself, I likely would have done it, but I would have felt too uncomfortable to achieve climax. Had pushing me to the edge and leaving me dangling there been his goal? To see me get off by myself?

It wasn't the first time I'd seen him naked, but the sight of it still felt new and dangerous. Predators were the most beautiful creatures by design. His sinewy form encouraged my gaze downward, to where he was fully erect, angling out from his body. He wrapped a hand around the head of his dick and stroked. He looked at ease like this. Powerful and in control, the one hundred and eighty degrees from me. I'd felt scattered and frantic as he had watched me touch myself. Luka was confident.

When he climbed on the bed, I retreated, giving him as much room as I could. Only, I'd forgotten about the long metal chain attached to the leather band padlocked to my throat. He could grab it at any time and flex his control.

He didn't. Instead he lay down on the bed and faced me, putting a hand on my shoulder. His voice was whisper-soft. "Come here."

I wasn't sure what he wanted and I was too afraid to ask. I inched closer with my breath held and my body tense. Luka studied my cautious approach, scooped an arm under me, and yanked me awkwardly on top of him, so I had one leg between his and our chests were pressed together. Naked flesh to naked flesh.

Like my bold act a few moments ago, this also felt shockingly intimate.

"Christ, Addison." His eyes were heated. "Can you feel how hard you made me?" I could, since his erection was nudged against my hip. "You're sexy as fuck."

He caressed his hand up and down my back, stroking. Each pass it dipped lower, until he finally curled it around my thigh and shifted beneath me. Now I was straddling him and the contact of his skin on mine sent a delicious shiver up my spine.

"I knew you'd do it," he said, and I could feel the deep rumble of his voice reverberating through his chest. "You'd be perfect, because you want to be the best at everything."

I turned my head to the side and stared at the straight lines on the elegant wallpaper. I hated how he had me so figured out when I hadn't a clue about him.

His lips pressed against my neck, just above the leather collar and beneath my jaw. He breathed the words and they soaked into my skin. "I want to do it right this time. Let me make it perfect for you."

He was actually asking for permission, more or less, which struck me deep. He didn't need my permission—I'd already agreed to surrender, so his statement threw me off-balance. His hands were fitted on my waist, holding but not trapping me.

Luka's approach today was as it had been Friday night. Like the living frog in a pot of water, slowly increasing the heat on the burner until it was too late and he was boiled alive. I'd been the oblivious victim then, but now I went into it with eyes open. I saw Luka's hand turning up the heat and chose to stay in the water anyway. I was a stupid girl and deserved whatever I got.

It was weird being on top since it gave me the illusion of control. It was only an illusion, though. His kiss engulfed me. When

I moved my hips to line him up, he took over. He put his hand between us and held himself steady so I could slowly lower down.

I grimaced as he began to intrude.

"It still hurts?" he asked, halting my progress.

"Yeah." The ache hadn't been noticeable until I tried to take him inside.

"Go as slow as you want."

His expression was confusing. It was the same concern I'd seen from him once before, mixed with something else . . . It was surprise. If I had to guess, he was surprised he was feeling concern, probably because he wasn't used to having feelings at all.

I was anxious and nervous in the position. As if I were on display, but there was a sliver of excitement as well. I was about to have sex for the first time by *choice*, even if that choice was twisted and warped.

It hurt a little, but the pain was more discomfort rather than true pain as I eased myself further down on him. Luka's eyes hooded, but he watched me, engrossed. The stretch between my legs was bearable, and I pushed down further.

Going slow was . . . strange.

I was hopelessly out of breath and trembling, unsure whether or not I could go on, but like everything else, I wanted to be good at this. A slow hiss crept out of Luka as I took another inch inside me. My hands gripped his arms ferociously. What did his hiss mean? Did he like it? My gaze connected with his, and time froze.

He'd said I stared at him like I wanted Luka to bad things to me, and now I was seeing that same look from him. His eyes were filled with profane desire, and they were a loud plea for everything I could give.

"Fuuuuck," he uttered when I'd made it all the way down and he was fully seated inside my body. His expression twisted with lust, focused only on me. It was crazy how he made me feel. He acted like all of my inexperience was a benefit, not a drawback. He was eager to show me *more*.

My breasts flattened against his chest and he reached up, tucking a wayward lock of my hair behind my ear. His fingertips lingered, skimming down over my lips. When he lifted his head up to bring our mouths together, he began to move, pushing his dick deeper.

Oh. My. God.

His mouth was fire and passion. All of his kisses before had been a warm-up and this was the big show. He'd drugged me on Friday night, but his kiss this morning was far more potent. I moved my lips against his, seeking his tongue, and moaned when he took control. His hands on my waist encouraged me to rock back and forth.

The slow, deep penetration was shocking, not just in sensation, but in how much I enjoyed it. His dick was so hard, and it felt . . . good. The contact of his body both inside and against mine was much more pleasurable than I'd expected.

"Do you like this?" I asked him between two painstakingly slow thrusts.

He shot me a look like I'd asked a ridiculous question. "You feel fucking *amazing.*"

Maybe I needed to give up thinking altogether, since I couldn't sort out my feelings. His praise made me consider a shy, bashful smile and I longed for the confidence he always held.

He moved cautiously. Each thrust was gentle and paced, and he seemed to scrutinize my reaction, watching for any sign from me to stop. Luka cared now? I could handle him being callous and mean, but this version of him? Not so much.

His slide in and out of me sent electricity dancing along my nerve endings, and I gripped his arms, holding on as the onslaught began. His mouth walked over my skin, finding the perfect spots to cause shivers, and his fingers dug into my hips, driving me down on him.

"Do *you* like this?" he said softly, teasing my words back at me.

Did I? He'd built to a steady rhythm and it pounded away the sensible voice in my head. I shoved my face into the side of his neck. He smelled wonderful, all woodsy and manly. I whispered it against his skin. "It feels good."

Deep inside me his muscle flexed. My mouth rounded into an O. *That* felt really good.

We were naked, and not moving all that fast, but in no time we were both slick with sweat. Luka was a furnace, and his hot mouth had me dizzy. So hazy, I didn't notice his hand curling the silver chain around his fist. The chain was slack as he set his metal-wrapped hand on the small of my back.

There was pressure on my neck, tugging me up. His control on the leash gently forced me to sit upright on him, and my eyes went wide with panic. I didn't like the distance between us. When I'd been over him, I'd been too close for him to really look at me, but now he was easing me back and going to see all of it.

"Grind on me," he said. He squeezed my waist, showing me exactly how he meant. I tentatively swiveled my hips, and he groaned. "Yeah, just like that."

His dark brown hair was askew, and his expression was raw. Primal. His body, glossed with sweat, was corded with lean muscle. Perhaps having to sit upright wasn't so bad. I was supposed to hate him, but I didn't right now. I'd suspend my hate until this was over, and enjoy looking at him until then.

The choker kept getting tighter, though, and I leaned back, having no choice but to reach behind and put a hand on his knee for support. My back arched and I stared up at the ceiling. It presented my breasts to him, and his hand slid a line up my belly and chest, until his palm cupped a breast.

What did we look like? I was riding him with my head thrown back, the roots of my hair damp with sweat, and his arm flexing as he pulled the leash, arching me like a bow. I lifted myself up and down, pumping on him, and . . . hell. I felt so sexual, and it was undeniable how much I liked the feeling.

He used his fingers to tease my nipple, while beneath me he matched my frantic thrusts. His dick drove into me at a different angle. It created a new kind of ache and a dark craving my body whispered only he could satisfy. It was all building too fast to stop, not that I wanted to now.

I gasped and panted, desperate for more but not sure how to get it. My worry was unnecessary. He'd said I was an easy read, after all. Luka must have known. His hand on my breast trailed down over my curves, coursed over my belly, and touched me. His thumb rolled circles on my clit.

"Luka," I moaned. The leather was constricting around my throat. His control was wrapped all around me, but it added to the experience. If I wasn't in command, I couldn't be held responsible. I was about to come, but it was only because he demanded it, I told myself. There wasn't guilt or shame in doing what he said, because I was only trying to survive.

"Yeah?" he said in a hurried voice. "You like that?"

My eyes fell shut. Emotion and sensation overwhelmed me. "I do."

The tempo increased, and the sharp, repeated slap of our bodies meeting filled the room. He was like a piston between my legs, and coupled with his devious thumb, I wouldn't last much longer.

"Put your hand on your tit. Pinch that pretty pink nipple."

His command sent a rush through me. I palmed my breast, and pinched the distended nipple between my thumb and index finger.

"Harder. Until it hurts." His gaze was locked on my hand. "Do it like I would, if I wasn't playing with your pussy right now."

I quivered. He was so filthy and unapologetic. It sent a shockwave of pleasure up me, melting my thoughts. I clamped my fingers hard, obeying his order, and it made my breast feel heavy. The focused, localized pain was enjoyable, but his thumb . . .

I'd never come with something inside me before. A few times I'd fingered myself, but it hadn't done anything for me, so I stuck to stimulation on the outside. This felt amazing, and I was sure my orgasm was going to be huge. My hand gripped his leg and he yanked hard on the collar. I was going to lose my mind. It felt too good with his hand stirring me.

"I'm gonna come inside your tight pussy and fill you up."

His dirty words sent me over. I cried out at the crest of my ecstasy, and moaned the whole way down. The orgasm bloomed from deep inside and traveled outward in powerful waves, rendering me immobile. Every muscle in me locked down, trembling at the assault of bliss, and finally surrendering.

Luka moaned, louder than I heard from him before, and shuddered. I'd just finished recovering when he started to come. His groan of satisfaction was loud and punctuated with labored breath.

I gasped at the rhythmic jerks inside me, followed by heat. Even though my orgasm had dissipated, this felt nice. And his expression as he came was captivating. His dark eyes were closed and his lips parted, and a vein by his temple pulsed. He looked . . . peaceful. Were these few short seconds as he came the closest to happy Luka got?

He wrapped the chain around his fist once more, brought it in front of me, and jerked me forward, crashing his lips against mine. My head was a jumble of thoughts, but he kept them isolated and quiet while his mouth was on mine.

I was still trembling as he backed me off of him. His fingers went to the padlock at the top of my spine, and a few seconds later the leather band was pulled free from my throat. I exhaled in relief, and my newly exposed skin was cold in the fresh air. His lips traced where the collar had been.

"Wasn't that better?" he asked on a low voice as he lingered at the base of my neck.

I turned my head to the side and pressed my ear against his chest. Of course it was better—I'd allowed it this time. Maybe even more, I'd sort of *wanted* it. I barely said the word. "Yeah."

"Go take a shower." His voice was unassuming and his hand brushed along my arm. "I'll get you some clothes and then we'll have breakfast."

It was all so bizarre. What we'd just done, and how comfortable he seemed to be about it. I rolled off of him, and heat creeped up in my face, annoying me. We'd just had sex, and he'd made me come. Why the hell was I still so shy?

"Your father?" I asked like a timid mouse. Luka had been awful to me, but also sometimes verging on sweet, and it was Dimitrije I feared more than the man beside me.

"No, he's hardly ever here. He stays with the whore. They left after dinner last night."

Luka got out of bed and then helped me to my feet. My legs were weak and uncooperative, but I managed. He stayed true to his word. Luka watched me wobble toward the bathroom, but didn't follow, choosing instead to get dressed. It didn't take him long. Moments after I shut the bathroom door between us, I heard the bedroom door open and close as he left.

I was empty as I stood under the stream of water from the shower. Not numb, not angry, not scared, just . . . empty. I decided to think about nothing at all, rather than analyze the last two days and how I felt about it. I focused on the menial tasks. *Lather, rinse. Shut off the water. Dry your hair.*

When I emerged from the bathroom with a towel wrapped beneath my arms, there were clothes laid out on the bed—a pair of jeans, undergarments, and a soft orange sweater. The boatneck top was older, but comfortable and flattering, and one of my favorite pieces. I dressed quickly and then eyed the doorknob.

Did he trust me somewhat, or would I find the door locked when I tried to open it? I held my breath, grasped the brass handle, and turned. Luka waited in the hall and seemed pleased to see me. He noticed the surprised expression I had, but said nothing, and nodded toward the stairs.

Every step I took beside him without running inched us closer to some sort of understanding. I sat across from him at the table in the kitchen that was once again set for us with a full spread. A lifetime had passed since the last time we'd been here.

"After breakfast," he said, pouring me a cup of coffee, "I assume you have stuff you want to work on. Homework or whatever."

I almost fell out of my chair. "I'm going to class tomorrow?"

His eyes clouded. "I didn't say that."

I made a face. "Well, what's the point of doing it if—"

"Tell me you don't want to do your homework." His expression was direct. "Regardless of whether you have class. Tell me it won't eat at you to leave it unfinished."

I set my coffee down with force. *Damn him.* "Yeah, okay, it'll make me crazy not to do it, but why does it matter?"

"Just do it, Addison," he grumbled and turned to look out the picture window at the bright, sunny day. He frowned. His gaze turned back to me and hardened. "If it matters to you, it matters to me."

He was so confusing, but I could tell there wasn't anything else informative coming from him, and I couldn't keep pushing. We ate as the conversation went silent, and the only sound was the scrape of silverware against china. It was tense, but not uncomfortable. I had a hard time starting a conversation and didn't mind the quiet, and Luka seemed to be the same.

When we finished our meal, his gaze settled on me and his head cocked to one side.

"What?" I asked.

The corner of his mouth hinted a smile. "I like this on you."

I glanced down, and back to him. "My sweater?"

"You wore it the first time I heard you speak. You correct-ed professor Kwon when he'd written the wrong variable on the whiteboard. You beat me to it."

My heart marched along at double-time. He remembered not only the event, but what I was wearing?

Luka appeared unfazed. "Tomorrow, I have to work." He rubbed a hand along the faint scruff on his face. "I'll have to leave the house by seven. There'll be someone here though, until I'm back for lunch."

I swallowed back my mounting irritation at missing my morning lecture. It wouldn't do any good to lose control of my emotions around him, but I still said it with my teeth clenched firmly together. "And what would you have me do tomorrow? Since I won't be at class?"

"You need better clothes. I'll get someone over here to fix that."

I choked. He was going to *what*? "I'm sorry?"

Despite it all, his annoyed look still did something to me. It made me feel excited and eager to see the expression on the op-posite end. Any hint of emotion from him was nice, but a pleased Luka was the most intriguing.

"We'll have lunch together. If all that goes well, you'll have further privileges."

But he wouldn't elaborate on them. My ingrained manners had me trying to clear my plate and set it in the kitchen sink, but Luka waved his hand, dismissing my actions.

"The housekeeper will get it."

Housekeeper. Where, exactly, was this mystery staff? The house was immaculate, but I hadn't seen so much as a shadow of them.

I was escorted upstairs, only this time he guided me to a new door. When he pushed it open, I sucked in a sharp breath. Luka hadn't been lying about packing up my dorm room. It appeared to all be here in this bedroom, which looked as generic as mine was. My clothes hung in the closet. There were open boxes set on the bed and I could see my belongings in there—pictures of my family, the packet from Duke, and my used textbooks.

Luka gestured to the boxes. "Get what you need and follow me."

I loaded my text books in my arms, only for Luka to take them from me.

When I reached for my laptop, his voice was sharp. "No."

I froze. "I need it for online stuff."

He shook his head. "Not today, you don't."

My fingertips slid over the cool metal case of my laptop, longing for everything I could access from it. I wanted more than anything to look up information on Luka Markovic, rather than figure out how to send a cry for help. How twisted was that?

I collected my planner and another book, hugging them close. My fingers curled around the bindings made me feel normal again, if only for a minute. Luka carried my books under an arm, and gestured to the hallway. This time when we descended the stairs, he turned right, and I followed him across the hardwood. We went past what seemed to be a formal sitting room, and then he pushed open a door.

There was one oversized arched window on the front wall, casting morning light across the bookshelves that lined the room. A large, ornate desk sat in the center, perched on top of an

Oriental rug. It seemed to be the focal point, but my gaze went to the shelves, where books and odds and ends had been carefully displayed, even over the fireplace opposite the window.

Luka set my textbooks on a tufted couch, but I drifted to the built-in bookcase, where my attention had landed on a framed photograph.

"Your mother?" I asked before I could think better of it. The image was of an attractive brunette holding a baby, while a young boy hugged her legs. His dark hair and darker eyes were instantly recognizable, even when he was five years old.

Luka's posture went rigid. "Yeah, that's her." He pointed to the couch. "You'll do your homework here."

His mother had a slender frame, big brown eyes, and long, sleek hair the same color as his. Her high cheekbones made her look elegant, and her bright smile announced where Vasilije's dimple came from. The picture filled me with sadness. What had happened to her? "She was beautiful."

Luka took in a deep breath. I wasn't sure if he was frustrated or caught off balance by my statement, so I hurried to the couch. I sank down beside the books and grabbed my planner, not wanting to make him angry.

"Yes," he said quietly. "She was very beautiful."

His expression gave nothing away, but his voice . . . the hurt there was unmistakable. I desperately wanted him to tell me more, but he didn't. His face was shuttered as he went to the desk and sat behind the computer. I had a ton of reading to do for developmental biology, so I dug the textbook out of the stack, cracked it open, and got to work, refusing to let my thoughts wander toward the man sitting across from me.

After a while, I no longer noticed the clicking of his mouse or keyboard. I retreated into the science, shutting the world out.

We fell into a strange pattern the rest of the day, working in silence in his library, largely ignoring the other person. Yet, we were still intensely aware of each other. When he got up to take a phone call in the hallway, the room became cavernous and cold.

It felt like it was simply a room, and not a space we were sharing together.

Luka was gone for a while. Was this another test? The computer was right there, and he was probably still logged on. I kept myself rooted to the couch. I'd already made my choice to play the long game with Luka. Attempting escape would only make it take longer.

When he finally reappeared, he carried drinks in one hand and balanced two plates of sandwiches on the other. Grilled chicken croissants with honey mustard dressing, which tasted amazing. "You have a personal chef," I said, "when it's just you here at the house?"

Luka set his napkin on the plate and pushed it aside. "Whitney only works on the weekends. She prepares everything for the week ahead."

"Oh." I shouldn't have been surprised that even Luka's meals were planned and controlled.

After lunch, he went back to the computer and I moved on to organic chemistry. The day rolled on. At one point Luka rose from the desk, opened the trunk that doubled as a coffee table in front of the couch, and retrieved a quilt. He cast it over me, and I glanced up, surprised.

"You were shivering."

I was so busy I hadn't even noticed until he said so. The sweater I wore wasn't very thick, and I'd been sedentary. How did he expect me to deal with him like this? The caring action was so confusing. I curled up under the warm blanket, and struggled with what to say. "Thank you."

He said nothing.

When my coursework was done and the sunlight was fading, I closed my book and peered at him.

He hadn't flipped on any lights, so the room was growing dark and he was lit by the glowing computer screen. Stubble shadowed his jaw. His black eyes focused on the screen, and then he picked up a pen, scribbling something down on a pad of paper. Yet he must have sensed my gaze because his attention swung abruptly my direction.

"What do you need?"

If I'd gone back to my dorm Friday night, I would have finished polishing my secondary applications this weekend. "I have some applications I was working on."

"For Michigan and Johns Hopkins." His face was emotionless.

"Yeah," I snapped. "That's right, you know because you went through my stuff when you were packing it up."

He sat back from the desk and quirked his eyebrow. "Some of it I did then. I finished going through the rest of it last night."

My eyes narrowed to slits, but he kept talking.

"That's upsetting?" he mocked. "Did I cut you with a broken piece of glass?"

My gaze dropped down to his forearm. The scratch wasn't as red or noticeable today, but it was still there. What he'd said was true, but . . . "You've done worse to me."

"Yeah. So I don't think me reading something you're planning to send to strangers is that big of a deal."

It wasn't, and yet it was. I'd put personal information in there about my vision for my future. My advisor had urged me to speak candidly about my goals. *"Let them feel your passion,"* she'd said. I hadn't written the essay for Luka, and it filled me with unease to know he'd read it, which I was sure he had. I'd printed out a draft for better proofreading.

"You look fucking hot when you pout."

My hands tensed into fists beneath the blanket, stifling back the irritation and the rush his words gave me. He was pushing my buttons on purpose.

He stood and gave me a hard look. "Again, what do you need?"

"I need to polish them and put them in the mail."

"All right. I'll help you get them ready and drop them off on my way to the office in the morning."

I pushed back the blanket and rose to my feet, not wanting him to look down on me. "What's the point if I'm not going to graduate?" In fact, Duke could rescind my acceptance if my grades slipped. Their medical school would not tolerate a senior slump.

He stared at me as if I were throwing a tantrum. "What did I tell you this morning?" He shifted his weight, and set his hands on his hips, signaling visible annoyance with me. "Does getting into med school matter to you?"

Yes, of course it mattered. He knew just how much it did. "It matters more than anything."

"Then, guess what? It *fucking matters* to me."

Chapter
SIXTEEN

I SWALLOWED A BREATH. "You have to go to class to graduate."

Luka rolled his eyes. "I understand how it works, but we're not there as far as trust goes. That should be your primary focus right now." He collected the plates from lunch. "Stay here, I'll be right back."

He left, and I plunked down on the couch, fuming. Despite how he'd worked me up, I was still cold. I aggressively yanked the blanket over myself, feeling powerless and frustrated.

Luka returned with my applications and my laptop. He set it on the desk, plugged it in, and hit the power button. Then, he handed me the application essay. "Read it out loud to me."

It seemed to be so he could multi-task. He went over to the fireplace and turned on the gas, then lit the ceramic pile of faux logs. The blue-orange flames licked over the realistic looking wood in a mesmerizing pattern.

Reading it out to him was weird, but helpful as well. I could hear the awkward phrasing I'd used in the opening paragraph. "Cut that last sentence," he said. "It's repetitive."

He was right.

I made the changes to the document on my laptop while he watched, and then he set up the printer and printed out copies to attach. When I was done addressing the envelopes he'd given me, he stuffed them with the applications, sealed them, and dropped them into the briefcase resting beside the desk.

When he shut my laptop, my gaze casually wandered to his screen and—

"You're looking at porn?" I asked, shocked. There was a black and white picture on screen of a topless woman, whose head was turned down and her hands tucked behind her back, or perhaps they were tied.

"That's research." He was quick to click the window closed, though.

"Is that what the kids are calling it these days?" I said, my voice flat. "Research?"

His hand dipped under my arm and he yanked me to my feet, bringing us face to face. "It's research about your training, Addison." His eyes flooded with something raw and sexual. "I've spent the whole day working on our plan."

Well, that was terrifying. So why did a thrill shiver down my spine? And . . . *our* plan? I tucked a lock of hair behind my ear and forced out a confident voice. "Okay. You need to get a hobby."

Luka's evil smile made my blood run cold and got me hot in the same instance. "I have one." He slipped a hand beneath the hem of my sweater and ran his warm fingers over my belly, causing me to flinch. They skated upward, tracing the cup of my bra. "It's this," he whispered.

He loomed overhead and didn't tip his head down, choosing instead to look over his long lashes at me. I was sure he noted every hurried breath I took, and saw my pupils dilate, a perfect response to his touch. My skin tingled beneath his fingertips and I studied his mouth. It said dirty, sometimes awful things, but it was beautiful, too. His sexy, cruel mouth was addictive.

The fireplace burned quietly. There was only a faint hiss of gas as it flickered in the now-dark room. Luka lowered his mouth almost to mine, but didn't claim it. He breathed over my lips and dipped down further into the crook of my neck. There, the tip of his nose brushed over my sensitive skin. He moved from one side to the other, teasing his kiss but not delivering it. I licked my lips instinctively, craving what he denied.

It wound me tighter each second as his hot breath streamed over me, and the faintest brush of his lips grazed my neck. I was itchy and agitated. No, those weren't the right words. *Eager* was a better fit. Perhaps even *desperate*.

"Luka," I said, verging on a plea. I was weak. How could I want him? I'd been tainted, like he'd poisoned me. Sinking down to his level was the only way to alleviate the symptoms.

"What do you need?" he asked. He was a vicious cat, sadistically playing with the mouse he'd caught. He'd toy with his prey before devouring it. "Ask me."

I sighed while he continued his torment. Was it possible to die from anticipation? How the hell was I supposed to ask him to kiss me, and why? Luka was a taker. He'd get whatever he wanted, use me up, and discard me when he was done. He wasn't bothered with right or wrong, and certainly didn't care what I thought.

"Are you shaking because you're cold?" His tone was rhetorical. We both knew I wasn't. The fire had warmed the room, and there was plenty of heat between us.

It felt a little like dying, or at least sacrificing a limb to save the body. I was surrendering more control, and soon I'd have nothing left. I stared into his intense eyes, and my voice was a whisper. "Kiss me."

"Louder."

My chest expanded as I pulled in an enormous breath. "Kiss me."

He obliterated everything. His mouth moved urgently against mine, and then his tongue got involved. Powerful, sure arms swept me up and dropped me down with a thump on the end of the desk. He didn't even stop kissing me as I heard the sharp snap of his fingers. There was no hesitation this time as I pried my knees apart and welcomed him to step between them. I curled my hands beneath the cotton of his t-shirt, finding his skin burning hot.

We were wild, thrashing against each other.

His kiss turned up to a new level of aggression, and I moaned with a hint of pain as he bit down on my bottom lip. I scored my nails down his chest, but it only caused him to escalate. A heartbeat later, his hand was wrapped tightly around my throat.

"Was this the plan?" I asked. "Making me ask you to kiss me?"

"No." His wet tongue traced the edge of my ear. "I just wanted it, and now I can't seem to stop kissing you."

He felt out of control? *Yeah, Luka. I know exactly how that feels.*

I was panting when he abruptly stepped back and pulled me to my unsteady feet. "It's a thousand degrees in this office."

I fell into his arms, letting him support me. "Is that you telling me to take off my clothes?" It was a half-joke, half-truth.

His gaze flitted downward and his eyes went hazy with lust, but he blinked it back. "No. We have other shit to do. Come on."

Dinner was served in the kitchen, thankfully not in the dining room. I shuddered when we walked past the long table where Luka had spanked my bare bottom in front of everyone. I had a purple-yellow bruise from it—I'd seen it in the mirror after my shower this morning.

He poured us each a glass of red wine to go along with our filet mignon.

"Your parents will be calling you soon," he said, "so we need to discuss the rules."

I'd been turning the base of the wine glass, but paused. "They'll be calling? How do you know that?"

His expression stayed flat, giving nothing away. "You'll put the call on speaker, so I can hear everything said." The table groaned as he leaned his elbows on it. "You can tell them you've met someone, but you don't give them my name. If you try to ask for help, or get them involved in any way, I'll revoke your privileges. That means you go back to naked and chained to the bed."

It reminded me how tired I was from last night, both physically and mentally. I leaned forward on my elbows as well. "I'm not going to try to escape, for my safety and theirs." The words burned as fire in my throat. "You and your father made it perfectly clear what the consequences are if I disobey."

He winced. Luka *actually winced* at how I'd lumped him together with his father. "I didn't want that to happen."

"Which part? Where you humiliated me, or where my life was threatened?"

He scowled. "All of it."

"Why? You don't give a damn about—"

He slammed his fist loudly against the tabletop and the place settings jumped. Wine sloshed in my glass, and I clamped a hand over my lips to mute my sound of surprise.

"I don't, huh?" he demanded. "You have no idea what I fucking gave up for you."

What the hell was he talking about? "Oh? Okay, then tell me."

"No."

I closed my eyes and pinched the bridge of my nose. "You get how trust works, right? That it's a two-way street?"

He exhaled loudly and his eyes turned stormy. "I don't want the life my father lives. I worked hard and earned my degree, and then I did it all over again for my master's." Luka glanced away and grumbled under his breath. "Not that my father doesn't work hard. He has to, to stay ahead of the Russians."

Part of me wanted to dig into his statement, but I was smart enough not to ask. It was doubtful he'd tell me what kind of business his family was really in, and it was probably better if I just assumed the worst. I didn't need the dirty details, so instead I evaluated his words critically. Was he saying he didn't want to be a part of the organized crime his father was involved in?

"I've been upfront with him," he continued. "Vasilije's like my father, and he's fucking eager to help out with that side of the Markovic *business*." Luka's voice dripped with disdain.

There was a long pause, prompting me. "So you're trying to protect Vasilije?"

Luka gave a short, ironic laugh. "No, if he wants to get into that shit, he will. My brother's an asshole. Just like my father, remember?" He took a quick sip of his wine. "When Vasilije got busted, it was for weed. It mellows Vasilije out and, seriously, that's a good thing. Most of the time he's a psychotic. He's a perfect fit to step up."

I failed to understand. "Then, what's the issue?"

"All that money needs to be kept track of. Why have an outsider cook the books when I can keep all our dirty secrets within the family?"

The realization washed through me and a sharp pang stabbed inward as I thought about Luka's situation. "You got your degree to try to escape, and instead it made you more valuable to your father."

He shook his head. "To my uncle. He's the one my father answers to. I've been working legit for them up until now."

My heart hurried along with concern. "Until now? What changed?"

"My father has leverage."

I gripped the edge of the table, knowing the truth already, but I needed to hear him confirm it. "I'm the leverage."

His dark eyes were empty, and for the first time, I noticed the faint lines at the corners. He was hiding the emotion locked inside him. He spoke softly, almost as if defending himself. "I had to make a deal."

Which had been to save my life, I was sure of it. He was trapped just as much as I was. "Why'd you do it?"

His lips turned down into a scowl, and he glared my direction. "He was going to have you killed."

"I understand, but I'm asking *why you* made the deal. He wasn't threatening your life."

There was no label to put to the emotion on his face, but it made my heart ache. While I tried to figure it out, the expression faded and returned to his emotionless mask. "I agreed to it because of what I did to you. I was the one who made the mistake. You shouldn't have to pay for it with your life."

He'd punched the air clean from my lungs. His admission was stunning, and it was an apology, not in words, but in actions.

"Christ," he groaned, smoothing a hand back over his hair. "I'm not any good at this shit, Addison. I don't think you understand how badly I wanted you. I've had you, and I *still* want you." His words made me feel weightless. "Every time I touch you, I just want more."

I blinked in disbelief, at a total loss.

"Say something," he demanded. His chest rose and fell with his hurried breathing.

My voice was uneven. "What do you want me to say?"

"Tell me you feel it, too."

My guts twisted inside, and I banded my arms tight around myself. He'd raped me. He was holding me here against my will. And yet, I *felt* it. "I . . ." He'd said no lies, and I was already in over my head. I was sick. The last, tiny hold on my control slipped from my grasp. "I feel it."

He was capable of expressing relief. His face softened as my words fell on him, and the smile spread across his lips like wildfire. God, he could be so beautiful when he wanted to. Like any event you waited for with excited anticipation, the smile was over much too quickly.

I wasn't sure exactly how it happened. He didn't give me a command, at least not verbally, but I sensed what he wanted. I'd admitted it, so it was too late for me to save myself. I stood from my chair, stalked around the edge of the table, and stepped into his waiting arms. I was pulled down into his lap.

As we were kissing, I was aware I was the dumbest girl in the world to let it happen. I'd already allowed him in my mind and my body—how long would it be before I allowed him in my heart?

His lips roved over mine and his tongue slipped into my

mouth. I gripped his face, holding on against his dominating, yet needy kiss. I was spinning, drunk off of him.

"I'm gonna fuck you on this kitchen table."

I closed my eyes and imagined it. I'd be sprawled out beside our half-eaten dinners with him thrusting powerfully between my legs. I grew damp, and my pulse kicked. "Okay."

Aggression flickered in his eyes as he stood, dumping me on my feet. "I wasn't asking permission."

He put a hand on my shoulder and shoved me to sit on the tabletop, causing it to groan in protest. I expected him to have me flat on my back, or order me to take off my clothes, but he grabbed his glass of wine and drank while he stood casually between my legs. His gaze didn't deviate from mine, though. His free hand found my knee and rested there, his palm warm.

"You feel that?" he asked as his hand squeezed. "My goddamn hand is aching for more. It wants to be on your tits. Touching your pussy. Inside you."

Maybe my wine was drugged. There wasn't any other reason why I suddenly felt so brave, despite the tremble in my core. I put my hands flat against the tabletop, leaned back, and spread my legs wider. I was signifying he had full access and could do whatever he wanted. There were warning alarms screaming in my head, but I willingly ignored them.

My gesture of submission had quite the impact on Luka. His hand tensed on my leg and he seemed to stop breathing. It was nice to catch him off guard and know I had such an effect on him, but I didn't get to enjoy it for long. His wine glass was set down with a quiet thud. One hand slid around my back while the other cupped the side of my neck, and his lips captured mine.

His kiss was mean and delicious. I sighed softly and tried to scoot my body closer—

My cellphone rang, interrupting us. I froze. He'd been carrying my cell all day? Luka dug my phone out of his back pocket and handed it to me. Sure enough, the screen announced it was my mother. My heart was pounding, and it was impossible to switch gears so rapidly. To come down off of the high of him.

He stared at me expectantly, and I dry swallowed.

"Hey, Mom," I said after answering it. "Hold on, I need to put you on speaker." I tapped the screen.

"—father's on the line, too." Her voice blared from the phone. "Addie, are you there?"

"I'm here," I said. "What's going on?"

Luka took the phone from me, placed it on the table, and his hands trapped my hips, sliding me to the edge. It fitted me against him and his arousal pressed against mine, both of us held back by clothes.

My mother's voice was bursting with energy. "We got some exciting news today!"

"Well, really, Jonathon did," my dad interrupted.

Since they couldn't see me, I made a face. All of our conversations lately seemed to revolve around my brother.

Faint amusement flashed through Luka, but it was overpowered quickly with lust. He ground himself against the seam of my legs, and his hands burrowed under my sweater. My mouth dropped open. It felt good, but I didn't want my parents to hear what he was doing, and my voice tightened with nerves. "Yeah? Did he get another scholarship?"

My mom giggled. "No, he won a car!"

Suspicion corded my muscles into knots, making me stay perfectly still as Luka's fingers followed the curve of my breast above the edge of my bra. My body wanted to focus on his touch, but my mind was pulled elsewhere. "What?"

"I know," she said, "it's crazy! Jonathon just left to go over to his girlfriend's house and show it off."

"It's not like it's an expensive sports car," my father added. "It's a Ford Fusion. But it's brand new, drives great, and looks good. He's very excited."

"And it's so much safer than the Buick. That car's almost as old as he is."

Luka worked his fingers inside my bra, and my nipple snapped into a sharp point on contact. I stared at him, silently asking him to wait, but my reluctance only seemed to appeal to him more.

"How?" My word was clipped.

My parents spoke over each other, until my father relented and my mother spoke. "A drawing. He doesn't even remember when he entered it, and your father was worried it was a scam."

Luka's hips moved, gently thrusting against me and forced a reaction. I let out a stuttering breath and put my hands on his chest, mouthing the word, *"Wait."* He didn't. He gripped my wrists and eased me down onto my back, pinning me to the table.

"It wasn't a scam," my father said. "We drove down to the Markovic dealership this afternoon and picked the car up."

I bucked against Luka, but his hands had me cuffed tightly to the wood, and his heated body smothered mine. He'd given my brother a car? Why? I was filled with dread. The opulent house Luka held me captive in suggested the Markovics weren't overly charitable, so this had to be a calculated move.

My mom babbled on about the car, telling me the color and its features, but I couldn't comprehend. I stared up at Luka and tried to understand what his play was. His expression wasn't any help. He seemed to be staring back at me with the same curiosity, as if wondering how I was going to react.

He let go of my wrist and tapped my phone's screen, muting it. "It's an insurance policy in case you try to run," he said. "The GPS tells us where he is."

"I already told you, I'm not going to run." Wait a minute. He'd said *us*.

"It's not my insurance policy." Luka's voice was soft. "As long as you do what I say, your brother will be fine. Better than fine, he gets a new car out of the arrangement."

There was no more discussion to be had because he turned off the mute, silencing me. I pressed my lips together to hold back my words. I was scared enough for myself. I didn't want to add worry for Jonathon on top of it.

My mother's voice was still bubbly and excited. "Anyway, enough about all that. How are you? How's school?"

I tensed, hating the lie. "It's fine."

"Is Avery around?" she asked casually, probably fishing to see if she could speak freely.

"No," I said.

"Oh. Is she still driving you crazy?"

The wooden surface wasn't comfortable, and it grew even more so when Luka's fingers fumbled at the snap of my jeans. The word came out forceful and meant for him. "No."

Like it mattered. I squirmed and shoved his hands away, but

he shot me a dark, serious look. It turned my body to stone.

"No?" She sounded perplexed. "That's good. What did you do this weekend?"

He leaned over me, one hand on the table beside my head and the other tugged down my zipper. I was trapped under his heavy, powerful gaze. "I, uh . . . went to a party with Avery."

My parents spoke at the same time. "You did?"

Luka's hand was inside my pants, touching me through my underwear, and his mouth lifted in the slight, pleased smile when he discovered how turned on I was. I quivered, and my hands splayed on the tabletop, trying to grip the flat surface.

"Did you have fun?" my mom asked.

Fun? I couldn't process a response and then I couldn't breathe as Luka began to peel the jeans and panties down my legs. I shook my head and gazed up at him with wide eyes, but he smirked and kept going.

I had to say something. My mom had asked me a question. "It was loud. And . . . kind of crowded."

When Luka pulled my jeans off my hips, my lower body thudded on the table and made the plate closest to the phone bang.

"You okay?" My dad sounded concerned.

"Fine," I said, hurried. "I dropped something."

Cool air wafted over my exposed skin. Since he'd gotten the clothes past my knees, it was easy for him to take them the rest of the way off, even as I twisted and tried to make it difficult. He tossed the jeans and underwear across the room where the microphone was less likely to pick up on it. Then, his gaze started at my ankles and slithered upward, lingering at my knees I'd pinched tight together. There was no doubt what he was thinking about.

Oh, shit . . .

I was shaky with trepidation, and maybe a miniscule amount of excitement. Luka was bad, and the worst part of me hoped he was going to make me be bad along with him. Naughty, slutty, and wrong. I teetered at the edge, wanting him to push me over.

"Were there any boys at this party?" my mom teased, probing.

My heart was beating in my throat as Luka's hand appeared in front of my face and his middle finger pressed against his thumb, only to move abruptly and produce a soft snap. I dragged air in through my nose, taking a deep breath as I parted my trembling legs. His face was evil and triumphant.

"Yes," I said on a low voice. I wasn't sure who I was speaking to.

"Yeah?" My mom couldn't keep her interest even from the one word. "Tell us about him. What's his major?"

Warm palms smoothed up my thighs, all the way to my center, and Luka's thumb grazed my clit. It was a jolt so powerful I bit my tongue and choked back my moan.

"He's, uh, older." Could they hear my frantic energy? "He graduated last year."

I placed my hands on my forehead as he bent at the waist and licked all the way from my entrance to my clit. Holding in the sigh of pleasure was nearly impossible and I was sure I was going to burst. My legs shook desperately. He repeated the action, and this time he stayed at the end, fluttering his sinful tongue which made heat dance along my body like fireworks.

"He's older?" There was surely a frown on my dad's face to go along with his question.

Luka's mouth was insane and swirled bliss all through me.

"Yes," I moaned, then tried to steel my voice. Did they have a clue what their good little girl was doing right at this very moment? "I know him," I said, trying to soothe away the concern. "He was . . . the TA of my calculus class my sophomore year."

My mom sounded happy for me. "Oh, you mean Luka?"

Chapter
SEVENTEEN

I froze, and Luka's head snapped up, his gaze finding mine. *Oh, shit!* I'd forgotten how I'd mentioned him, and the realization hit me rapid-fire. I'd told my mother about my plan to buy him coffee, and how I'd chickened out. She knew all about my stupid crush on him.

My face burned hotter than the surface of the sun. "Um . . ."

His smile was different this time. Still amazing, but he looked as if he'd conquered me. Which was exactly how I felt.

"Wasn't that his name?" she continued. "The boy you were head over heels for?"

Mom! "I wasn't!"

Luka buried his lips into the side of my leg, planting kisses and silencing a laugh. I was doubly annoyed with my mom, not just at how she'd unknowingly embarrassed me, but how I'd been denied the sound of his laughter. It was such a rare occurrence.

"Okay, Addie," she said. "Whatever you say. Are you going to see him again?"

Luka's indecent kiss had rendered me honest. I threaded my hand through his hair and locked my gaze with his intense one. "Yes." *Oh, yes.* I had a feeling I'd be seeing a lot more of him in another minute. "Hey, I gotta run. Tell Jonathon congrats for me."

Luka looked disappointed as we said our goodbyes, but the second I disconnected the call, his hands began to work his belt.

"Head over heels?"

"I didn't even know you."

Did I now?

It was awkward being half naked on the dinner table while he stood beside me, but then his pants were sliding down his thighs and his hard dick was nudging between my legs, readying to make good on his earlier promise.

He pushed inside, giving me just an inch. "You don't have to know me to want this. Which you do, don't you?"

The fit of him inside my tight body was still a lot to handle, and it hurt. Yet it felt good. A beautiful pain. The stretch was achy, but it shifted into a new sensation as he pushed deeper inside, sealing the connection between us closed.

"Yes," I breathed. *Yes.* It felt so good to confess it out loud.

His eyes reflected everything I felt, every drop of lust and pleasure and need, but there was more in his look. He had rage and darkness. He was scary, and perfect.

This morning he'd been almost gentle, probably as gentle as Luka got, but his first harsh thrust now set the tone for the session. I cried out. Pain stabbed into me as he impaled me on his firm dick, but it slid easily into my slick body. The sensation was darkly satisfying, as if he were claiming me all over again for the first time.

The force of his body fucking mine had the table knocking against the floor, scooting along.

"Get your shirt off," he demanded. "When my cock's inside you, you'll always be naked. I want those goddamn tits available to me."

I frantically yanked at my shirt, lifting it up over my head, and as I cast it over the side of the table, I knocked over my wine glass. It didn't spill much, as I'd already drank most of the glass. Luka set it back upright as I hurried to undo my bra, and the straps tangled briefly in my arms. It dropped to the floor with barely a sound.

He pinched my nipple so hard there was pain. "Be more careful."

He drove into my body, punishing me, but the initial hurt was gone, and now I felt heat and pleasure. Every inch I took inside me heightened my craving for him, and I became incensed. I raked my nails down his arms, urging him for more, like I could scrape it out of him. His hands clamped around my waist, holding my thrashing body down.

"Perfect little Addison." His voice mocked disapproval. "Talking to her parents while I've got my head between her thighs, licking her sweet pussy." His thrust caused my eyes to roll back into my head. "Were you worried they'd find out what I've done to their good girl?" With my eyes closed, it made his voice sound treacherous. "That you're not a virgin anymore?"

I couldn't think about his words. I fisted a hand in the center of his shirt and pulled him down. Wait, no. His clothes were in my way. I wanted his heated skin pressed against mine. I reached over his shoulder and grabbed another handful of shirt, this time on his back, and jerked it up over his head.

He broke our devastating kiss just long enough to get rid of the t-shirt, and then his lips returned to mine, swallowing my moan. His smooth, soft skin was addictive, and he felt feverish. Maybe that was why his words and actions could be so cold. He used all of his warmth in his burning body.

My spine dug into the table as he continued to pound

relentlessly, and I sighed in anguish as his chest drew away. My eyes fluttered open in time to see him dip his hand in the spilled wine, and then he was smearing the wetness over my breasts. The action was followed quickly by his mouth and swirling tongue. It was enjoyable, the dual sensation of the cool wine and his hot mouth.

And it was all building toward a big finish.

"Maybe you should call them back," he said, nipping at the underside of a breast. "Let them hear you coming all over my cock."

Holy hell, I was terrified he'd make me do it.

"No." He said it like he was correcting himself, and stood upright. His eyes were possessive. "Forget it. That sound's only for me."

My legs gripped at his waist and my hands clung to his forearms. The table creaked loudly beneath me, and I was gasping for breath, each one a struggle. I'd been careless and spilled the wine, and now the words spilled from me with the same recklessness. "God, Luka. It feels really good."

I watched him break apart while he was surrounded by me. His broad shoulders pulled tight together, his eyes slammed shut, and he withdrew from me abruptly. I lay stunned as he gripped himself, pumping his fist over his dick. Ropes of thick liquid flicked onto my belly and breasts, and I flinched at the contact. There was a loud, deep groan of satisfaction, and his fist slowed. He moved until the very last drop had poured from him onto my lower abdomen, and leaned over, supporting himself on his free hand.

"You . . ." He hadn't quite caught his breath. His Adam's apple bobbed as he swallowed, and he seemed to finally even out. He said it softly. "Look what you do to me."

I propped myself up on my elbows, confused on what exactly he— *"Oh!"*

Luka eased two fingers inside, and set his other hand on my clit, stirring. I collapsed on the table with an enormous bang.

"Holy shit," I moaned. He was touching me in a spot I hadn't felt before. It was so deep and intense, my body burst into flames. He studied every minute move I made as his fingers pumped in and out and worked me into a frenzy. The orgasm threatened, and then it abruptly barreled down on me. My arms flayed, searching desperate for something to hold onto, and I clawed at the wooden tabletop.

"Yes," he said, his voice coated in power. *"Yes*, Addison."

I unleashed a cry that verged on a scream as the climax obliterated. I seized and contracted, one intense wave, then another right on its heels. The pleasure was on a whole new level from anything I'd had before, and it just kept going. I shivered in ecstasy, and the uncontrollable writhing kept me moving on his hand, prolonging the orgasm.

And after a lifetime, the pleasure began to ease away and I began my journey back down to earth. Back to the reality where Luka Markovic had just fucked me on his kitchen table, his come all over my breasts, and given me the greatest orgasm of my life with his skilled hands. I'd been with him two days. The longest two days of my life, but still only *two days.* What would happen after a week? Or a month?

How much further down would he take me?

π

Not going to class on Monday nearly made me sick.

I sat on the bed in the green-striped guest bedroom that was mine now, apparently, and chewed at my fingernails. It was an old, disgusting habit I usually only fell back into during finals or the week leading up to the MCATs, but I was more anxious now than I'd ever been for a test. At least those I could prepare for and felt in control. There was no control now since Luka had stolen all of mine away.

I didn't try to escape, but I fantasized about it. I made plans and different scenarios, more than anything to give myself something to do. I needed a distraction to keep from thinking about the class I was missing out on.

After dinner last night, Luka had led me to a half bath off of the kitchen and instructed me to clean up. Then he'd taken me upstairs, allowed me to pick out some sleeping clothes and things for tomorrow, and returned me to my bedroom.

There'd been no mention of the shiny silver deadbolt that had been installed on the outside of my door, but I'd noticed it immediately. Luka must have had it done while we'd been in the office working.

He'd kissed me goodnight and left, and the distinct clunk of the deadbolt turning made my heart sink. We had a long way to go with building trust.

I'd slept better than the previous night, and when I woke, there was breakfast waiting on top of the dresser, right beside my stack of books, and I was grateful for both. I ate quickly, showered and dressed, and curled up in the loveseat with my organic chemistry book in my lap.

He'd removed the ticking alarm clock, so once again I had

no idea what time it was, and it was beyond irritating. It was overcast outside, making it difficult to judge. At one point I got up and peered out the window, staring at the pretty front lawn and long driveway that curved to disappear into a heavily wooded forest. There were no other houses in sight. I went back to reading and taking notes.

I was nearing the end of a chapter when a soft rap on the door broke the silence and startled me.

"Addison?" a female voice asked. "May I come in?"

Like I had any control over that. I couldn't exactly let her in. "Uh . . . yeah, that's fine."

I closed my book and stood, straightening my clothes. Was this the person Luka had said would be at the house with me? The lock on the door was turned, and it swung open slowly, revealing a petite woman who looked to be thirty. Blonde and fair skinned, with big doe eyes and a white, perfect smile.

"I'm Jennifer," she said as she came in and shut the door. "I'm married to Alek." She said it like I should have a clue who that was, but my vacant stare must have announced I didn't. "I'm Luka's cousin-in-law."

She set her purse down on the dresser, and placed her hands on her hips, zeroing in on me. "Let's have a look at you."

"I'm sorry?"

"Can you turn? Luka said you needed new clothes and a dress for Goran's Christmas party."

I walked in a slow circle. "Who's Goran?"

When I came back around, there was a tight smile frozen on her pleasant face. "He's Luka's uncle."

The head of the Markovic family, the one Luka said everyone

answered to. I threaded my nervous hands together. Luka had sent Jennifer to pick out a dress for me for Christmas, and it was barely November.

She went to her purse, retrieved her phone, and held it up. "Can I take a few pictures?"

Could I say no? "Uh, sure." I didn't smile and stood awkwardly as the camera snapped away.

The phone was set down and a measuring tape retrieved next. Jennifer went about her business as if I were more an object than a person, taking my measurements and recording the information in her phone. She asked how tall I was and my shoe size, and when she look satisfied, she picked up her purse.

"I'll be back later in the week with some options."

Jennifer left as abruptly as she'd arrived. She'd seemed on a mission, and I wondered if Luka had ordered her not to socialize with his prisoner. She knew I was his captive because she locked me in as she left.

A while after Jennifer's visit, the door was unlocked, pushed open, and revealed Luka standing in the hallway. He wore black pants, a gray patterned dress shirt, and a black tie that had been tugged loose. I was instantly anxious.

"I've got lunch ready." He turned, not waiting for me, and headed back to the stairs.

He'd set out the food his chef had prepared, because I could see the marked containers stacked beside the sink. He sat down at the table he'd fucked me on last night, and began to eat. How could he be so indifferent to it all? I sank down into the seat opposite him.

There was no conversation, making me tense. Why had he

bothered to come home for lunch if we weren't going to say anything? I couldn't handle the silence another moment.

"How's work, darling?" I asked, my tone pointed.

His chewing slowed and his gaze tightened on mine.

Since I didn't get a response, it pushed me further. "My day's been great. Nothing to do but sit around and wait for you."

He set his fork down deliberately, and his expression hardened. "I don't care for the attitude."

"Well, I don't care for missing class when I'm not sick."

"You want to miss class because you don't feel well?" His words were laced with the threat. "I can make that happen."

I blew out a breath and my shoulders slumped. Luka had trapped me in this awful position, but he was also trying to make the best of it. He could have taken the easy way out and left me at that dinner table with his father. Not only would he be rid of me, but he wouldn't have been forced into making the deal with his uncle.

So I shouldn't be lashing out at him, since my goal was to earn his trust. I sighed. "I'm sorry. This is . . . hard for me."

Luka blinked and his gaze drifted away from mine. His voice came out less confident than usual. "I know it is."

We plunged into silence once more, but this time it wasn't quite as oppressive.

He picked up his fork, but hesitated. "Eat your lunch. I have something for you after that might make it easier."

"A time machine?" I asked.

His eyebrow pulled upward. I looked down at my plate of chicken parmesan and got busy eating so it would keep my mouth occupied.

The lack of conversation wasn't uncomfortable. It was clear Luka was a man of few words, but I longed to know more. He'd gone through all of my stuff, had read my application essay, and prodded me for information. He knew a lot more about me than I did about him. My heartbeat picked up as I attempted a conversation.

"You look nice," I eked out.

His eyes clouded with suspicion. I couldn't blame him, but it wasn't a lie. He looked great in his professional clothes. He'd rolled back his sleeves, showing off an expensive watch, and the dress shirt fit him expertly.

"Do you have to wear a tie, or choose to?"

He appeared to consider his answer carefully. "I don't *have* to, but I like to look my best." His coal-colored eyes deepened. "Just like you." He'd finished his lunch, and now I seemed to be his primary focus. "But you should be aware you look your best when you're not wearing anything at all."

My mouth went dry. I thought the same of him, but there was no way I'd say it out loud.

Luka's phone, which rested face up on the table, chimed with a text message. He scooped it up, typed out a response, and set his gaze on me. Something sexual lingered in his dark eyes, and it made me pinch my knees together.

"Your time is my time," he said, matter-of-factly. "So you're going to use my time to bring yourself right to the edge of orgasm, but you won't come. You'll do it twice before I'm back at six fifteen."

My mind stumbled over the assignment. "I . . . there's not a clock in my room."

"I'm about to give you one." He took the napkin out of his lap, tossed it on his plate, and turned toward the doorway. "Vanessa?" he called, his voice raised.

A woman appeared carrying a black book. Her long, straight brown hair was pulled back in a low ponytail, and matched the rest of her. Efficient, no nonsense. She had dark skin and her face was pretty, and she looked to be the same age as Luka. But her frame wasn't the standard delicate feminine one—she was more muscle than curves.

I imagined when she wanted to, Vanessa could be downright intimidating.

"Did you finish?" he asked.

"Yeah." Her curious, distracted gaze wandered over to me, and then she must have realized how unprofessional her answer had been. "I mean, yes, sir."

"That's weird, don't call me that." Luka scowled. He took the black book from her, which wasn't a book. He flipped open the cover, examined the iPad inside, and seemed satisfied. "Thank you," he said, dismissing her.

She nodded and disappeared through the doorway.

"Your assistant?" I asked.

"No. She's new." He slid the iPad across the table toward me. "This is yours."

"What?" I stared at the tablet with disbelief.

"It won't connect to the Internet, but I put some books on there, and also this." He tapped an icon that led to the videos stored on the device, and then tapped again. The video went fullscreen and began to play, and my mouth fell open.

"Is this from today?" I grabbed the tablet to examine it closer.

208

It appeared to be video of my molecular biology lecture.

"Yeah," he said. "Vanessa will video your classes every day and bring the footage to me."

I paused the video and stared at him, trying to sort through the competing emotions. I was thrilled he'd arranged this so I wasn't really missing the lectures, but less pleased that he could hold the videos for ransom. He could get me to do almost *anything* for those videos, and he knew it.

"Notice your new iPad has a clock at the top of the screen." Luka's eyes gleamed. He was excited about doling out the assignment to me.

The tablet suddenly felt heavier in my hands.

After lunch was over, he glanced at his watch, and it was clear it was time to return to my prison cell. I fought not to drag my feet up the stairs. I was already sick of the green striped wallpaper, and I longed for Avery's garish Christmas lights duct taped to the ceiling.

Luka hovered in the door, looking unsure of how to proceed. We hadn't touched. The distance between us should have been reassuring, but it wasn't. My betraying body wanted him closer. It desired his warm skin against mine, and I cursed myself.

"I'll be back at six fifteen," he said.

I lifted my chin, trying to look unaffected. "All right." It was supposed to sound snide, but my voice weakened and turned breathless. "I'll be here, waiting for you."

His shoulders tightened, and it looked like he was wavering. Was he going to step into the room, shut the door, and start something? And, did I want that? No, I told myself, clutching the iPad closer. He'd already given me what I needed.

His decision had been made and the faint desire in his expression drained away. "See you later." Luka was halfway out the door, and lobbed the comment over his shoulder. "Have fun with your assignment, but . . . not *too much* fun."

Chapter
EIGHTEEN

AT LUNCH ON THURSDAY, Luka announced he'd leave my room unlocked. The doors to the bedrooms were to remain closed, and the computer in the office was password protected, but I could move about the first floor as I wished. Being from a family of criminals, the whole house was wired with a sophisticated security system. If I entered a room without permission, he'd get his text alert, and I'd go back to square one.

"Naked and chained to the bed," I'd repeated, exasperated. "Yeah, I know."

His 'assignments' had gotten progressively more challenging, but also thrilling, and I always completed them. I couldn't shake my ingrained desire to please and succeed, and needed to ensure my class videos would keep coming.

Monday's task hadn't been too bad, at least not until Luka had returned and quizzed me on it. He'd wanted to know exactly what I'd thought about during my two sessions, and made me describe in detail my memory of the previous night on the table. He'd also had two fingers inside me, coaxing both the words and the suspended orgasm from me.

Tuesday had two assignments. He gave me back my razor and instructions to go completely bare below the waist. The second task was to wait naked for him in a specific position on the bed so he could inspect my work. I had to sit with my legs wide open and feet flat on the mattress, leaning back on my hands, so everything was clearly on display the way he thought I *looked my best*. He'd come home from work, carried in a glass of wine, and sat in the loveseat staring at me. Butterflies had fluttered in my stomach, but his heated, lustful stare made me feel powerful and desired, too.

It was also the most conversation we'd ever had, as he seemed to want to prolong our mutual anticipation. Or possibly just to make me uncomfortable. We talked about his job, mostly. When he'd gotten his undergraduate degree, he'd struggled to find work that wasn't public accounting with low pay and long hours, and although he'd been concerned about pressure to help with all sides of the Markovic business, he'd accepted the legit job offer from the dealership. Plus, they'd offered to pay for grad school.

Luka glossed over the details, but I could read between the lines. His uncle's personal accountant was now slowly bringing Luka into the fold regarding the criminal activities. As ridiculous as it sounded, I was worried for him. He'd worked so hard to be better than that, but his family was sinking him, dragging Luka down into their dirty world.

Wasn't he doing the same to me?

Wednesday's assignment had been to take video while I brought myself to orgasm. I'd been mortified to film it, but when I was done, I'd been surprised by how hot the video turned out. And it had stolen my breath as he'd watched it in front of me last night.

"What would you like me to do today?" I asked, my voice tight with nervous energy, when we'd finished our lunch. He hadn't given me a dirty task to complete yet, which set me on high alert.

"No assignment. I'll be home late." His eyes clouded over. "I've got a dinner meeting with my uncle."

I felt the chill all the way to my bones. "Oh."

The silence was heavy with all the questions I wanted to ask, but didn't.

"Dinner is in the fridge. Whitney puts the heating instructions on the label. Don't try to burn the house down."

I wasn't sure if it was a joke or not.

He stared vacantly at the table, and I couldn't help myself. "Luka . . . are you okay?"

His gaze connected with mine. It was anything but convincing. "I'm fine."

"All right." I swallowed thickly. "You can, I don't know, talk about it if you want to." The words were shocking, coming from me. I sucked at being a friend, and this was Luka. Why would I want to encourage any kind of relationship? I forced myself to sound light and carefree. "And really, who am I going to tell?"

His head tilted slightly, evaluating me like I was a suspect.

I shrugged. "Or don't tell me. You do whatever you want."

Because he made it clear each night where I stood when he locked me into the green striped bedroom alone. I was a toy for him to play with, and when playtime was over, he put me away. He'd fuck me, but not sleep with me, and *that* bothered me. After all that had happened, him refusing to share his bed was what made me angry.

I was clearly losing my mind.

"I need to get back to work," he said, rising from the table.

I did the same, took a step toward the stairs, and stopped myself. If I had free rein over the main floor of the house, I didn't need to return to my room. I was the timid animal released from captivity, unsure of how to adjust to the wild. "I guess I'll hang out down here?"

"That's fine." He smoothed a hand down his tie, and his forehead creased like he was deep in thought. "Fuck, come here."

I'd only made it one step to him before he had me wrapped in his arms and his mouth covered mine in a desperate kiss. What on earth was happening? His hands caressed my back and pressed me against his chest, and his lips were needy. He tasted of longing, and kissed me like a man on borrowed time.

Holy shit. The realization was like being shot in the chest. Luka was nervous, and this kiss was a potential goodbye. It also explained why he was giving me freedom to move about the house. If he didn't return, eventually I could try an escape.

"Don't go," I whispered when the kiss was over.

I'd never heard him shocked before. "What?"

"The meeting. You're *worried*." Worried for his life.

He pulled in a long breath. "I'm sure it'll be fine. If I don't go, that . . . would not be fine, for either of us." He cupped my face in a hand, and his thumb brushed softly, tracing my cheek. "I'll be back later tonight."

He kissed me once more, and then pulled himself away, leaving me adrift with emotions I didn't want to have.

The rest of the day dragged more than normal. I watched the lectures Vanessa had recorded from the previous day, did my required reading, and then set about exploring the parts of the house that were available to me.

Pictures of Luka's family were scarce. I lingered over the one in the office, wondering what had happened to his vibrant, healthy-looking mother. Would he open up about her death someday? I scowled. Every day that passed where I was locked in this house made my feelings for him hazy and unfocused. How the hell had my hate evaporated so quickly?

The sun set outside, and the absence of light exaggerated how empty and cold the house was. I knew there was someone here, though. Luka's trust had grown considerably through the week, but not enough to leave me on my own. How long would I have if I tried to escape right now? How long would I have if I found Luka's room and went inside?

I couldn't bring myself to read any of the books he'd uploaded to the iPad. My eyes had glazed over at the covers and "A Submissive's Handbook" mocked me. Without ever discussing it, I understood my role beneath Luka, and although I wanted to be the best at everything, I struggled with this.

I ate dinner alone at the kitchen table, not tasting the food Whitney had prepared. Lightning flashed, bathing the kitchen in bright white for a split second. Outside, thunder rolled and rattled the large window on the back of the house. The clouds gathered, blotting out the moon, and rain fell in torrents against the glass. The sound was deafening.

I waited at the kitchen table for a long while, until my eyelids grew heavy.

What if he didn't come home?

Logic said I'd return to my life. This would be just a blip in my timeline, one week of madness, and then everything would be back on schedule.

Could I really do it, though? Return to my life like none of this had effected a monumental change in my core? I was naïve, but not stupid. Regardless of what happened, Luka's imprint would be a lasting one.

When he hadn't returned by ten o'clock, I shuffled upstairs, brushed my teeth, and prepared for bed, although I left the door to my bedroom open. I hoped he'd let me know when he came home, but the open door would help if he didn't.

I curled up under the covers and watched the hallway. The winter storm outside raged on, battering the house.

π

"Addison."

Luka's deep voice startled me awake. I sat up, disoriented, and spied him in the doorway, backlit by the hallway light.

He's back. I should have been afraid, not filled with relief.

"Hey," I said, rubbing the sleep from my eyes. "What time is it?"

"Two thirty."

I blinked against the light, adjusting. Luka wasn't wearing his work clothes from earlier. He wore a pair of boxers that clung to his lean body, and his hair was messy, as if he'd been sleeping. He must have come home and I'd slept through it. But now he was awake in the middle of the night.

A bright flash lit up my bedroom, followed by an enormous crack of thunder. It was so strong, the room vibrated, and I flinched.

"Get up," he demanded.

I hesitantly rolled out of bed and shivered when I left the warmth of my covers, tugging at the hem of the tank top I wore over a pair of pajama pants. I padded out to join him in the hallway, confused. He wrapped his fingers around my wrist, and his hot skin against mine was scorching as he pulled me down the hallway, all the way to the door which was ajar at the opposite end.

My heartrate quickened. I'd figured out from the sounds in the morning that this was most likely his room.

The room was dark, so I didn't get a good look until he snapped off the hallway light. There was another crack of lightning. Gray faux stone covered the accent wall, and jutting out from it was a large, low platform bed. The covers had been cast off to one side.

His warm hand cuffed my wrist and tugged me across the plush carpet to the bed. Rain beat against the window, punctuated by the deep grumble of thunder.

"When did you get home?" I whispered.

"Around midnight."

"Did everything go okay?" Why did I care?

"Yeah." He leaned over and pulled down the covers on the side of the bed that had been made, then glanced at me expectantly, waiting for me to climb in. I disliked the breathless feeling his actions gave me and shoved it down, turning to get in bed, only for him to stop me. "Wait."

He undid the ribbon at the waistband of my pants, and his gaze pinned me in place while the soft fabric slid down my legs. The cool air gave goosebumps to the goosebumps already on my skin. The lighting flickered across his face, exacerbating the sexual, dangerous expression there.

I stepped forward out of the pants pooled at my feet, bringing us chest to chest, and I stared back at him. Beyond the window, there was electricity slashing the sky in jagged bands, but in the space between me and Luka, it crackled with intensity. His eyes flared with desire.

I swallowed a breath as he lifted me up in his arms, putting his hands on my ass. His command was dark and urgent. "Wrap your legs around me."

His hip bones dug into the insides of my thighs as I locked my ankles behind his back, and my arms draped around his shoulders. Even though I wore only panties and a thin tank top, I wasn't cold anymore. I couldn't feel anything but his heat.

His lips branded me with kisses of fire. They seared across my mouth and throat, and abruptly we were moving. He took a knee on the bed and lowered me onto my back, letting my head sink into a soft pillow. His mouth erased all thoughts from my mind. He'd told me I was his, and when he kissed me, it was never truer.

His erection was growing between my legs and pressed into me, sliding cotton against cotton. It was a wicked, delicious tease of what I knew was to come. When his tongue surged into my mouth, I answered, showing him I wanted what he was going to give me, and my body told him how ready I was. Surely he could feel how soaked my underwear had become.

His hands worked up under my shirt as more lighting flooded the room. God, he looked intense. I knew it was going to happen, but I still jumped at the delayed boom of thunder. I was nervous. I thought I wanted this, but being in his bed threw me off balance.

"Christ," he mumbled, presumably about the storm. His hand slid over my breasts, his fingers gliding from one to the other, moving under the fabric of my shirt. My nipples tightened uncomfortably, aching for more attention. I subtly arched beneath him to encourage it. Could he tell? I'd given up on feeling guilty. He was going to take whatever he wanted, so I'd might as well enjoy it.

"I can't believe the storm didn't wake me, too," I said.

His hand continued to skim across my breasts, circling and tracing patterns. "It didn't wake me, I couldn't sleep."

I tensed. "Because of your meeting?"

His hand stilled. "No." It drew hesitantly away, and I felt the shift go through him. "My mother died on a night like this."

I controlled my intake of air so it didn't sound like a gasp. He rolled onto a hip and stayed to one side of me, propped up on an elbow. Someone else was in command of my body, not me, because my hand lifted and touched his face, cupping his jaw. It was a tender, reassuring gesture, and I thought myself incapable. When someone else got emotional, I usually felt awkward and inept. But with him . . .

"What happened?" It was just loud enough over the driving rain. I wanted him to tell me about the event which had clearly shaped the man.

His chest expanded as he took a deep breath. It was dark in the room, but I could still see him. He looked reluctant, but not angry that I'd pried.

"My parents . . . fought a lot," he said. "She knew he was screwing other women behind her back, but she let it happen as long as my father kept it discreet." His gaze drifted away from mine and lingered on the pillow beside me, staring vacantly. "My mom came home to find him fucking the whore in their bed."

The whore, not a whore. "Tori?"

He nodded slowly. "She was just nineteen. My mother loved

my father but she wouldn't stand for it. They fought like I hadn't heard them before. Screaming, and breaking shit, and saying things a nine-year-old shouldn't have to hear."

My heart twisted.

But his expression turned to stone. "She said she was going to the cops and would tell them everything about my uncle's business. It was storming like this, but she got in her car and took off. It was the last time I saw her." His hand glided over my waist, holding me. It felt possessive and imprisoning, but I didn't mind being his prisoner right now. "She only made it halfway there before she lost control and hit a tree. My father said she wasn't wearing a seatbelt and died on impact."

I covered my mouth with a hand for a moment, catching my breath. I didn't know what to say, but there was a desperate need to say something. *Anything*. I was filled with sadness. "Luka."

"That was the story I believed." His voice was cold and detached. "I believed it because I was a stupid kid and that's what everyone told me."

The pieces began to come together, and my stomach dropped out. *Story* implied fiction. She hadn't been killed in a car accident? "What really happened?"

"My father couldn't have her talking, so when he told his brother what happened, my uncle sent someone to kill her." There was so much contempt on Luka's face, I could see the words tasted vile to him. "My father knew what was going to happen, and he didn't do a fucking thing to stop it. He may not have put the bullet in her, but he killed my mother."

I jerked in Luka's hold, a physical reaction to his horrifying words. All of his hatred toward his father made terrible sense now and disgust roiled in my belly. Dimitrije had chosen his brother over his own wife, the mother of his children.

I knew the answer, but asked anyway. "When did you find out?"

"Two years ago. After my cousin's trial, when he was celebrating his last night of freedom before going to prison, he got drunk, and high, and it all came out." Luka's hand twitched against my bare skin. "He doesn't remember telling me."

"What about Vasilije?"

"He doesn't know. No one knows I've been told the truth."

I swallowed hard. "Except me now."

His guarded eyes peered into mine, and he looked sort of pleased to share the secret. Relieved, even.

"And who would you tell?" He'd spoken it like a half-joke, but it was too serious to hear anything but the real question.

Who would I tell? "No one."

"I can't tell Vasilije. He idolizes my father, but he loved our mother even more. It'd destroy him."

So, even though the relationship was strained between the brothers, there was still love there. Luka was trying to protect his younger brother emotionally.

"You asked if I'd ever killed someone." He settled down so his head was beside mine on the pillow, and his arm on my waist tightened. He was *holding* me.

My pulse sped. "You said you came very, very close once."

"I blamed him for her death, even before I knew all of it. And after, I wanted to kill him like I'd never wanted anything in my whole goddamn life."

The air in the room went thin. Luka took what he wanted,

didn't he? I barely squeaked out the words. "Then why didn't you?"

"I don't know." His uneven breathing ghosted over my skin. "I had the gun, and he didn't know I was behind him. I thought I was ready, but I . . . I don't know," he repeated. "I hesitated. He's my father."

I turned my head toward him, and a lock of hair fell in my eyes. He brushed it back, his fingers skimming over my forehead and tucking the hair behind my ear.

"Don't get any delusions about me being soft," he said quietly. "I could change my mind and pull that trigger tomorrow."

I gazed at him. The sharp angles of his sculpted face and serious eyes were beautiful. "No," I whispered. "Soft isn't a word I'd use to describe you."

As if to emphasize my statement, thunder cracked and rumbled, making me jump while he remained unfazed. His gaze was heavy. It trapped me as he closed the tiny space between us and pressed his lips to mine in a slow, seductive kiss.

"Shit," he whispered. "It's so fucking late." His mouth moved against mine lazily. "I need to get some sleep."

It sounded like a dismissal. I blinked, and pulled back. "Oh. I'll go."

He looked pissed at the idea. "No, you won't. That's not what I meant." He curled his arm around my shoulders, but looked uncomfortable with the embrace. It probably felt as foreign to him as it did to me. "You'll sleep here tonight."

I wasn't supposed to want this. I certainly wasn't supposed to have nervous flutters of excitement about it. He was my captor, controlling all aspects of my life, and had admitted he might be a murderer someday. But as he shifted closer and found a position that was more comfortable for both of us, I couldn't ignore how I felt. Over the course of one week, my perception of Luka had changed dramatically. We were so similar in other aspects of our lives. Would I have turned out the same as he had if I'd lived his life?

Chapter
NINETEEN

LAST NIGHT HAD A POWERFUL effect on me, and I was aware I was falling deeper under Luka's spell. The good news was it seemed to have an impact on him as well. Luka was nearly late for work. When his alarm had woken us both, we'd blinked our sleepy eyes at each other. It was followed immediately by our mutual realization that my arm was around his waist and my leg thrown over one of his.

"You're really warm," I said on a hurried breath, scrambling across the sheets to put distance between us. I could claim I was just using him for body heat, but it was a lie.

He chased me across the bed and pinned me down, burying his lips against the side of my neck. He must have known what he did to me, and kissed me that way on purpose. A shiver shook my shoulders.

When he took me all the way to the edge and made me crazy for him to do more than just kissing, when the plea was on my lips, he commanded me to get up and follow him to the shower.

He'd wrapped his hands around my throat while we were soaked by the rainfall shower head. "Repeat it."

There wasn't a belt around my neck, and I was confident we had enough trust, so he was only making me repeat the mantra to exert his power. My voice was steady. "You get pleasure or I get choked."

I knelt on the tile and sucked his dick while he twined his

hands in my drenched hair. His deep moans of pleasure created a dark craving in me, and I was only half satisfied when he reached his end. He sensed it, of course.

"Don't use any of my time to touch yourself today. I want you aching for it tonight."

After the shower, he'd had to hurry to get out the door, and left me feeling restless and needy.

I was still sitting at the kitchen table eating a late breakfast when Jennifer appeared, garment bags draped over each arm.

"Oh, you're eating," she said without giving me a greeting. "I'll go get these ready for you to try on."

Jennifer had unwrapped several dresses by the time I plodded upstairs to my room. She noticed my appearance in the doorway and waved me in.

"Let's start with these," she said, pointing to the clothes laid out on the bed.

I gathered them up in my arms and went into the bathroom, feeling uncomfortable changing in front of her. I tugged on the outfits, one after the other, and paraded out into the bedroom like it was a bizarre fashion show for one. Two, really. Jennifer snapped pictures with her phone, and texted them to Luka.

The clothes were nice—they looked expensive and well-made. They weren't things I would have picked out for myself. Some were a tighter fit than I was used to, and some were low-cut, but overall she'd done a good job.

"What's Goran's party like?" I asked her as she passed me a green dress on a hanger.

She hesitated. "It's nice. Good food and good booze, and an excuse to dress up."

The dress was slinky and much too sexy for me. As soon as I stepped out in it, Jennifer pursed her lips to one side. "No, that won't work. Let's do this one."

It was navy blue, simple and elegant in the front, but backless, plunging all the way to the base of my spine. Lace trimmed the edges where it gave way to skin, and the dress fit me perfectly.

I tried to pry more information from Jennifer, but she gave tight, short answers to every question. *Where is the party? Goran's estate. How many people will be there? A lot.* When there were no more clothes for me to try on, she hung what I was keeping in the closet and took back the others.

She glanced at the text message that popped up on her screen. "Luka's downstairs."

It was already lunchtime. I grabbed my iPad and followed her out of the room. Luka waited at the base of the stairs, his attention fixated on me, but his expression was unreadable. "The blue dress," he said to Jennifer. "Does Addison have everything she needs for it?"

"Yeah." She adjusted the strap of her purse, fidgeting.

"Good, thanks for your help." The corner of his mouth pulled up into a smile. "She'll look *perfect.*"

He used the word specifically to get under my skin. Why did I allow one innocuous adjective to hold so much power? It was a compliment and it made me feel warm and proud, but it also felt like a lie, too.

He held out his hand, wordlessly asking for my iPad, which I passed to him. He said goodbye to Jennifer and then we went into the office. I watched as he hooked the iPad up to the computer so he could download the new videos while we ate.

Did he notice the change between us during lunch as much as I did? The conversation flowed seamlessly for the first time as he asked about my family's holiday traditions, and told me about his. Then, he dropped the bomb that if I wanted to go home for Thanksgiving break, I could, but it'd be with him in tow. He was my new boyfriend, after all.

"I don't know if our relationship is serious enough," I said, "to introduce you to my parents yet."

He blinked slowly. "Is that a joke?"

"Maybe," I whispered. "The truth is, I don't know if I can prepare my parents for you. You're . . . pretty intense."

For a fraction of a second he seemed amused. "We'll be fine. I can dial that back if I have to." The word *we* lingered. Strange, but not unpleasant. Luka's expression returned to his serious one. "Your task for this afternoon. Hold on, I'll go get it."

My nerves swirled. What sinful, dirty assignment was he going to give me? I waited with held breath as he left the table, disappeared through the doorway, only to return a moment later carrying the iPad.

"Memorize this as far as you can."

He set it in front of me and the screen was full of numbers. I gave him a skeptical look. This was what he wanted?

"You look disappointed." He smirked as if he could tell I was expecting a different kind of chore. "Is this too hard for you?"

"Rote memorization? Of course not. I'm just thinking about the last time you had me reciting pi." Since that horrible morning, Luka hadn't been as cruel or scary.

His expression gave nothing away. "That, like the bathtub, was necessary. Neither of those were fun for me either, but

I had to break you, Addison." He sighed. "*I had to*, so my father wouldn't."

π

The house seemed to grow twenty degrees colder when the sun set, but I wondered if his absence contributed as well. He burned hot enough to heat whatever room we were in together. So I was curled up on the couch in the office, the blanket covering me, when Luka arrived home from work.

"How's school, *darling*?" he asked, throwing my attitude laced comment from Monday back at me. I couldn't tell if he'd meant it to be light and teasing, or mocking. He walked the perfect line between.

"Fine," I said. "I finished a while ago, so now I've just been sitting around, waiting for you."

He gave me a dark look. "I gave you an assignment, so I hope that's not true."

I pushed the quilt off and stood, setting my hands on my hips. "You want to hear about your assignment? Three point one four one five nine—"

"Stop." He held up his hand, then pointed to the doorway. "Upstairs."

I marched behind him, wondering if he meant my room or his. He turned left at the top of the stairs, and I slowed a step. Since he'd given me freedom from my prison, I spent as little time as possible in the green striped bedroom.

When I stepped inside and turned, his hands closed on my waist, and he walked me backward toward the bed. My nerves twisted in my stomach.

228

His expression was authoritarian. "Undo your pants. Everything down to your knees, and lean over the bed."

My legs went weak. "What?"

"I want your ass in the air by the time I get back."

He strode quickly from the room, leaving me spinning. My fingers were made of lead as I undid the button of my pants, and clawed both them and my panties down. I set my elbows flat on the mattress and forced myself to control my breathing. The tremble was already working its way up my legs. Being exposed like this was almost worse than being naked. My hands itched to pull the fabric back up and cover myself. Instead, I stayed as I was, staring at the green stripes that were symbolic bars.

I was short of breath as he returned and shut the door, closing us in together. He was carrying a small black bag, and he dropped it by my feet with a thump. His hand curved over my bare flesh, and a soft sound of appreciation slipped from him.

"I've been thinking about this all day," he said, his voice low. "Did you?"

His fingers brushed over my slit, making me swallow a breath.

"Hmm?" The fingers became more invasive, and he teased my clit. "I didn't hear you. Were you less than perfect today? Did you waste any of my time and disobey me?"

"No." It came from me hurried.

"Good."

He sank a finger inside my body, all the way to the knuckle. I opened my mouth to gasp, but I didn't make a sound. I arched back into his touch. It was shocking how immediately the pleasure came. I may have been shy and nervous, but I was also incredibly aroused. He was in total command, and when that happened, I was free to feel however I wanted.

"So wet for me."

I closed my eyes and enjoyed how he stood beside me, one hand on the hollow of my back and the other pressing slowly inside my body. A moan escaped, and it sounded like a desperate whine. But it cut off abruptly when his damp fingers slid upward through my valley, coursing through my cheeks.

Luka's wicked chuckle threw me into chaos, and he pressed his hand firm against my back. "Do you want me to tie you up, or can you hold still?"

What the hell kind of question was that? I couldn't answer without tacitly giving my consent to whatever he was planning. So I said nothing at all. And I was well aware it didn't matter anyway. He'd get his way.

His fingers stirred over my pussy and repeated their path, skirting a line upward. Maybe it felt good, but the sense that it was dirty overruled everything else. I jolted from his obscene touch.

"This body is mine." His tone was firm. "Repeat it."

His dominance had so much weight, I sank forward and turned to rest a cheek against the mattress, keeping my eyes closed. "This body is yours."

Luka moved, kneeling behind me. My heart was pounding up in my throat, blocking my ability to breathe, and then it wasn't a problem. I stopped breathing completely as he licked me, all the way from front to back.

My knees went weak. It felt good, but it was horrifying. I whimpered and balled the comforter beneath my hands into fists, clutching at the fabric as my knuckles turned white. This time when he did it, he *stayed*. His tongue moved at the tight circle of muscles, and I gave a cry of panic. Holy fuck, what was he doing? I reached a hand behind me and tried to ease him back.

"I'm asking again." This time his tone was razor sharp. "You want me to tie you up, or stay still?"

I was so flustered by his actions I couldn't think straight. I had no idea which was the right answer, and my muscles were so tense I couldn't move. "Luka."

His hands were warm on my ass cheeks, lifting and separating, and this time when he leaned in and sent his tongue wandering over my flesh, I groaned. My body delivered the signal loud and clear to my mind it was pleasurable, but my brain fired back I was disgusting.

I clawed at the sheets as he tore me apart with his ruthless mouth.

My legs rattled against the bedframe as his tongue ceased, giving me a reprieve. I was vaguely aware he was moving. I heard a strange sort of click, but couldn't place the sound, not until something cold and wet was dripping on me. He'd uncapped a bottle, and . . . oh, no. He was putting lube on me.

"W-Wait," I cried. "What are you doing?" I pushed up on my elbows and tried to stand.

His hand came down on my ass with a loud crack, and pain thundered up my spine. "Whose body is this?"

I stayed on my elbows and breathed through the stinging heat his punishment had left me with. My voice broke on the word. "Yours."

His shadow fell beside me on the bed as he stood. "Mine."

Something cold and smooth like metal was nudged between my cheeks, prodding for entrance.

"No!" I jerked up.

He was ready for my reaction. I was shoved down on the bed at the same time he dropped something beside me. As I scrambled up, he twisted my arms behind my back, just as he'd done a week ago. He secured my wrists with one hand and scooped the toy up, but not before I got a look. The small silver plug had a heart-shaped base, and the jewel at the end glittered the color of sin.

"Yes," he said. "Mine. Mine to have any way I want, *anywhere* I want."

The plug moved through the lubrication he'd put on me, and when he'd found the spot he wanted, there was pressure. I choked on air, swallowing huge gasps as it began to intrude.

"That's it," he said, his voice low and carnal.

My body pushed back, not wanting the penetration, but there was nowhere to escape, and the uncomfortable stretch grew. I whimpered as the toy slid deeper, every fraction of an inch burning worse than the last. I struggled against the hand holding me down, but my twisting made it hurt more.

"Hold still, *luče*," he whispered. "That's right." The pressure began to ease, and the intrusion stopped. "Oh, fuck me. Good girl."

He released me, and both of his hands smoothed over my back, caressing. It was lodged inside me, the heart-shaped base against my skin. I felt uncomfortably full, and . . . heavy. I lay still on the bed, my chest heaving, as Luka's hands continued to trail over me. I endured his sensual touch while I pulled my mind back together.

Slowly, the burning sensation began to fade and shift. I could feel it with every breath, but it didn't hurt. It was . . . odd. I blinked and tried to decide if I hated it, but, no. Hate was too strong of a word. I wasn't even sure if I disliked it.

"Addison."

I blew out a shuddering breath.

His command was spoken softly. "Stand up."

Hell, that I could *really* feel. I pushed up on my shaky arms, lifting myself off the bed. The fullness and weight was stronger now, and each movement made me aware.

He lingered to the side and his words traveled over my shoulder. "Get dressed."

I clamped my teeth tight together to hold in the question. How long was he going to leave me like this? I fumbled with my pants, gingerly pulling them back in place, and did up my fly.

"Look at me."

I turned and faced him. His expression was drenched in desire, and his eyes burned with power. I stood stock-still as he trapped me in his embrace, one hand twisted in my hair and forcing my gaze up to meet his.

"You have no idea how fucking hot you look like this. Your cheeks are flushed and your eyes are wild, trying not to show what's going on inside. But I know. I'll always know." His grip pulled my hair taut with an edge of pain. "Go downstairs, pour a glass of wine, and bring it to me."

My shoulders tensed.

His lips turned up in a cruel smile. "Make sure you ask Whitney for her recommendation."

Chapter
TWENTY

As my body grew accustomed to the plug, it became easier to move around, but every step down the staircase made my anxiety grow, just as Luka had intended. Would his personal chef know about the dirty secret in my body the second she laid eyes on me? I used to have a great poker face, but that was cards.

She stood at the kitchen island, a pair of tongs in her hand as she supervised dinner. A pot steamed on the sophisticated gas range, but her focus was on the grill top, where lamb chops were cooking.

"Hello," I said over the grill's ventilation fan. My cheeks were burning.

She glanced up and did a double-take. Whitney's bright gaze scanned me and a smile stretched on her face. "Why, hello, Addison."

Luka's personal chef appeared to be in her late thirties. She had rich brown hair, cropped short and it swept across her forehead. I was instantly struck by how maintained she was. The exceptional organization of her meals should have shown me how organization extended into all aspects of her life. Even her apron was a perfect white.

"I was wondering when I was going to meet you," she said, her eyes glittering. "Luka wouldn't let me ask, so I've been making extra meals in case you have any dietary restrictions."

"Oh," I said. "No, I'm not allergic to anything."

"Yay!" she joked. "Shellfish is back on the menu." She picked up one of the chops and turned it. "I'm Whitney, by the way." The tongs were set down and she extended her hand for a shake.

I'd swear I could feel the toy more the longer I remained in her presence. "Nice to meet you." I didn't want to seem rude and tried not to speak in a rush. "Luka asked for a glass of wine before dinner. What do you recommend?"

She thought for a moment. "There's a California cabernet that'll go nicely with this lamb."

I stood in silence as she went to the wine fridge, checked labels, and pulled out the bottle she was looking for. Whitney moved with precision while she opened the wine, and thirty seconds later she handed me the poured glass.

"Thank you," I squeaked out.

She noticed my hand trembling, but said nothing. Instead, she gave me a friendly, curious smile, and nodded.

I trudged up the stairs and down the hallway back to him, careful not to spill the red wine. I lingered with my hand on the door knob, drawing in a deep breath to calm my nerves before pushing it open.

Didn't matter, I wasn't prepared.

Luka must have moved the new piece of furniture in while I was downstairs. I wasn't sure what it was exactly, and I stared at it with dread. The piece was black and similar to a construction sawhorse, only there was padding covered with vinyl at the top. Buckle cuffs decorated all four legs.

I almost spilled the glass, but Luka snatched it out of my hand just in time.

"Breathe," he ordered, setting the wine down on the dresser

and locking me in his arms, keeping me from bolting. "This is like the clock. It's another tool to help us get to where we need to be."

I couldn't rip my gaze away from the damn thing. He was going to restrain me to it and do unspeakable things. That fear was paralyzing.

"Look at me." It took an enormous amount of strength to comply. His expression was serious. "This experience can be as pleasurable as you want. I'd prefer that." His eyes flooded with lust. "You sound so amazing when you come. I've watched the video you took, like, fifty fucking times." He turned me in his arms, pressing me back against his chest so we were both looking at the thing and his lips were beside my ear. "It's just a bench. There's nothing to be scared of."

Was he serious? "What about you?"

I couldn't see his knowing, evil smile, but I sensed it. He brushed my hair off of my neck and out of his way, planting a slow, lingering kiss there. "When we're doing this, you're not scared of me, you're scared of how you feel when you're with me."

"Nope," I said. "Pretty sure I'm just terrified of you." It was a lie and I was certain we both knew it.

He picked up the glass of wine, turned his head to the side, and drank. "Then, get over it during dinner."

"Dinner?" New dread poured into my belly. I'd thought we were going to continue whatever he'd started and use the new *tool* he'd moved into the room. "What about the . . . the . . ."

"The plug in your ass?" He said it so casually I hated him a little again. "It stays. I want you thinking about how my cock's going to feel there later."

He had to hold me up as I sagged in his arms. I couldn't

catch my breath. And he was absolutely right. I was plenty nervous about him doing that, but it wasn't half as scary as the idea I might end up liking it.

π

It was the most uncomfortable dinner yet. Not just because of the toy, but because I couldn't focus on anything. Trying to hold a conversation with me was frustrating for Luka, and he often had to repeat himself. But he was the one to blame for my flustered state, which he was clearly enjoying.

He ate his dinner slowly, savoring me more than the meat. I picked at the food, just wanting this part over. The sooner we got through dinner, the sooner we'd get back to the bench and on with it. I told myself there wasn't a single molecule of curiosity in me about what was going to happen. I wouldn't fucking allow it.

I did, however, drink the wine he poured for me. Both glasses. When he poured himself the last of the bottle, I held my empty glass out to him.

"You're already smiling," he said, "so I think you're done."

Crap, I'd already gotten to stage one. "You didn't care I was wasted our first time."

His expression hardened. "That's because I was wasted, too. I already told you, I want you to enjoy this. Not get sick and feel like death tomorrow. You ever had a wine hangover before?"

"No," I fired back, getting mouthy from the alcohol. "Just tequila and rohypnol, Luka."

He exhaled loudly and the muscle along his jaw ticked. "Upstairs, now."

Luka carried the glass of wine with him, and pushed open

the door to the green bedroom, gesturing like a gentleman for me to go inside. My buzzing brain prayed the bench had magically disappeared, but no. It sat, waiting for me. Or maybe . . .

"Is there a chance you're going to be strapped down to that and not me?" I said, my voice slurring.

Amusement passed through his expression, gone as quickly as it arrived. "No. Take off your clothes."

I'd wanted to get dinner over with, and now I wished I'd stalled. I moved achingly slow as he sat in the loveseat and watched me with a lustful gaze. I discarded my clothes one at a time on the bed until I had nothing left except what he'd put inside me.

The room was freezing, and got colder when he pointed to the bench.

I swallowed a gulp and forced my feet to move. But as I stood beside the bench, I wasn't entirely sure what to do.

Luka was up in a flash. "You lay on it face down, length-wise. Your head goes here." He pointed to one end, and then helped me lower myself awkwardly on it. The cold vinyl squished and ran between my breasts, down along my stomach, and between my legs.

His warm hands took hold of my wrist and gently placed it in the first cuff. By the time he was securing my final ankle, I was shaking like a leaf. I rasped for air and gripped the legs of the bench, driving my nails into the wood. Fingers ran the length of my spine and I shivered. His touch was electricity, shocking my nerve endings awake.

The first spanking he gave was nothing in comparison to his others before, and the next was the same. Almost gentle, like he was warming me up.

"I'm going to turn your ass the *perfect* shade of red."

He built up the intensity slowly, following a pattern where he'd spank each side, then circle his fingers on my clit. My head was buzzing, and I moaned softly as he manipulated me. As his slaps got harder, I could feel them inside and out because of the plug.

The rhythm filled the room. *Slap, slap, moan. Slap, slap, moan.* My body responded to him, becoming eager for his touch, whether it was delivering pain or pleasure. The lines blurred together. My backside was on fire, but it was a tingling, interesting feeling. Once again, I wondered how much I could take. And this time, I also wondered how much he'd give me. Was he . . . pleased at how I handled his spankings?

He paused at one point to finish his wine, and then stepped back up to my burning skin. I flinched at his soft caress. He whispered under his breath, "So fucking gorgeous."

It flooded me with heat. Then, two fingers speared into me and I cried out. It was startling, but not painful. The sensation with the plug already inside me was different and exciting. I glanced up at him and he watched me right back, his faint smile twitching on his lips.

Wait a minute, was I supposed to feel good about pleasing him? Goddamn him. Maybe I'd pretend I didn't like it just out of spite. But what good would it do? It wasn't punishment for him and the only control he'd given me was over how much enjoyment I'd take from tonight. I moaned louder as his fingers drove deep, touching the spot that felt incredible.

I was reeling as he abruptly withdrew, and this smack, the one which came without warning, was like the one from the horrible dinner with his father. I gnashed my teeth together and sucked in air through my nose.

"That was for the way you talked to me downstairs." He grabbed a fistful of my hair and pushed his face right up to mind. "And this," he said, his eyes smoldering, "is for how you make me stupid." His lips crashed into mine, and the kiss was *intense*. Brutal. "You make it so I can't keep my hands off of you, or think about anything else."

His tongue swept in my mouth, and I welcomed it. His kiss made me fall apart and feel stronger in the same instance. Every tiny adjustment of the angle, or movement of our lips together deepened the madness. I sighed against his mouth, wanting to breathe his confidence in. He tasted like sex and desire. What could I learn from him?

Luka was breathing as hard as I was when it ended. His pupils were large and skin flushed. I wanted him to kiss me like that again, or touch me, or . . . shit, for him to connect his body with mine. Or do all of those things at once and send me into oblivion. My muscles strained from the grip on the bench legs.

He rose up but stayed near my head and in my sight, letting me watch him undress. He had a habit of tugging his tie loose as soon as he came home, but leaving it that way. Now he undid the knot and slid the end free from his collar, tossing it onto the bed. Then, he worked the line of buttons on his dress shirt, and pulled the shirttails free from his waist. It was added to the pile. He moved faster after that.

When he stood before me completely naked, my lungs squeezed in my chest. Luka was a rush to look at normally, but naked? It was almost too much.

"Tell me you want this." He stroked his hand over his hard

dick, twisting his grip.

I ached for him, but when my lips parted, I was unsure if I could say the words.

His tone was dark and imposing. "Addison."

"My family and friends call me Addie," I said. *Shit.* Had I skipped over phase two, and gone straight to phase three, where logical thought was abandoned? Did I want him to use my abbreviated name like he was my friend? Like we were close?

He froze, and then his thick eyebrow arched. "Good for them, *Addison.* I don't like nicknames."

I flashed back to the moment at the frat party before we'd gone upstairs. Vasilije's frat brother had called him Vas, but Luka had used his full name.

"In fact," he added, "only the whore gets a nickname."

I blinked my drunk eyes. "Why do you call her that?" If Tori had only been nineteen when she'd wound up in bed with Luka's father, she probably had been seduced. Or worse. Maybe she had been placed in the same situation Luka had put me in.

"Because she's a whore. She'll tell you she fucked half the guys at the dealership before my father started fucking her for money." "Oh."

He scowled and spanked my bare cheek with a loud smack. "We've gotten off track here." His fingers traced my entrance, spreading around my arousal. "Focus. This is what you should be thinking about."

I bit down on my bottom lip as he moved behind me. The tip of his cock teased between my folds, and I issued a soft sigh. Last week I'd been petrified when he'd done this, and now I wanted it. He'd turned me into a slut in a week flat.

"Tell me what you learned today," he ordered.

I wanted my voice to sound confident, but it wavered. "Three point one four one five—Oh!"

Luka drove deep inside me, all the way to the root. My back bowed and I tried to get away, but the cuffs answered back, holding me down. It was still so much, and too quickly, plus the plug made me feel tight.

But, holy hell, it felt good, too. The warm skin covering his hips pressed against the heated flesh of my stinging backside, and he ground himself into me. I groaned with both discomfort and dark satisfaction.

"That's right," he said. "You're not scared, you like it. You like how you feel with all that inside you, don't you? My cock deep in your pussy," his fingers grabbed the heart of the plug and turned it, "and *this* in your ass."

When he began to move, I couldn't control my moans. They fell from my lips, one after another, making me sound desperate and needy. He was right. So terribly right. I was bound to the spanking bench so I couldn't hide from my shame, but I couldn't escape my pleasure, either.

He was panting in no time, and his thrusts quickened to a steady, controlled pace. The bench creaked with his movements, but most of the time it couldn't be heard over me. My lower body was in ecstasy with the different sensations, and I gave myself over to them as willingly as I gave myself over to him now.

"Oh my God," I moaned.

Bliss rolled from my fingertips, down to the ends of my toes as he thrust himself inside, repeatedly hitting the spot I craved. My body moved by its own choice and wiggled on the bench, restless and anxious for release.

But when he slowed and his fingers closed around the base of the plug, my heart ground to a painful stop. I grimaced as the toy was retracted and thudded to the carpet. Luka wasn't moving inside me, but he was pulsing.

I pinched my eyes tightly shut as he withdrew. Footsteps carried him away and there was rustling. I didn't want to know what he was doing. Anxiety gripped me so tightly, it squeezed out a panicked noise.

"Pi," he demanded. "Go."

Chapter
TWENTY-ONE

I FORCED MYSELF to picture the numbers, and began to recite them in a trembling voice. It pitched upward when he touched my clit, and something slipped inside my pussy. It wasn't buzzing this time, but I recognized it from before. The black U-shaped vibrator.

"Shit," I said, realizing I'd lost my place.

"Start over."

I lost my place a second time when he uncapped the lube and smeared more of the cold, thick liquid on me. "Wait," I pleaded, so nervous my throat closed up.

"Focus." His hand rested at the spot right where my cheeks began, and there was a noise as his other hand lubed himself, preparing. "I want to hear how far you *perfectly* memorized it."

"Three point one four," I whispered, drawing in a deep breath.

And then he was there. Not just with his dick pressing against me, but with his words, reciting the numbers along with me. The pressure built and the burning stretch was worse this time, but his voice was steady, keeping me on track.

Distracting me as he pushed the head of his cock inside. I gasped at the aching discomfort, but he pressed on, chanting the numbers in unison. I tried to reach back to stop him, but the cuffs held me still. I came to the end of the string of numbers, unable to think of anything else. Only the sensation of him owning me.

"Jesus Christ, it's so fucking tight."

I was going to fall apart. Fracture into a million pieces until there was nothing left. But he moved in slow strokes, pushing just a little deeper each time.

"It hurts," I whispered, not sure what good it would do. He'd told me to tell him that our first time, so maybe—

Holy *fuck.*

He reached between our bodies and squeezed the vibrator, activating it. The steady buzzing was a magnifying glass on my pleasure. A cry tore from my parted lips, filled with surprised enjoyment.

Luka's breath came and went, deep yet rapid. I didn't have to ask if he liked this, it was evident by his moans, and he didn't have to ask me either. The vibrator shook away the discomfort, and as he buried himself all the way inside, I felt the first wave of pleasure threatening.

I could like this. Holy crap, I could come from this. The longer he continued to ease his dick inside and out, made me believe. Powerful need consumed and took over. I gasped as he found a rhythm we both seemed to enjoy.

"Does it hurt now?" he whispered.

"No." I answered as quickly as possible, focusing on the heat building in my core. I hungered for the release clawing its way up. I didn't give a fuck about how wrong or dirty it was. He had me pinned down, completely at his mercy, and the sordid part of myself liked everything about this experience.

My moans swelled as he moved faster. My body was firing on all fronts, heading toward ecstasy, ready for him to cast me over the edge. When I swiveled my hips, I found I could press the vibrator up against the padded bar and position it exactly as needed. *Oh, shit!*

I might have groaned it out loud, but paid no attention.

His punishing tempo made it hard to breathe, and then his filthy words caused it to stop all together.

"I wish you could see how good it looks, watching your ass eat my cock."

Jesus! My stomach twisted, and the muscles low in my belly contracted, and it was enough to catapult me into my release. I screamed as I came, my voice hoarse and dry. The room was a sun-baked desert. Luka's heat had sucked all the moisture from the air.

He followed me into my orgasm. His hand clenched tight on my shoulder and he convulsed, pulling himself from within me right as he started to come. Thick, heated liquid struck my clit, and flicked onto the backs of my legs, dripping down as he gave a tremendous sigh.

"*Fuck!*" His cry of satisfaction was intensely hot.

It took us both several moments to recover. When his breathing was under control, he set about undoing the bindings at my ankles. As he freed my wrists, his mouth was on mine, kissing me seductively. His languid kiss was the most powerful one in his arsenal. He helped me rise up off of the bench, and then lifted me up in his strong arms, tucking me against his chest.

Luka carried me into the bathroom, where we showered together under the stream of hot water. Would it scald away the filth he'd put on me?

I hoped not.

It was buried under my skin, too deep to come clean. He rubbed my aching shoulders, and massaged away the marks left by the cuffs. My eyelids grew heavy as he shut off the water and handed me a towel, banding another one around his hips.

"Stay here." He pushed open the shower door and disappeared.

The exhaustion in me whined. I wanted to collapse into bed, not go another round, which was what I assumed was going to happen. I eyed the small seat in the shower. If I sat down, would I still be awake whenever he returned?

The door swung open. "Come on," he said.

Surprise made my feet clumsy and I tripped as I stepped out, latching a hand onto his shoulder.

His eyes widened. "Okay?"

"Fine." Although, not really. Luka held out a long, white bathrobe for me. I glanced from the soft, fuzzy looking garment to him, and back again.

"You're always cold." He said it plainly as he helped me slide it onto my shoulders, then tied the sash at the waist. He kept his grip on the ends and bound me in place. "You won't sleep in this room anymore."

My pulse quickened. "Where am I sleeping?"

Luka's eyes were black ink. "With me."

"Why?" I had to lick my lips to combat my dry mouth.

"Because this part of your training is over." He tugged on the ends of the robe, cinching it tighter and pulling me close. "Monday we start a new phase."

"Which is?"

"You go back to class."

π

I was back two weeks before we had our first issue. I settled into my new routine almost seamlessly. Vanessa drove me to class and stayed with me wherever I went, and after school was over, she delivered me back to the house. I never considered escape. I told myself I was in it for the long run, until Luka truly let me go.

It'd been weird at first with Vanessa, but Luka said she was there for my protection as much as his. If word got out that he was handling his uncle's finances, his family's enemies might show interest in me. That was scary as hell, but he reassured me I was fine. The likelihood was microscopic, and Vanessa was working for him to support her amateur MMA career. She made an excellent bodyguard, he'd said.

Bodyguard.

I didn't ask, but Luka volunteered the information. When his cousin had gone to prison, the Russians saw an opening and took it. Every month they pushed further into Markovic territory, both the guns and sex trafficking business. It turned my stomach, and I was overwhelmingly relieved when he didn't offer specifics. No wonder Luka wanted nothing to do with his uncle's real trade.

Despite my fear, the arrangement with Luka worked out better than the first half of the semester, because I had my own space to work without Avery around, a chauffeur, and a personal chef. Whenever I was working on homework at night, Luka either left me alone or sat quietly beside me, on his iPad or phone.

It'd been more of the latter this week. We tended to gravitate toward each other. I'd sit on the couch in the office while he worked at the desk, and when I was done, he'd take me upstairs to what had become *our* room.

Not every night was filled with sex. A week after returning to class, my period arrived. Luka and I stayed up late, just talking. He seemed fascinated by my boring, normal life. We had conversations about all sorts of things, but he'd only let me pry so far before finding other uses for my mouth.

I tried not to dwell on how quickly I'd adjusted to life with him, or how easily I had bent to his will. The shocking truth was I didn't *hate* my time with Luka. Sometimes I even looked forward to it.

It was a Thursday when I sat on the couch with the quilt on my lap, reading a textbook. The far-off growl of the garage door signaled he was home, and I straightened in my seat, quelling my smile. But footsteps thundered loudly up the hall, much too fast to be anything but angry. I bolted up from the couch, concern flooding through me. What had happened?

My suspicions were confirmed when he threw open the office door and his eyes burned. I backpedaled and collided with the desk at the same instant his hands seized my shoulders.

"Tell me what you did today, Addison."

I stared at him with total confusion. "Nothing! I went to my physics lecture, and organic chem lab."

His dark eyes were narrow. "Tell me about your lecture."

My brain filtered through the morning, trying to figure out what had set him off. "It was what you'd expect—" Then, it clicked. "This is about the coffee?"

"Yeah," he snapped. "It's about the fucking coffee."

I almost laughed, but caught myself in time.

I hadn't made many friends in college, but I'd gotten to know most of the other pre-med students who were on the same track. Gavin was bright, and friendly, and like me, a bit awkward. After two years of seeing each other at nearly every class, we'd become friends. We sat next to each other, exchanged lecture notes, and had a friendly competition on our tests.

Vanessa had mentioned he was the first to ask what had happened to me when she showed up in my place, requesting to video the lectures. She'd told him I was sick. Once I'd returned to class, he'd lingered even closer, offering to help catch me up.

"Luka," I said softly.

"You think a guy hitting on you isn't noteworthy? Did you not make it clear you're unavailable?"

His possessiveness was stunning, and if I was honest, I sort of liked it. I was petty and stupid, but I enjoyed knowing he didn't like anyone challenging his claim. As if they could.

"He bought Vanessa and me both a cup of coffee this morning," I said. "He was just being polite." Luka's scowl intensified, spurring me on. "He didn't buy the coffee for me." It'd been apparent right away how badly Gavin was smitten with Vanessa. "He's such a nerd, and she's a badass. You should see them together, they're adorable."

Gavin had been waiting for us this morning in the lecture hall, three cups of coffee resting on the long table before him. He was sweaty and nervous as he'd passed them out, trying to sound casual and failing. I'd watched him attempt to flirt with the woman with whom he had hardly anything in common, but he did it anyway.

I'd been proud and envious to see my friend take a risk and go after what he wanted. In spite of all that had happened, a part of me wished I had done the same with Luka.

"He's interested in Vanessa?" Confusion painted Luka's face.

I gave a light smile. "Oh, yeah."

"I had her describe him to me," he said, releasing me. "It sounds like she could snap him in half with one finger."

My smile grew. Gavin was a twig. "He'd probably like that."

It took Luka several seconds to adjust to the information, and I was surprised at how much emotion he'd displayed. It was disarming, and I shut off my mind, avoiding all consequences. My hands gripped his strong jaw, and I pulled him to me, planted my lips tentatively against his, showing him he had nothing to fear.

"You've made me say it enough times," I whispered.

He blinked, looking affected by my kiss. It was the first time I'd *ever* initiated it. "What?"

"That you own me. I understand that, Luka."

His kiss was powerful, deadening my thoughts, all except for one. Would I ever want to own him?

Thanksgiving was a disaster.

It started off well enough. My parents were skeptical of the older man I introduced as my boyfriend. Luka was five years older than I was, and his serious demeanor announced he was anything but a boy, but my family rolled with it. Jonathon didn't care at all.

We ate turkey and stuffing, and held conversations about current events over pumpkin pie. My brother showed off his new car, unaware my boyfriend had orchestrated the whole thing. I gave Luka the tour of my family's house, only because he insisted. He'd enjoyed me showing him the barn where our equipment was stored, at least the stuff we didn't co-op. Up to that point, the day had gone much better than I expected.

It went downhill when I'd led him to my bedroom, leaving the door open, of course, since my parents were conservative. Luka's gaze had scanned the room, assessing the mathlete trophies and valedictorian sash clinically, and then he'd told me in graphic detail how he wanted to bend me over my bed and fuck me while my parents were downstairs.

Only my dad wasn't downstairs. He'd heard the whole thing.

My father's face had turned a terrible shade of purple as he told Luka to leave. We tried to calm him down and tell him it had been a joke, but eventually Luka's true self broke free, and he announced I lived with him now.

"Addison's twenty-one," Luka said, standing tall under my

father's angry glare. "An adult."

"And she's also our daughter," my father snapped back at him. "It's our responsibility to keep her from making poor decisions."

Luka's expression soured. His hand wrapped around mine, tugging me toward the closet so we could retrieve our coats.

"Addie," my mother pleaded. "This is crazy!" She stared at me with disbelief, probably wondering what the hell had happened to make their smart daughter move in with a serious and imposing man she'd only really known for a month.

"I know it's kinda fast," I said. How on earth was I going to explain it? Luka's and my relationship was like an arranged marriage where our lives had been thrust together, and we were doing our best to make it work.

My father didn't need an explanation and wasn't intimidated by Luka. He put his hands on his hips and puffed up his chest. "You're just kids. You're both too young to be playing house."

The hand on my wrist tightened and I sucked in a breath. Outwardly, yes. Luka appeared young, but he wasn't, and I sensed how annoyed he was with being called a *kid*.

Luka's tone was edged with controlled anger. "I'm four years older than you were, when you married your wife, sir."

My dad's shoulders pulled back as if Luka's statement was a verbal slap. But it was true. My parents had been high school sweethearts and gotten married at twenty-two.

Luka held my coat for me to put on. "I think it's best if we head out. I'm sorry if I upset you, but the truth is I'm selfish and greedy. I enjoy coming home to her every night. I like Addison . . . very much. Can you blame me for wanting to be around her?"

His gaze found mine and he flashed a full-out grin.

It was a miracle my eyes didn't fall out of my head. A tiny voice inside said he'd only done this for effect, playing the role of the love-struck boyfriend, but dear God . . . When his face lit up, it was hard not to believe this was truth.

His smile drugged me. I was marginally aware he delivered our goodbyes to my parents, apologizing once more for making the holiday uncomfortable, and telling my parents they were welcome at *our* home anytime. I genuinely had no idea how they would handle that. The exterior of the house was just as impressive as the interior. Would my parents' jaws hit the floor as they pulled up in the circle drive of the mansion?

"That didn't really go as I'd planned," he commented when we were seated in the car. His long fingers rested on the leather-wrapped steering wheel, and I wondered if he'd put his hand there so he could have a sense of control. "But they needed to know eventually."

I stared out the window, waiting for him to put the car in gear and back out of my parents' driveway, but he didn't. We sat in cold silence for an eternity.

"Addison." He placed his hand in my lap, gently squeezing my thigh. "I meant what I said."

"That you want to fuck me on my high school bed with a thumb in my ass? I'm sure."

He glared at me. "You *know* what I'm talking about." He exhaled, signaling frustration. "I told you, I'm not good at that shit, but I like coming home now, okay? People usually get on my nerves, but not you." He looked so different when he was unsure. "I like being with you."

I stared at the hand in my lap. It was the same for me, but I couldn't admit it. He'd steamrolled right over me; how could I confess to liking it? To liking him?

He waited impatiently for my response, so I dropped my hand on top of his, encasing his warm fingers. It was the best I could do. I was sure he wasn't overly pleased, but it seemed to satisfy him enough, because he put the car into gear.

π

I hadn't heard Luka come into the office because I'd been too busy studying. It wasn't until he cleared his throat that my head snapped up and my gaze locked on to him. He leaned back against the desk, his arms crossed, and a rich blue tie hung loose at his neck.

"Go change into something nice," he ordered. "We're going out to dinner."

Was he insane? He'd never interrupted me before, and it was finals week. I shook my head. "I'm studying." I pointed to the textbook in my lap to reinforce my statement.

"Which one?"

"Developmental biology."

He made a face like I was being ridiculous. "Like you need to study for that one. You can take two hours off. We're going out to celebrate."

"Celebrate?" There'd been a weird pitch to his voice that I couldn't place.

"Yeah." He gave me half of a smile. "Your early acceptance to Johns Hopkins came today."

It took me a moment to process the words, and once I got over the initial thrill . . . "You opened it?"

It wasn't the invasion of privacy that bothered me, it was that he'd taken the moment away when we could have shared it together.

"No, I didn't open it," he scoffed. He pulled a thick envelope off the desk and held it up. "I'm assuming. Unless this is an unnecessarily detailed rejection letter."

"Holy shit."

"Open it. Then get your ass upstairs and get dressed."

I stood, snatched it from him, and tore open the envelope. I didn't mind when he moved to stand behind me so he could read over my shoulder, or when his arms wrapped around my waist, holding me close.

"I told you," he whispered as we scanned the letter, confirming my acceptance.

Johns Hopkins. My dream school.

I couldn't stop smiling as he led me upstairs to our bedroom and picked out a dress for me to wear. Luka watched me get ready, amusement playing in his eyes. Maybe even a little bit of pride. He knew how badly I wanted to get in.

I practically galloped beside him as we walked down the hall toward the garage, unable to contain my excitement. Tonight the six-car garage was completely loaded with cars. Often Dimitrije stored his newest acquisitions for his pre-owned luxury dealership here, and Luka examined the selection as if facing a difficult choice.

"BMW or Lexus?" he asked.

It was the most elegant of the cars in the garage, and its black paint gleamed. "The BMW." He seemed pleased at my choice. I relaxed into the soft leather in the passenger seat, marveling at the interior. "It's like a spaceship."

He paired his phone with the large screen and plugged the restaurant's address in.

"We're going into the city?" I asked.

He nodded, but didn't elaborate. As we drove, I called my parents and told them the good news. The conversation was stilted when they realized Luka was listening in on the car speakers, but they were happy for me. After, Luka and I chatted about our days, and then we lapsed into a comfortable, easy silence.

We were exiting the freeway into the city when his phone rang. I stared at the screen, and went cold. Dimitrije Markovic was calling.

Luka's expression turned to stone as he pressed a button. "Hello?"

"Where are you?" Dimitrije's tone was annoyed.

"Downtown."

"Did you take the new BMW?"

Luka's eyebrows pulled together. "Yeah, why?"

There was a loud sigh on the other end. "Don't get pulled over, and if you do, don't let them search the trunk. I've got stuff in there."

Luka's hand tightened on the wheel at the same time the muscles along his jaw flexed. In his head he was surely cursing his father's name. "All right, understood."

The call disconnected and blanketed the car interior in tension. What kind of stuff was back there? Guns? A dead body?

"Should we turn around?" I asked.

"No," he said. "We're almost there. We'll be fine."

The restaurant was Serbian. I could tell from the fact Luka

spoke in Serbian to the host, who greeted him by name. It was always surprising when the foreign language rolled out of him. Unexpected, but pleasant.

The day Luka started to let me have supervised internet access, I'd queried *luče*, spelling it incorrectly as he'd pronounced it, *luche*. He'd grimaced, and then typed it in for me. He'd been embarrassed at calling me a term of endearment, most closely related to 'baby.' He'd only slipped and done it the one time, but when I'd read the translation, warmth spread down through me. It shouldn't have. I wasn't supposed to like how he'd whispered to me in his mother's native language.

We were seated at a table near the back, and from the way the host fawned over us, it was clear he knew *exactly* who Luka was. A bottle of wine was poured for us and left on the table, and as I reached for my glass, Luka spoke abruptly.

"Congrats, Addison. I'm happy for you."

I held my wine in stunned surprise as he clinked his against mine, and then brought his glass to his lips.

"Are you?" I asked quietly.

He looked confused. "Of course. This is what you wanted—"

"No." I was on an emotional rollercoaster, and it made me reckless and brave. "Are you happy?"

He set the wine down and his fingers remained on the bell of the glass, as if he were too distracted to move while thinking about his answer. "Yes," he said finally. His gaze captured mine and stole my breath. "You make me happy."

I could barely get the question out. "Do you trust me?"

He paused.

Oh, no. Slowly his expression melted into his cold,

emotionless mask. He'd seen right through my attempt to ask for freedom. The phone call from Dimitrije had reminded me of my true goal. Luka's family were criminals, and I needed to escape.

"I trust you . . . enough," he said. "Not enough to let you go yet, if that's where you're heading."

I took a sip of my wine and glanced away. He could always tell what I was thinking. I was determined not to let my failed attempt ruin my night. Eventually he'd have to let me go. Johns Hopkins was in Maryland, not Chicago.

Our food was excellent, and I liked the cozy ambiance of the restaurant. Even though the tables were close to each other and the place was busy, it seemed like we were secluded near the back. It felt . . . intimate. It was the closest thing to a real date we'd ever been on.

"Order dessert," he said, when he noticed me eyeing the cart loaded with all sorts of pastries. "The chocolate torte's like my mother used to make—"

Commotion near the front drew our attention. In fact, it seemed to draw everyone's attention in the restaurant. Two men lurked at the host's stand, and the host turned to Luka, giving us a good look at his angry face.

Luka motioned to bring the men back to us. He straightened in his seat and didn't look at me as the men hurried through the aisle, grabbed the two empty chairs at our square table, and sat down.

"Luka." It came from the smaller of the two men. "We heard a Markovic popped by. Wasn't expecting it to be you."

There was an undercurrent of tension to the man's words. He'd been trying for a friendly, casual tone, but there was malice buried there. The larger man was perched on his chair, and his eyes scanned around the room like he expected it to burst into flames at any moment. Was he security?

Luka smiled as much as he typically did, only this one didn't even reach his eyes. "Sorry to disappoint, Ivan."

Ivan leaned back in his chair like he was getting comfortable, and crossed his arms over his chest. "I've been hearing things about you."

Luka raised an eyebrow. "What things?"

"You've had several meetings with Goran. What's going on?"

"Nothing you'd be interested in. Family stuff."

Ivan's scrutinizing gaze swung toward me. "Who's this? You going to introduce your friend?"

"No." Luka's tone was clipped.

Ivan uncrossed his arms, and the change in posture was a signal to the man beside him, who shifted as if going on alert. Ivan's expression screamed he'd been offended. "I thought we were friends. You won't tell me her name? That's rude."

Luka didn't hesitate. "You're right. Her name is Avery."

Chapter
TWENTY-THREE

ICE CREPT ALONG MY SPINE. Whoever this Ivan was, he wasn't a friend. The entire restaurant had gone quiet at the two men's appearance.

"Avery," Ivan repeated. His eyes were beady and his face unattractive. "I'm sorry for interrupting your date."

"It's not a big deal," Luka said. He refused to look at me, and his focus rested squarely on the silent man beside Ivan. "If anything, you're saving me from it. She's dumber than a box of rocks."

I sat still, unsure of what type of reaction to display. The real Avery would lose her mind being called that. Even though it didn't apply to me, it still kind of stung.

"Ouch!" Ivan chuckled and stared at me incredulously.

"See what I mean?" Luka said. "I just insulted her and she's still just sitting here."

He wants you to go. I shot to my feet and channeled Avery as best I could. "You know what? Go fuck yourself."

I hurried out of the restaurant and into the cold night, striding past the shops decorated for Christmas. What now? I didn't have a phone. Should I use this opportunity to run?

No. There was no running. They'd come after Jonathon or perhaps all of my family, and I didn't know the first thing about how to disappear. And . . . Johns Hopkins. I wasn't ready to give up now that I was closer than ever.

What if Luka's in danger?

I wrapped my coat tighter around myself as the winter wind lashed at my bare legs, and I made my way toward the BMW in the parking garage. Not that I had a key. When I reached the car, I leaned on the front end and huddled for warmth. At least here I was out of the wind.

How long should I wait for him beside the car carrying the terrifying *stuff* in the trunk? Ten minutes? I considered my options. I could go back to the restaurant and act like I'd forgotten my purse. Or maybe I could return and say I wanted to give Luka another piece of my mind. I hated the worry that balled in my stomach and weighed me down like a stone.

What happened if Luka was gone? Would Dimitrije send someone to kill me?

I was torn with what to do, until I heard fast approaching footsteps. Someone was running. I sank down, trying to hide between the wall and the front bumper of the car, making myself as small as possible.

"Oh, Christ," Luka said, relief coating his voice. "You're here."

I put my hands on the hood and pulled myself to stand, feeling the same relief he had on his face. "I wasn't sure where to go."

He sprinted forward and swept me up into an embrace. His kiss burned across my lips, and warmth crawled through my body, heating me all the way to the tips of my toes.

"Who is he?" I asked.

"It's complicated." Luka released me and pulled open the passenger door. Once we were both seated inside and the heater was going, he gave me his full attention. "Ivan used to work with my uncle. Now I think he works for the Russians. Even if he doesn't, he had some big ol' balls to walk in there."

We didn't talk much on the ride back to the freeway. Once we were heading for the suburbs under the orange-yellow lights of the highway, Luka spoke again.

"I'm sorry our dinner ended like that."

I wasn't sure how to feel about how the evening played out, and forced a joke. "Hey, I did get to tell you to go fuck yourself."

He grinned widely, and I wished I could see all of it rather than just his profile.

"You should do that more often," I said.

"What?"

"Smile. It's so rare, but you look amazing when you do it."

He took his eyes off the road for a moment, glancing at me. "Maybe I will."

My pulse flared. What was happening to me? Everything was hopelessly twisted.

We were still twenty minutes from the house when Luka suddenly exited the freeway. I sat up in my seat, confused, and saw how on edge Luka appeared. "What's wrong?"

"The same car has behind us for a long time."

Anxiety tightened my voice. "You think someone's following us?"

"No." His gaze locked on the rearview mirror. "Fuck, maybe. He's exiting, too."

There wasn't enough air in the car to breathe. I clenched my hands around the seatbelt strap and hung on as Luka drove the car down the dark and rural road. A single pair of headlights followed behind. We crested a hill and he turned off into a new subdivision that was in the beginning stages of being built. Only the model home was up, the rest had probably been cornfields three months ago.

The car didn't follow us.

Luka snaked the BMW through the maze of roads, circling in a cul-de-sac, and parked. We waited for someone to appear, but after a stressful minute, it seemed unlikely. He undid his seatbelt and massaged away the crease in his forehead.

"I'm all wound up," he said. His hand came down, and he adjusted as if an idea had just occurred to him. "Get in the back seat."

"What?"

"I'm not waiting until we get home. I'm gonna fuck you with my fingers right now." His voice grew with intensity on each word. "Work you until your pussy's dripping wet."

It sent a rush of heat straight between my legs, and my mouth fell open. Would I ever get used to his vulgar mouth?

"Then," he added, his gaze on my parted lips, "when you're good and ready, you'll slide down on my cock and I'll fuck you until you're screaming."

My chest rose and fell with each enormous breath I pulled in. The desire for him was overwhelming. Too powerful to resist.

"And I know how to make you scream, don't I?" His voice was velvet. "Answer me."

"Yes," I breathed.

"Get in the back seat."

I shrugged out of my coat, got out of the car, and darted into the spacious back. He moved just as quickly as I did, and we were both sliding over the leather bench of the back seat at the same time. I heard the snap of his fingers, and instantly my legs parted. I spread wide for him as he covered my mouth with his.

Being with Luka was insanity. I was crazy and perverted, but

I *liked* the feeling.

He'd raped me. He controlled me. And I was beginning to wonder if he might love me.

"Oh," I whimpered. He pushed my panties to the side and drove a finger deep inside while his tongue traced the edge of my ear. I clutched at his arm, holding on to his strong bicep while his finger pumped in and out.

"You need another," he said. A second finger pushed inside. "Such a good girl. You love how my fingers fit inside you. You're clenching so tight on them." Because his mouth was close, it was like his words were inside my head. "Say it. Tell me how much you love it."

I gasped. "I love it."

"You love what?"

I undulated my hips to make him move faster. "Your fingers inside me."

"Anywhere, too, you fucking slut. You go wild when I press my thumb against your tight asshole. You squirm, just begging me to slip it in."

I closed my eyes against the rush his visual gave me. "Yes."

"You're so goddamn perfect." He growled it. "There's no one else like you. No one," he took a breath, "except for me."

I trembled right on the edge, but Luka didn't keep me waiting long. His other hand got to work, stirring and teasing, hurling me into chaos. I came hard, bearing down on the fingers buried inside and moaning his name.

Bliss was still dissipating from my core when he grabbed my panties and yanked them down. "Off."

I lifted my hips, slipped the underwear down my legs, and

abandoned them on the floorboard. Outside it was freezing, but under Luka's intense look I might as well have been standing in the Sahara. I was so hot, I wanted to rip my dress off. He had entirely too many clothes on, too.

But rather than remove anything, he fitted his hands on my waist and urged me to get on top, straddling his lap. He pushed the curtain of my hair out of his way and kissed me with his hot mouth. Beneath me, he was hard and ready, and I ground against his erection, but it didn't satisfy. It only made the want in me stronger. His hands crushed against my breasts, pinching and twisting, stealing my breath. It made me swivel my hips and slide my tongue against his.

His tone was sinful. "You're making a mess on my pants, rubbing on me like that. You want me to go to work tomorrow wearing your dirty cum on me? Are you marking your territory?"

I'd done it because it felt good, but his corrupt idea got my blood to boil. "Are you my territory?"

His teeth were sharp at my neck. "Like my cock wants anyone else. Undo my pants. I fucking need to be inside you. I'm about to run out of patience and I won't be nice when it happens."

"You're not nice," I said.

His mouth curled into an evil smile. He'd warned me of that our first night together, and now I believed it, but I also knew I didn't want nice. I slipped a hand between the space of our bodies and fumbled with his belt buckle. He didn't help me. Worse, he got in my way as he tried to undo the zipper at the back of my dress, making the space to work in smaller. I slid the end of his belt free, dropped his zipper, and shoved my hand inside, closing it around the hot and hard bar of flesh.

The windows had frosted over so we could no longer see out of them, but foreign white light grew from outside, lighting the car interior. Another car was coming.

Suddenly, bright light poured in, and not just white. It strobed red and blue as well.

Chapter
TWENTY-FOUR

LUKA DUMPED ME out of his lap and hurried to do up his pants. "Fuck, *fuck*!"

I yanked up the zipper on my dress so quickly it jammed, and smoothed my hair down, tucking the sides behind my ears. Blood roared through me and my heart pounded. When my gaze went to the floorboard, I saw my discarded underwear. There wasn't time to put it back on. The cop car had parked and a door thudded shut as the officer got out. I kicked the panties under the seat and pressed my hands into my lap.

Luka was all the way on the other side of the back seat, sitting still and calm, even though he was breathing rapidly. He looked emotionless, as if whatever was in the trunk wasn't a terrifying concern.

The cop, a man in his forties, hadn't reached the BMW when Luka rolled down the window as much as the safety feature would allow. The officer accessed the situation, peering into the back seat with his blinding flashlight.

"Evening, folks," he said, his voice gruff. "Are you having car trouble?" His tone left no doubt he knew what we'd been up to when he'd arrived.

"No, sir," Luka said. "We just stopped to have a conversation."

"Hmm. You kids have IDs?"

Luka dug his wallet out, and handed over his driver's license. "She left her purse at home."

The cop stared at Luka's ID, and then the flashlight focused in on my face. I squinted against it, unable to see anyone. *Don't look guilty, Addison.*

"Everything okay, miss?"

I swallowed thickly. All it would take was one word from me. I'd had an opportunity to run tonight, but this . . . This could end it all. Not just set me free, but put Luka away. His fate rested entirely in my hands, and as my vision adjusted and I saw his face, it was clear he knew this. His eyes were desperate chaos.

I could tell myself I was doing it for trust, or out of worry for my family, but it was a lie. Faced with the sudden decision, my dark connection to Luka had grown too powerful to sever.

"Yes, sir," I said. "I'm fine." I squeezed out a tight smile.

It did the trick, because the officer handed the plastic card back to Luka. "You can't park here. Find somewhere else for your conversation."

"Yes, of course. Thank you."

We hurried to the front seat, and as soon as I was buckled, we were off. We rode in total silence until he was back on the freeway and I could breathe again.

His word was gentle. "Why?"

"What?"

"I could be sitting in the back of his squad car right now."

I watched the reflectors on the guardrails blur past as I assembled my thoughts in my head. "I don't want that."

"Why?" He repeated it with more urgency, and perhaps it was tinted with hope.

Because I *cared* about him. "Because you and I," I said, taking a deep breath, "are similar creatures."

He rewarded me with his perfect smile.

π

Goran Markovic's Christmas Eve party started in less than an hour. I put on my blue dress and finished getting ready, but apprehension bounced around inside me like a dozen pinballs. Luka was in the walk-in closet, his collar up, and he was balancing the ends of his tie when I appeared in the doorway.

"I'm not sure I can do this," I admitted. His family was criminals, and I wasn't anxious to meet any more of them.

"Why?" He looped the end of his tie over the other.

"I don't know. Probably because the last time I saw your father I was naked from the waist down. And, oh yeah, he threatened to kill me and my family."

"That won't happen." Luka slowed to a stop, abandoning his goal, and the tie fell open. He encased me in his arms so his hands were warm against the exposed skin on my back. "That's over. You're mine, and they know it. No one would touch you, so don't even think about them."

It was hard to do. I had a lifetime of caring about other's opinions to brush off. His family was going to look down on the poor farm girl who had no business being in their lives.

Of course Luka could read the thoughts going on in my head. "Fuck them, whatever they think. You're smart, and beautiful, and *pure*." His eyes filled with intensity. "They'll be envious. Maybe even jealous of what you have, but it doesn't matter, because they're beneath you, Addison. Every last one of them, including me."

I squeezed my grip on his shoulders to support myself, and

gazed at him with disbelief. He was the most confident person I'd ever met, and he thought I was better than him?

"We make an appearance," he added, "and then we're out of there."

The party was strangely normal. The Markovic family was large, and the main living area was packed with adults talking while kids darted through parents' legs and stole cookies from the dessert tray before dinner. The nine-foot-tall Christmas tree was decorated exclusively in gold and looked like it belonged in a department store rather than a home. I'd always preferred the trees littered with homemade ornaments in various states of wear. Plus, the gold was gaudy and over the top.

Luka kept his arm around me as we made our rounds. I was introduced to dozens of people, but never spoke unless directly asked a question. Not only was I extremely uncomfortable, but this would speed along our exit.

Vasilije lingered in the kitchen, drinking a beer and talking with two men, one of whom I recognized. Michael, Dimitrije's bodyguard. Vasilije glanced at his older brother, then to me, and a smile quirked on his lips.

The relationship between brothers was strange. Luka rarely talked about Vasilije. He'd seemed just as envious of his younger brother as I was mine, when it came to being popular and well-liked. But like me, he was also fiercely protective. Vasilije was eager to get involved in the criminal side of the family business, but both Dimitrije and Goran made it clear they wanted Luka to step up. As reluctant as Luka was, I sensed he'd do whatever he could to prolong the inevitable for his brother.

"Hey there, naughty schoolgirl," Vasilije said. His gaze

wandered over my dress, and . . . holy crap, was he checking me out?

I tried to emulate Luka's confidence. "Hey there, Satan."

Luka laughed. It was brief, but it was amazing to hear the gen-
uine sound. Vasilije laughed as well, but his was wicked. His expression was lecherous, and instinctively I shifted closer to Luka.

"Her name's Addison," Luka said.

"Yeah, I know." Vasilije's face melted into boredom. "Dad's
told me all about your *wife*. I'll try to keep out of your way."

"What?"

Vasilije took the final sip from his bottle of beer and dropped
it into the recycling bin nearby with a loud clank. "I'm coming
back to the house after the break's over."

"Why? What's wrong with your frat?"

"Nothing. But you have to be a student at Randhurst, and I'm
currently not anymore."

Anger seeped into the corners of Luka's face. "You flunked
out? Jesus Christ, Vasilije."

His brother was indifferent. "College isn't for everyone. I
tried it, and determined it's not for me." Displeasure smeared on
Luka's face and Vasilije rolled his eyes. "It's a big fucking house,
get over it."

The hairs on the back of my neck lifted and tingled. Someone was watching me. I glanced over my shoulder and instantly found Dimitrije, who stared at me with disdain. His attention
slowly drifted back to the man he was talking to. The conversation seemed . . . intense.

Vasilije must have noticed what I was looking at. "The fucking Russians. They keep pushing, and Dad's gonna have to do

something."

"Be quiet." Luka's tone was stern.

We all watched the exchange in silence. When the man left, Dimitrije's attention returned to me, and under his exacting gaze, I shivered.

"You're cold?" Luka's palm slid up and down my arm, trying to warm me.

I pressed my lips together and nodded. Around Dimitrije, my bones turned to ice.

"All right." Luka pressed his hand into the small of my back, urging me deeper into the kitchen. "I have to introduce you to my uncle, and then we can go."

Goran Markovic was as intimidating as his younger brother Dimitrije. Goran's nose wasn't perfectly straight, as if it had been broken and never healed right, and his eyes were cold and intelligent. He stood taller than his brother, with more gray in his hair, but it made him look distinguished. Wise, and calculating.

"This is my girlfriend," Luka said.

"Addison." Goran gave a similar smile as Luka's. Only a corner turned up. He extended a hand. "It's a pleasure to meet you."

There was no way to stop the tremble as I shook his hand. My voice was choked, barely able to be heard over the party. "You too, Mr. Markovic."

His hand was like iron, and he didn't release his grip. "I need to say thank you."

"Thank you?"

"For getting Luka to agree to look at my finances. I'm not sure if he told you, but he discovered my last accountant was stealing from me."

"Oh?" I glanced at Luka, but his expression was flat. His eyes were tight, disguising whatever emotion he was feeling. "No, he doesn't talk about that with me."

Relief took over when Goran released my hand. Again he flashed the pleased smile. "Well, I'm glad to finally have someone I trust looking after my investments."

"Is that what you're doing?" Luka said. "Are you investing in a private wine club downtown? I was putting together the tax documents this morning and you spent five figures there this year."

Goran's expression shifted as if recalling a good memory. "No, not investing. They carry an exclusive wine I can't get elsewhere." His gaze turned to me. "Talking taxes on Christmas Eve? While I appreciate his work ethic, do you?"

I wasn't sure what to respond with, and looked to Luka for help.

But it wasn't needed. Goran chuckled softly. "You probably do. Luka says you're driven. And he told me you're going to medical school. Congratulations."

"Thank you."

His gaze held mine just a fraction too long, and my shiver was back. He eyed me as if assessing my potential, and all I could do was think about how this man had ordered the death of Luka's mother. Goran reached abruptly into his suit jacket pocket and retrieved a buzzing phone, then motioned to the party.

"I'll let you kids get back to it. Excuse me."

We drifted toward the main room, and exhaustion slammed into me. I wasn't sure how much longer I could handle being the doll in a pretty dress on Luka's arm. I whispered to him. "Can we go?"

"I already texted our driver."

I sagged into the warm back seat as soon as the car arrived—my dress of silk and lace weighed a million pounds under my coat. Luka loosened the knot at his neck, and his hand came to rest on my knee. I shifted closer and leaned into him.

It'd been two months since we'd sat in costumes in the back seat of one of his cars, heading toward his house. We were still in costumes now, but everything else was different.

"You look beautiful tonight," he said.

My breath hitched. "Thank you."

I set my hand on top of his, and traced patterns on the back of his palm. The only sound was the pavement steadily rolling beneath tires as the car carried us through the night. He looked beautiful tonight, too, but then, he always did.

"I paid off your student loan."

I stopped tracing my patterns. "You did what?"

"Your interest rate was ridiculous, and it pissed me off. So I paid it."

My mind floundered. What was his motivation? What angle was he working? "I can't let you do that."

"Yes, you can." His eyebrow bent into an upside-down V. "It's already done, anyway. They're not going to give me my money back."

"Luka—"

"I didn't do it to trap you. There's no strings attached, so you'll accept this from me, understand?" His voice was quiet, yet firm. I nodded slowly, too stunned to render an answer. His displeased look softened. "Good. Merry Christmas, Addison."

Holy crap. His hand beneath mine turned over, and he laced

his fingers with mine. Such a simple action, and yet it carried so much meaning.

"Merry Christmas, Luka."

Chapter
TWENTY-FIVE

VASILIJE MOVED IN the week after New Year's.

His room was in the middle of the second floor, and I was grateful there was an empty guest bedroom between the brothers as a buffer. Since Vasilije had failed out of school, Dimitrije got him a job in sales at the dealership. Luka was in the back office, so he said he didn't see much of his brother.

I didn't either. Luka asked me to steer clear of him, and I had no problem following that order.

My spring semester was a lighter load than the fall, but still kept me busy, and I spent most of my afternoons in the office, which Luka had forbidden Vasilije from entering. It had become our space as much as Luka's bedroom had.

"He finally asked her out," I said to Luka one afternoon.

He looked up from his desk to spy me curled up on the couch. I still had the blanket over my lap even though the fire was going in the fireplace.

"Gavin?"

"Yeah. He's in my psychology lecture."

Luka sat back in his chair, intrigued. "What'd Vanessa say?"

"She said yes. You'd think it wouldn't work between them, because they have nothing in common."

"They like each other," he said. "Sometimes that's enough."

I supposed that was true. I stretched my arms up above my head and closed my textbook, setting it on the table.

"Are you done for the night?" he asked. To anyone else, his tone would sound benign, but I knew better.

He had plans for this evening. My blood pressure rose. "Yes."

"Good." He stood from his chair and his expression thickened with desire. "Come here."

I followed his order without a word. I stood still and allowed him to methodically strip off my clothes, each removal exposing more of my flesh to his lust filled eyes and greedy hands.

I wasn't nervous, and I wasn't cold—the fire was putting out enough heat. But I shook anyway from the excitement and anticipation. He took his papers off the desk and put them in a drawer, which left the top of the enormous desk bare.

He trapped my waist in his hands and moved me to the center of the desk. "Sit."

The smooth wood was cold against the backs of my legs.

Rope had been stored in the bottom drawer of the desk, which he retrieved and dropped down beside me with a quiet thud. Luka's eyes gleamed as I found his gaze. He hadn't tied me up since the first day I'd been at the house. He'd told me one day I might want it, and now I looked at the coiled rope with surprise. The blackness inside me *did* want it. There wasn't any other feeling like being at his mercy.

It was a rush when he eased me onto my back, urging me onto the center of the desk. There was no conversation. No discussion about rules, or safe words, or feelings. The realization washed over me. There was no need for it, because I trusted him.

He snapped his fingers and I obeyed. I held perfectly still as he worked, threading the different sections of rope around the desk legs and then winding the ends around my wrists. Occasionally his gaze would wander to mine, checking in on my status.

I'm fine, I hoped my expression told him. *I want this.*

His warm hands positioned my feet flat on the desktop, and then there was more rope. It was lashed around my thigh, just above each knee, ensuring my legs stayed open wide to him, and the other ends were anchored beneath the desk.

When it was done and I was bound to the desk, firelight played over him, and a lazy grin swept through his face. I was a vibrating, exciting mess, and enjoyed being on display like this for him.

"Maybe I'll leave you like this all night," he said on a low voice. "You look too fucking perfect not to."

I licked my lips. Once again, his heat filled the room and evaporated all the moisture.

Luka freed the tie from his neck and dropped it on the chair. Then, he worked the buttons of his shirt, peeled the sleeves down his arms, and tossed the shirt on top of the tie. He rolled the chair back to the corner, giving him plenty of workspace.

"You look so good," I said, unable to contain it. His lean chest was hard and toned in all the right places, and I craved to have his smooth, hot skin against mine.

He paused. "Who said you could speak?"

I sucked in a breath. Luka liked to control all things when we were together, and I should have realized he expected to control my voice as well. "I'm sorry," I whispered.

Which was clearly the wrong thing to do. Displeasure arrowed his eyebrow up. He repeated it in a demanding tone. "*Who said you could speak?*"

I knew better than to say anything else.

When he seemed satisfied I wasn't going to talk, he put his hands on my breasts, caressing them. His warm palms kneaded and traced my curves, and I reveled in his touch, closing my eyes to enjoy the sensation better—

There was a sharp smack of fingers against skin as he slapped my breast.

"Eyes on me."

I fluttered my eyelids back open. The sight of him shirtless and standing between my bound legs was intensely hot, and his dark, lewd expression in the flickering shadows was incendiary. I had to press my lips together to hold in the moan.

He moved lower. His fingertips drew a line down my belly and glided further along, continuing all the way through my center and up to a bent knee. Then, they trailed back down to where I was quivering. His feather light touch caused the muscles in the insides of my thighs to contract and flinch. I withstood his teasing for a lifetime, growing hot and more desperate with each passing moment. When was he going to really touch me? When was he going to fuck me?

He yanked a drawer open and searched around inside. It was shut with a thump beneath me, and he held something silver in his hands. A short strand of tiny silver beads. Clamps gleamed at either end. I watched with apprehension as he studied the clamps.

I was fairly sure where these were going, and when he gripped one of my breasts in a steady hand, it confirmed it. The jaws of the rubber tipped clamp pinched open, and then bit down on my hardened nipple.

It hurt. Not badly, but it was a burning ache. I gulped down breath as he fastened the clamp on the other nipple and dropped the cold chain connecting them onto my abdomen. His gaze flitted to mine, checking my reaction.

"I'm okay—" *Wait, shit!* I wasn't supposed to speak.

His face turned to stone. "Congratulations. You've just lost the privilege of my touch."

My heart sprinted. What did he mean? Again, he jerked the drawer open and something else was dug out. When Luka shut it, my mouth fell open. He dropped one on my stomach while he pulled the other on—a black latex glove. He tugged it up to his wrist, and then retrieved the other and shoved his hand inside. There was the tiny cloud of powder as it was snapped on. He laced his fingers together and settled the latex tightly in place.

It wasn't like his rubber-coated touch was all that different than his regular one, but the implied idea was what got to me. This barrier between us, denying pure contact and dulling his heat. His black hands squeezed and gripped at me, while his bare chest shone faintly with sweat from the fire, and his belt buckle glinted against his black pants. He looked dangerous—no, *lethal*—this way. Fucking gorgeous.

I moaned when he pushed two fingers deep between my legs. *Finally.*

The chain between my breasts was clenched in a black-gloved hand while the other fucked me. His voice was commanding. "You'll say my name when I pull on this chain."

There was a small pull, generating heat and a sting on my nipples. "Luka."

Pleasure rippled over his expression. "Who owns this body?"

Tug. "Luka."

"Who's the only man you've had inside you?"

281

Tug. I gasped at the sensation. It was painful, but in the way I enjoyed. "Luka."

"Tell me who your greedy, wet pussy aches for?"

Tug. "Luka," I moaned.

"Tell me," he said, his words stronger, "who you belong to."

Tug. I was half out of my mind. "Luka."

His fingers drove into the spot, and his thumb circle above, giving me dual pleasure. His expression shifted into one that was beyond lust, into something I hadn't seen before. It made my heart stop.

"Tell me the name of the man you love."

Tug.

My mind went blank.

His second tug was more of a jerk, and I gasped against the acute pain, but no words spilled from my lips.

"Goddamnit, Addison. Answer me."

He pulled so hard, I cried out and jerked against the rope. Emotion swirled and tumbled. I cared deeply about him, but *love*? I had to come up with a response. "You said no lies!"

The chain crashed against my skin as he dropped his hold and stumbled backward, staring at me with disbelief. He looked wild and . . .

Holy. Shit.

Luka looked crushed, and it was heartbreaking.

His gaze swung away from me, and he stared at the fire, coursing a dark hand through his hair. I wondered if he was trying to calculate where he'd made an error in his equation since he hadn't gotten the answer he was expecting.

The night after that horrible dinner with his father, I'd told

Luka I'd never love him. Somewhere along the way, I began to wonder if he could do the impossible. *Had he already?* No. I couldn't be in love with him. He'd marked me as his and stained my soul to match his perfect shade of black, but I wasn't ready to be in love with Luka Markovic.

His attention snapped back to me, his eyes focused. His pants were undone, and within a heartbeat, his dick pushed inside. I groaned at the intrusion, but I was happy. I wanted our bodies fused together.

The chain was snatched up. "Whose cock is that fucking you right now?"

Tug. I was eager to answer. "Luka."

He began to pump his hips and injected me with his heat. "Who knows exactly how to make you come?"

Tug. "Luka."

Even though the ropes immobilized me, his free hand locked on my waist and pinned me down. His thrusts were rough and furious, jolting me. "Tell me who you think about all the time."

He didn't even have to pull on the chain. "Luka," I gasped in between his body slamming into mine. The desk banged against the floor and the ropes dug into my skin. "Luka, Luka, Luka . . ."

He pitched forward, fisting the chain tighter and brought us nose to nose. His eyes were full of darkness. Pools of liquid sin I would be thrilled to drown in.

"Who do you exist for?" he snarled, yanking the chain so hard my back bowed up and my chest met his.

"Luka!"

I came violently off of the pain and the pleasure, shattering beneath him. His lips sealed over mine, and I was sure he was sealing my fate with his devastating kiss.

π

We didn't speak about it.

He made me come a second time on the desk, and then he'd followed after. He'd untied me, we'd gotten dressed in silence, and went to bed.

It bothered him over the next week, even though he said nothing. We ate our lunches and dinners together when our schedules allowed, and spent our nights in his big bed, learning more about each other and our lives. Nothing was off limits to him when he got curious, sexually or intellectually.

It was a Thursday night. I tossed and turned in bed, unable to keep my mind quiet. My financial aid package had arrived this afternoon and I'd discussed with Luka. While it would help, I'd still be looking at massive loans. It was normal to graduate from medical school with one hundred thousand dollars' worth of debt, but that didn't make it any easier to stomach. He'd gone quiet when he saw the paperwork, considering it carefully, but there was little to be done.

It was what it was.

"You'll be fine," he commented. "You'll pay those off in the first few years."

But now it was after midnight and I couldn't shut off my brain. I had to get up and do something, even if it was just to stop disturbing Luka every time I shifted beneath the sheets. I didn't have class until noon tomorrow, but he had work.

I threw on my robe over my pajamas and padded down the hallway. I'd get something to drink and then surf the internet or

284

read. Anything to distract. Anything to keep from thinking about my future and whether or not the man I'd left in bed was going to be a part of it.

Light glowed from beneath Vasilije's door, but it wasn't surprising. He always seemed to go to bed late. I poured a glass of white wine, hoping it'd make me sleepy, or deaden my noisy thoughts. I was halfway to the office when a hulking figure appeared in the open hallway that ran beside the dining room.

"You're up late," Vasilije said. He stood casually, but he was blocking my route to the office, and I couldn't shake the feeling he was doing it on purpose.

"Yeah." I wasn't sure what else to say, and waited expectantly for him to move, but he didn't. It forced me to go into the darkened dining room.

"Hey, hold up. I want to talk to you for a minute about something."

Apprehension needled along my spine. Luka had an emotionless mask to hide what was going on inside, and it seemed as if his brother was the opposite. Vasilije's large, warm grin disguised the empty chaos beneath.

He hurried around me into the room, blocking off my exit once more. "It's about Luka."

I swallowed thickly. "What about him?"

"You don't have to be his prisoner. I can help you."

Tension corded my muscles. "I'm not his prisoner."

"It's okay, Addison." He stepped closer. *Too close.* His gaze roamed over my face, settling on my lips. "You don't have to be afraid."

"I'm not." I was afraid, but it had nothing to do with Luka.

Vasilije's grin was like the Cheshire cat's, showing his perfectly white teeth and dimples. "Come on. I see you walking around here, following him like you're his little pet. You don't have to be his fucktoy."

My blood roared in my veins and alarms blared in my head, but I did my best to not show any of it. "That's not how it is."

"What's it like, then?" He inched closer, and I took a step back. "Tell me what a pretty, smart girl like you is doing with a boring guy like him. Doesn't it make you crazy?"

"What?" I moved back again as he advanced on me.

His grin fell. He snatched the wine glass from my hand and set it on the table, and he affected his voice to a patronizing tone. "Luka's 'so smart,' and he's 'such a hard worker,' and so *perfect*. He makes me fucking crazy."

My insides churned as I bumped backward into the wall. "He's not perfect."

"Yeah," he said, annoyed. "He's probably perfectly imperfect." Vasilije reached out and slid his hand around my cheek, cupping my face. I jerked away from his unwelcomed touch and his hand was icy cold, in stark contrast to his brother's. "Gets whatever he wants. He wanted you, and takes you, even if he's gotta hold you here against your will."

"I can leave whenever I want," I said, my voice small.

He gave a humorless laugh, knowing it was a lie. Luka had given me a lot of freedom, but I still wasn't free.

"Come on." Vasilije's hushed tone was gentle, yet scary. "Let me help you. I can talk to my father." He moved so fast there wasn't time to stop him. He tugged open the knot holding my robe closed. "You don't have to be with Luka."

I tried to duck under the thick arms that trapped me against the wall, but his hands were inside my robe, sliding around my waist.

"No!" I said, loudly.

"Shh. I'm not perfect, but I'm better than him." The cold from his hands seeped through the thin fabric of my tank top. My shiver was instant, and I shuddered harder as he leaned closer, readying to cover my mouth with his. "And if you're free, you can be with whoever you want. Right now," he whispered, "in this moment."

"I want him," I blurted out. "I'm Luka's."

Vasilije halted, and looked unconvinced.

It urged me on. "I'm *his*, Vasilije, by choice. It didn't start out that way, but that's how it is now. I belong with him. I think he loves me," I said, startled by how strong and confident my words were. They broke free and poured from my mouth. "And I *know* I'm in love with him."

Vasilije's expression soured, and his thoughts were visible in his eyes. He did not like losing out to his brother. His hands gripped tighter, driving his fingers into my skin.

"You're hurting me," I gasped and tried to get free.

"Get your fucking hands off of her!"

I'd been so focused on the threat of one Markovic, I hadn't noticed the other when he appeared in the dining room. Luka was shirtless, with pajama pants slung loosely around his hips. He moved as a blur, throwing his brother off of me, sending Vasilije crashing against the buffet in the corner.

"Fuck, calm down," his brother said. "We were just talking."

There was no calming down for Luka. He got between me and his brother, using himself as a protective shield. His hands were clenched in fists and the muscles in his back and shoulders strained, tight beneath his skin. His deep voice was terrifying and believable. "Touch her again and I'll kill you."

"Whatever, Luka. I was testing her loyalty to you. You should thank me—"

"Get the fuck out of my sight."

Vasilije's angry footsteps plodded away and up the stairs. It wasn't until a door slammed that Luka spun to face me, his expression full of alarm. "Are you all right?"

Adrenaline snaked in my system, but relief was also working its way through, and I nodded. Luka pulled me away from the wall and crushed me into his arms. His urgent mouth locked onto mine as if desperate to confirm our connection, and I matched him, eager.

"How much did you hear?" I whispered.

He didn't answer with words. Instead he scooped me up and sat me on the dining table, and his kiss leveled me. He'd heard it all, and I blinked back the overwhelming tears that flooded my eyes. I loved him. It was my final surrender.

I flung the robe off my arms. I grasped at the hem of my tank top, lifting it up—

He broke the kiss. "We're out in the open."

He was worried about Vasilije? "Fuck him," I said. "Let him see you taking what's yours."

We tore at our clothes together, hurling my shirt and our pants to the floor. I wrapped a hand around his cock, stroking him, and in two pumps down his length he was hard as steel. I needed him inside me. I had to know what it felt like to be joined together with the man I loved.

He hurried, preparing to take me.

When he slid inside, our moans mingled together. My arms banded around his shoulders and I held on, wrapping my legs around his hips. His mouth never left mine as he began to move. He was fucking me on the dining room table in the same spot he'd bent me over my first day here.

The dark need roared inside. I'd looked at him so long ago and wanted him to do bad things to me, and he had. Making me fall in love with him was the worst of all.

Luka typically didn't do fast. He took his time and drew things out, but there wasn't time for control now. I groaned with satisfaction as he pistoned his hips, fucking me like he had to, before we woke from this beautiful nightmare.

"I love you," he breathed.

His words sent me soaring, and gave me the courage to admit the truth. "I love you, Luka."

We were two bodies moving as one. He eased me back on the table and moved inside, claiming me over and over again. The room was a million degrees, burning away doubt and guilt and shame at loving him when I knew he wasn't nice or good.

We erupted together. It was so hot I worried we'd scorch the tabletop.

He slowed to a stop, resting on top of me and still lodged deep inside, his face buried in the side of my neck. His hurried breathing was loud in my ear.

"You have to let me go," I whispered.

He tensed, knowing I didn't mean physically.

"I have to know this is real," I continued. Because Vasilije's words weren't wrong. Did I love Luka because I had no choice?

He rose up on his arms and peered down at me with an expression that was a mixture of unhappiness and . . . fear. He was afraid of losing me.

"No," he said.

"Give me space to find myself as this girl who can love you, and I'll come back."

"I need you here with me. How can I go back to how it was before you?"

"Please, Luka. This matters. You said anything that matters to me, matters to you. *Please.*"

Hearing me beg for freedom broke him a little. He retreated, and I followed him up, wrapping my arms around him.

"I don't know if I can do it," he said finally, his voice unsure. "Let you walk out the door and not follow you."

"You can. You got me to fall in love with you." I pressed my forehead against his. "You can do anything."

Chapter
TWENTY-SIX

AVERY WAS PISSED when I moved my stuff back into the dorm room that was microscopic in comparison to the mansion. She stood with her arms crossed over her chest and annoyance smeared on her face as the final bit of clothes were hung in the tiny closet on my side of the room. She'd been using both closets as her own in my absence.

Luka straight-out told Avery to leave when I was finally settled, so we could say goodbye without her angry glares.

He lingered and stalled, not wanting to leave, and part of me felt the same.

"You'll come back to me," he said, his order sounding less confident than normal.

"Give me this space, and yes, Luka. I will."

Would I be back at his house within the week?

His goodbye kiss was brutal. He lashed at me with his tongue, controlled me with his mouth, and made my knees go weak. When the words were on the tip of my tongue for him to stay, for him to take me back home, he abruptly released me and left without saying a word. There was no goodbye or *I love you*. He'd been reeling and unable to process this foreign feeling of relinquishing control.

The first week back was incredibly strange. It was like a limb was missing. We chatted nightly on FaceTime using the iPad he'd given me, and although his house wasn't that far from school, the divide was fucking enormous.

I almost caved my second week when Luka threw a temper tantrum. He was used to getting his way. So he started to give me assignments again, and when he had some control, even just for a few minutes, things improved.

He drove me home from school for spring break, and took my family out to dinner. His hand had curled around mine under the table in my lap, and he was every bit the doting, love-struck boyfriend we'd pretended he was at Thanksgiving. Only this time it was real.

Tensions had eased considerably for my parents when I explained I had returned to my own space at the dorm, and Luka had made it clear he was committed to me. We were in love, and my mother was thrilled. She'd beamed at Luka from across the table and winked at me when he wasn't looking.

After dinner, he'd turned down my father's offer to come in, and I stayed in the front seat of his car, waiting wordlessly for my parents to go inside.

"Come home," Luka said when we were alone. It tore at my heart, but I still wasn't ready. I needed to know he would let me stand on my own, and I had to have my independence back.

I spoke softly. "I will."

"When?" he demanded. "How much longer are you going to need?" Irritation tinged his voice.

"I don't know."

He exhaled loudly, and his hands rested on the steering wheel. "I fucking hate this." He turned to look at me, and his expression was hard. "The house is empty and I can't sleep at night."

Hearing those words made me weak. Sleeping in my tiny

NIKKI SLOANE

bed with Avery nearby instead of him was the hardest part about the decision I'd made. I both liked and hated that he had the same trouble with it.

"I know, I'm sorry." I put my hand on his leg, leaned over, and rested my ear against his shoulder. "Let me get through spring break and maybe I'll be ready."

"Or maybe I'll drag you back to my house right now and never let you leave again."

The reminder of what he'd done made me go cold. I straightened away from him and grabbed my purse.

"Fuck," he groaned. "Stop. I don't want to leave like this." Luka leaned over and threaded his hand through my hair, holding me into his kiss. "I'm trying, okay? I'll give you whatever you need, but what you want is . . . difficult. I miss you."

Every second I remained in this car was more dangerous than the previous one. I wavered horribly. I loved him and wanted to be with him, but then there was also the desire to be free, and to make him repent for what he'd done. I wasn't holding us apart to be cruel or punish, but he needed to learn to give in to my demands, too.

I wanted a partner, not a master.

"Why'd you do it?" I whispered.

"What?"

"Our first time." My voice was thick with emotion. "Why didn't you stop?"

His face contorted as he tried to assemble an answer. "I'd been thinking about you a lot recently, right before the party. So when you showed up, I don't know, I thought it was fate. And when you told me you hadn't been with anyone before, I told

293

myself you'd been waiting for me." He sighed. "I know that's stupid. I wasn't exactly thinking straight. I'm . . . sorry, Addison, about how I brought us together." His voice was soft. "I wish I'd done it differently." Luka paused, and then his expression went warm. "But I'm not sorry about us being together."

I kissed him with total abandon, and had to stop myself from climbing over the seat into his lap. I missed him, too. His mouth, his touch, the way he made me feel. My eyes were damp with tears when I scurried from his car and into my parents' house.

Every time I said goodbye, I wondered if it would be the last time I'd have to do it. The wall I'd placed between us was on the verge of breaking, and one more push would send it tumbling down.

π

I'd been back at school after the break three days before I'd decided I had to go back to him. I was sitting in my physics lecture, unable to focus on what the professor was teaching when I finally came to peace with it. His family was deep in organized crime and I wasn't sure if he could escape, but I knew I couldn't run from my feelings anymore.

I'd go into this relationship with eyes wide open.

So I held my cellphone hidden under my desk and texted a message to Luka, telling him I wanted to talk. I'd have to know how much shit his family was really into, and how Luka and I were going to figure a way to get him out. His reply was quick. He'd be at my dorm room in thirty minutes.

Class ran long, and I had to dash to my dorm. I flew down the hall to my room, only to pull up short. Air halted painfully in my lungs and my mind went into total panic.

Two uniformed cops were waiting at my door.

Oh, shit. What had happened? Were they here about Luka, or here for me? I forced myself to pull in a breath. *Act natural, Addison. Remain calm.*

"Addison Drake?" the taller of the two officers asked me. When I nodded, he gestured to door. "May we have a word in your room?"

I nodded hesitantly. I moved slowly to put my key in the lock and turn it. The door weighed a million pounds. "What's this about?"

The officer pulled the door closed behind his partner, shutting us together inside my room. He eyed my bed. "Can you have a seat, please?"

"Why?"

"I have some very difficult news for you."

Somehow my feet moved and I complied. I sat down gingerly, tension so tight in me I worried I'd shatter like glass if I moved too quickly. All I could think about was Luka. *Please let this be all right.*

The shorter officer stood motionless as the taller one began to pace back and forth, visibly nervous. Just as he was about to speak, there was a knock at my door. My brain went blank. What the hell was I going to do? What was Luka going to think when he walked in on two cops in my room?

I didn't get a chance to try to send him away. The shorter cop opened the door. Luka blinked. His gaze swept over the uniform and badge, but he hid the alarm from his face. Only I could see the danger beneath.

"Addison?" Luka said, his wide-eyed gaze turning onto me.

I said it on a hurried voice. "They said they need to talk to me." Could he hear the honesty, or did he assume this was an ambush?

"Are you a close friend with Ms. Drake?" the cop asked.

Luka took in an uneven breath. "I'm her boyfriend."

The taller cop stopped pacing and scrubbed a hand over his jaw. "Can you come in, please?" He motioned to my bed, wordlessly suggesting Luka sit beside me. Hyperawareness crawled along my skin as Luka sank down at my side. These officers had no idea who he was. So, why were they here?

The cop squatted so he was directly in front of me. "Addison. I'm terribly sorry to tell you that there was a fire last night at your parents' home in Mokena. It spread very quickly." The man's eyes were deep with sympathy as he drew in a deep, preparing breath. "Your family did not survive."

I blinked. "What?"

He didn't repeat it, probably knowing he didn't have to—this was a normal reaction and the person would need time to process. But I couldn't process. He was saying my family was . . .? He couldn't be right. I'd just seen them a few days ago, and everything had been fine.

The police had to be mistaken.

Luka's arms curled around me.

As I stared at the cop and the other officer who lingered beside, both of their expressions stricken, I began to worry they hadn't made a mistake. He'd said my name. They'd come here to my dorm room. What if what he said was true? An earthquake erupted inside and I shook with tremors.

Dead.

My family.

Gone.

"What?" I cried again, slamming a hand over my lips, trying to contain the emotion. I didn't know what to do. Cold crashed over me, sucking every last molecule of warmth.

When tears spilled from my eyes, Luka pulled me tight to him, and his fierce grip made me break apart completely.

I faded in and out of sobs, swinging wildly from grief to disbelief and back again. The cops went over the details quickly and said an investigation into the cause of the fire had been initiated, but I vaguely acknowledged what else was said.

Mostly I sat on the bed while Luka held me and I tried not to die.

The police left once he was done asking them questions, and confirmed he'd stay with me. I cried quietly, unable to function. Everything hurt and ached. For a long while, we remained on the bed, where I found him shaking almost as much as I was.

Time passed, slow and unforgiving.

"*Luče,*" he said, pressing his lips to my forehead. "I'm so sorry."

He held me so tightly, it hurt, but I was grateful. His strength held me together.

π

Luka took care of everything.

He notified my professors, made all of the funeral arrangements, handled the insurance and financial issues, and took care of the outpouring of support I couldn't deal with. I just wanted to be alone. No, that wasn't entirely true. I just wanted to be alone with him. I spent the next day in our bed, curled up in his arms, relieved he'd taken off work.

On Saturday, he made me eat something. Whitney was beside herself and had prepared a dozen dishes, wanting to offer comfort any way she could. I ate like a zombie and returned to bed.

My family was gone, as was the house. I had nothing left in the world.

Nothing except for Luka.

"You need to go back to class," he said finally one night, "after the funeral. Some people will say it's too soon, but they don't know you. You need the normalcy. You need to focus on your goal."

"Okay," I said, devoid of feeling.

Luka pressed his lips together and struggled to hide the worry from his face. I was cold all the time now. Not even Luka's heat could melt through the ice that surrounded me.

He sat beside me at the funeral visitation and forced me to do what I was supposed to.

"You're not the only one grieving," he'd told me softly. "It's important to go through the motions for other people, to offer them comfort as well. You're strong, Addison. You can do this."

"Is that what Vasilije said?" I asked. I'd come into the kitchen last night to see the brothers talking over beers, and had interrupted Luka asking his brother for advice.

Luka frowned. "We weren't talking behind your back. I'm shitty at dealing with people. He's not, so I wanted his help, and Vasilije's concerned about you."

I gave a humorless laugh. "Right."

"He knows what it's like to lose a parent, doesn't he?" Luka's gaze softened. "We get what you're dealing with."

"A parent, not an entire family. And you can't," I said. "Even I don't know what I'm dealing with. It's all just . . . cold."

I stared at Jonathon's friends bawling at his casket, and wondered if I'd ever feel warm again.

The day of the funeral was tedious. My bones hurt as I suffered through the service, and rode in absolute silence beside Luka in the back of the limo, trailing three hearses. When I stood at the gravesites, I got angry.

This was unfair. It was so *fucking* unfair I could hardly stand still. My grip on Luka's hand was ferocious, and I gnashed my teeth together. What had I done to deserve this? What the fuck had my family done?

I wanted to break something. I needed to hurl everything to the ground, to tear out my hair, and to lose myself completely in the madness. Better to feel rage than nothing at all.

Luka set me in the back seat of the limo and recognized the change in my demeanor. He waited until we were in motion before speaking. "Are you angry?"

"Yes."

"With me?"

"No."

"You should be." He stared at me like I was missing the obvious. "This is all my fault, Addison. None of this would have happened if it wasn't for me. I brought that down on your family, and you'll never know how fucking sorry I am about it."

"What the hell are you talking about?"

"My father is convinced this was the Russians. They figured out who you were, or followed me when I took you home for the break."

"Why?"

"We're not sure. He's still working on it."

I stared at him in his crisp black suit, and hated the guilty expression on his handsome face. The hate was a feeling I could respond to. I'd gone so long without any emotion other than sadness, it felt new and exciting.

So I leaned over and slapped my palm across his face, punctuating the silence with the crack of skin smacking skin. It felt good. A needed release. Luka's cheek flamed pink, but otherwise he had no reaction.

It only fed my anger. He should have been livid. Last time I'd slapped him, he'd threatened to destroy my hand, but now he just sat there with his gaze fixed forward. So I did it again. This time I hit him so hard my palm stung, and the force of it turned his head to the side.

But otherwise he was unfazed. He took my outburst without a word.

"Goddamnit, Luka. Stop me. Get mad. Fucking do *something*."

I reared back to strike again, but this time he caught my wrist. "You think I don't deserve this? We just put your whole fucking family in the ground. That was my fault. Everything that's happened to you, all the shit I put you through . . . I destroyed your life."

He had, there was no denying it, but how the fuck was I supposed to reconcile the fact that I still loved him? He'd taken everything from me, but he'd also become my everything.

His grip fell away from my wrist and he looked prepared to receive further punishment, but I didn't want to punish him. If it was true the Russians were responsible for the fire that took my family, Luka wasn't responsible. He didn't want to be a part of the

Markovics' dark world.

"Their death is not your fault," I said, my statement burning in my throat. "It's your father's."

Luka's head slowly turned my direction, and there was understanding in his eyes, perhaps even relief that I didn't completely blame him. But I needed to feel the burn of anger, to soak in the heat of my rage, so I could finally feel warm again.

I grabbed him roughly and slammed my lips over his, shoving my tongue in his mouth and catching him unprepared. He tried to slow the kiss down, but I wouldn't have it. Already tiny flames flickered in my body, and made me thirsty for more. We hadn't truly been together since I'd left him at the mansion, and the pent up lust mixed with my depression, creating a dangerous storm.

He issued a sound of discomfort when I bit down hard on his bottom lip. I wanted to draw blood and goad him to match my anger.

"Addison," he said like a warning.

I ignored. I hiked my black dress up and climbed on him, straddling his lap. I clenched fistfuls of his hair, tugged his head to the side, and sank my teeth into his neck. Once more he groaned, unhappy.

His hands seized my arms. "*Addison.*"

There was one trick left to try. I wrapped my hands around his throat and squeezed as hard as I could. I didn't possess enough strength to overpower him, but the dominance snapped his control. His eyes flared with darkness as he ripped my hands away. "What are you doing?"

"Fuck me," I said. "Be brutal."

His expression was pure shock. "What? No."

"Yes. I have to feel something else other than this numbness. I need it," I said, my voice shaking, "and you owe me."

"Jesus fucking Christ." He shook his head. But as he stared at me, he could tell I was serious. Luka could read what I was feeling, and see how desperately I wanted it. He glanced around the back seat of the limo. "What, right now?"

He liked to be in charge, so I had to push. "Don't make me wait another second."

Luka clamped his hands on my waist and moved us together, throwing me onto my back on the bench seat. The force was so great when I slammed into it, my head bounced against the upholstery and it knocked the air from my lungs.

Even though it was mid-afternoon, the tinted windows made the interior dim, and his intense eyes glittered in the low light. "You want it rough?"

"Yes," I hissed. Once more I sank my teeth into his flesh, biting him just beneath his jaw. I dove my hands inside his suit jacket, sliding them between the silk lining and his dress shirt. "I shouldn't have to repeat myself."

He drew back so I could stare up at him. His face was hard, all vicious lines and aggressive eyes. Was I pushing him too far? I was reckless and wild.

Luka rose up on his knees and latched one hand on the back of the seat to steady himself as the limo eased through a turn. His other hand tangled up under my skirt and jerked my panties down while I raised my hips to allow it. He pulled so hard, the fabric dragged painfully across my skin. I kicked it the rest of the way, and he threw them to the floor.

Lust mixed with danger, and hung thick in the back of the

vehicle. When he leaned down, I grabbed the collar of his jacket and peeled it off of him, desire and anticipation making me clumsy. The ache for him was a thousand knives stabbing me. I couldn't think over it.

He let me work his jacket off, but that was it. When I reached for his belt with both hands, he grabbed them and pinned them above my head, holding them against the cool glass of the window. He'd done it so his other hand could shove my legs apart and two fingers pushed so deep inside me, I gasped with a hint of pain.

"You want this?" His tone demanded an answer. Luka never asked permission before.

Warmth flowed from his hand, burning up my core and snaking out through my veins. I squirmed on his fingers and bucked my hips. "Yes," I babbled. "Yes, yes. I need it."

I needed him to do bad things to me. Make me deserve what had happened.

When he worked a third finger inside, I cried out, but the discomfort was welcomed. The fire crackled and burned hotter, warming the empty void I'd become.

"Quiet," he hissed. Maybe he was worried the limo driver would hear me. Luka's gaze focused in and his expression was vicious. He was exactly how I wanted him to be. His fingers pumped in and out, and I grew slicker with each thrust, showing him how much I liked it, even if my moans sounded otherwise.

He had to release me to undo his pants, and I used the opportunity to launch my own attack. I slapped him again, surprising him with the action, and snarled it out. "Hurry up."

His eyebrow went through the ceiling and anger swelled in his eyes. As soon as he had his pants shoved down over his hips and his cock out, his palm sealed over my lips. His other hand rubbed my clit in hurried strokes, taking me close to the edge, only for his fingers to come down hard in a strike directly across my aching center. The slap of his hand against my damp skin was a loud snap.

I cried out against his hand, and stared at him wide-eyed. He was a beautiful demon, made just for me. I scratched my nails down his neck, leaving bright pink track marks in my wake. Marking him as mine. The hand on my mouth shifted, so he could clench it around my neck, tight as a vise, collaring me beneath his warm fingers.

"You know what you do to me?" he growled. "You make me so fucking hard."

He stabbed himself between my legs, taking me in one enormous thrust and impaling me on his cock. The sensation of him inside me tore my mind from my body, and I went wild. I thrashed against him like a rabid animal, all teeth and claws. It felt *amazing*. For the first time in a week, I was alive. Filled with hunger and need, instead of endless sadness.

Luka fucked me like a savage. He grunted with his merciless thrusts, pounding into me, and I moaned, although it was choked off. His grip was intense and pressed hard against the pulse banging in my neck. He drove down into me, pushing me into the seat where a seatbelt dug into my back, but I didn't give a fuck. The fire consuming us was too powerful to fight, so instead I locked my ankles behind his back and held him to me.

Luka kept me right on the edge of orgasm, not allowing me to go over, so in frustration I reached down and touched myself. If he wouldn't get me there, I would. When he realized what I was doing, he looked scary. My hand was shoved away, and he tapped me hard on the face. Just with the ends of his fingertips, but enough to make my breath halt in my lungs.

"Whose pussy is this?" he demanded. "You'll come when I say so."

His soft, corrective slap had shocked me, but I loved it. I was going to explode. "Please," I rasped. "Fuck, Luka. *Please.*"

"I'll never let you go again," he said between enormous pants for air. "We belong together. Repeat it."

"We belong together," I agreed.

"Because I own you." His lips pressed to mine. We'd gone at it like people on the brink of insanity, and when we reached the top of the precipice, he flung us over with a final push. "And you own me."

Pleasure detonated. I screamed as I came, making the limo driver slam on the brakes, sending us tumbling, but Luka held on. He braced an arm on the floor to stop us, and as the powerful orgasm swept through me, he began to reach his end, too.

"I love you," I whispered through his loud moans, and gripped him ferociously as he shuddered and pulsed inside me.

"Fuck, I love you," he said, when he seemed to have regained the ability to speak. He lifted his head and smoothed a hand over my cheek. "Are you all right?"

The limo had stopped moving, and we could hear the driver getting out, probably preparing to check on me. Was I all right? "No," I said lightly, stroking a hand over Luka's thick hair. "Not yet, but I will be."

He stared into my eyes, and I knew he understood exactly how I meant it.

Chapter
TWENTY-SEVEN

I WENT BACK TO SCHOOL the following week as Luka had asked me to, and he'd been right. The normalcy helped to combat the unfamiliar life I'd been thrust into. I spent my days in class trying to catch up, and at night he helped distract me during the difficult first few weeks.

There were setbacks.

One night, the realization that my great-grandmother's crystal bowl had been destroyed had sent me into a deep depression. The only photos I had of my family were what I'd saved in my phone or online, so Luka reached out to my extended family and Jonathon's school to try to get me copies of everything possible.

And there were days when I had to remind myself they were really gone. Jonathon wouldn't graduate from high school. My parents wouldn't be there to see me walk across a stage and receive my college degree. Sometimes the pain was so acute I couldn't breathe, and I begged Luka to give me a different type of pain.

Which he did.

Other days, I coped. I survived by leaning on him. He arranged for a team to shift through the wreckage of my house and bring us whatever might be of value to me, sentimental or otherwise.

It was an early Saturday morning when a knock on our bedroom door roused Luka and me awake.

"Addison," Vasilije said.

I glanced at Luka with sleepy eyes. Vasilije and I hadn't said much toward each other since I returned to the house. He'd given me a sincere apology about the incident before I'd left, and then a heartfelt condolence, but most of the time I didn't see him. He was hardly ever home. So why was he asking for me and not his brother?

"Yes?"

"Can you come downstairs?" His voice was loud so I could hear through the door. "My father needs a word."

It was barely light outside, and his father was here? I froze as panic pumped through my veins. Luka's expression mirrored my suspicion, and we both climbed out of bed, pulling on clothes. "Yeah, just a second."

We trailed behind Vasilije down the stairs to the first floor, but he kept moving. It wasn't until he reached for the basement door that Luka's warm hand wrapped around my arm and jerked me to a stop.

"Wait a minute, what's going on?" His voice was uncharacteristically tight. Luka was nervous?

Vasilije's expression was stoic. "Dad's downstairs."

"No. We're not going down there."

His brother's eyebrow rose. "Dad didn't say shit about you. He needs to talk to her."

"No," Luka repeated, firm. He glared at his younger brother.

Vasilije's face soured. "Jesus, calm down. I promise, he just wants to talk to her. And he wasn't asking Addison to come down, he's telling her."

I'd never had a reason to go into the basement. It was unfinished storage, or so I'd been told, and I worried about discovering something down there I didn't want to find. Luka's tension confirmed my suspicion. Whatever was downstairs was related to the Markovics' true business. But I needed to know, didn't I? I nodded, signaling I'd go.

Luka seemed unsettled as he turned the doorknob and motioned for Vasilije to lead the way. He filed down the stairs next, taking my hand in his, so he could enter the basement first.

The stairs were bare wood, and the stone colored walls and poor lighting made the stairwell feel like a cave. It wasn't much better when we reached the bottom. It was windowless. Pipes snaked overhead and the cement floor sloped gently toward a drain at the center of the room.

I could smell the metallic scent of blood before I spotted it.

Dimitrije Markovic stood in slacks and a white dress shirt with the sleeves haphazardly rolled back, and red spots dotted his bare forearms and shirt front. The blood came from the crumpled heap of a man lying on the floor. Nearby, a bloody metal baseball bat leaned upright against the wall.

My grip on Luka tightened as my body went on red alert. Had Dimitrije brought me down here to help this man, knowing I wanted to become a doctor? His gaze spotted me beside Luka, and in contrast to the first time I'd seen him, Luka's father seemed pleased to see me beside his son.

The man on the floor groaned with agony, and Dimitrije glanced down. Disgust swept over his face. "Maybe I should burn you alive, like you did to this poor girl's family."

My knees threatened to give out.

Holy shit, was what Dimitrije said true? Was the man lying at his feet responsible for the fire? The police hadn't found the source of ignition or any evidence, but ruled the fire as starting under suspicious circumstances. I'd had to lie when they'd questioned me, asking if I knew of anyone that could have been involved, and it was the only time Luka hadn't been by my side when dealing with my family's death.

"What you don't realize," Dimitrije said, continuing to talk to the puddle of flesh moaning on the ground, "is this girl is *my son's*." His powerful tone was absolute. "It makes her part of my family, and I put my family above anything else. You've started a fucking war."

The man rolled onto his back and gazed up at the ceiling while he tried to pull his puffy, mangled face into a grotesque smile. "Good," he croaked. He laughed, but it was cut short when he coughed and a mouthful of blood erupted from him.

"Ivan?" Luka asked. His gaze swung from the man up to find his father, who confirmed it with a grim nod. "Why?"

"Because it was an easy first strike," Dimitrije answered. "They want us to retaliate. They thought we'd be too focused on that to notice they were moving a huge shipment over in Cicero." His mouth lifted in an evil smile. "We *let* it happen. I had someone slip a welcoming present inside."

Ivan coughed, giving a sharp noise of surprise.

Dimitrije put his foot in the injured man's chest. "Who's going to be there when that crate's opened, huh? I heard the boss is in town."

"Changes nothing," Ivan choked out. "The Russians have more. More men and more guns. More power."

"Shut the fuck up." Dimitrije kicked him in the ribs, forcing him to roll away from the blow. He gurgled blood and drooled it on the cement. I shuffled backward. It wasn't the sight of blood or Ivan's traumatized face that made my stomach turn. I was unaccustomed to violence.

"Addison." My name on Dimitrije's lips was a command for attention I knew I had to obey, but it was nearly impossible. "I didn't trust you when Luka brought you into my home, but you've proven your commitment to him. To my family."

My blood moved as slush through my veins. It was becoming clear why Dimitrije wanted to speak to me.

"This piece of shit took your family, and I brought him here to give you retribution."

Oxygen was leaking from the room, and I couldn't catch my breath. Luka stared at Ivan, and it looked like he was barely holding back his rage. Beyond him, Vasilije watched the scene with fascination and a sick gleam. And then my gaze returned to meet Dimitrije's. His bloodstained shirt was scary, but his black eyes were horrifying.

"You want a gun?" I wasn't sure who Vasilije was talking to at first, but it became apparent it was me.

Did I?

I peered at the battered man on the floor and a voice inside me answered back *yes*. My family had died a horrible death, and Ivan's life for theirs didn't even balance. Warm, sickly rage roiled in my belly and rose in my throat. What would I feel like with a gun in my hand? How powerful had I become now I'd been given the choice about this man's fate?

Luka's hand let go of mine, but it was so he could wrap it around my waist and pull me tightly against him, offering his support. Telling me he was okay with whatever I decided.

The blackest, evilest part of me wanted Ivan dead, but . . .
I couldn't.

I was going to be a doctor and save lives. How could I go on
to do that if I committed this dark deed? The rest of my life I'd be
atoning for it.

"No," I whispered.

Vasilije's gaze crept to Luka. "What about you?"

Since I was clinging to him, I could feel the tension and fury
in his body, all the way to his foundation.

"No," I said again, this time louder. I gazed up at Luka, hoping he could read everything I was feeling, because I couldn't find
the words. He hadn't crossed the line into total darkness yet and
I didn't want him to. If he did this, he might never come back. I'd
already lost everything. *Please,* I silently pleaded, *don't make me
lose you, too.*

His expression didn't change, yet I could sense he understood. "No," he said, affirming what I wanted.

Vasilije stared at us like he couldn't believe what he was hearing. Finally, he sighed loudly and glanced back to his father. "You
want to finish with the bat? It's making a big fucking mess."

"Please." I tried not to whimper, and failed. "I can't . . . Don't
do this. If you send him back to his people, what happens?" Could
Ivan tell them about the bomb and avoid the war he promised
was coming?

Dimitrije's cold stare said there was no chance of this man
leaving the basement alive. Perhaps Dimitrije was eager to go to
battle with his enemies. I stood paralyzed as he reached over and
curled his fingers around the grip of the bat. My heart pounded
in my chest and threatened to explode as he stalked toward Ivan,

dragging the weapon noisily across the ground, his eyes brimming with violence. Oh, God. *Oh, God!*

Luka yanked me, shoving me face first into his chest, hiding my eyes from what was about to happen as his arms locked around me. He held on tightly as the sound of the bat whooshed through the air, followed by a disgusting thump and crunch of bones.

The gurgling announced the blow wasn't fatal.

I balled my hands in Luka's shirt as I shook violently, barely able to stand. I sank as deep into his arms as possible, wanting to retreat inside him when another blow rang out. This one had more force to it from the sound of metal striking something more solid than just body alone.

The gurgling stopped.

For a long moment, it was silent in the basement, other than the water heater humming in the background. Luka had watched it happen, and some of the tension eased from him, but what the hell did we do now?

"Luka." Dimitrije's tone was full of disappointment. "You'll stand by and let it happen, but you can't do it yourself?"

Luka's chest lifted in a deep breath. "Turns out, I'm a lot like you."

"What the hell are you talking about?" The metal bat was tossed down, where it clattered and rolled loudly on the floor, making me flinch. "Did you have your goddamn eyes shut?"

"I'm talking about my mother."

I shifted in Luka's arms and made sure to keep my gaze up off of the floor, not wanting to see the result of his father's work.

Dimitrije didn't appear quite as distinguished when he looked guilty. His voice was grim. "That was different."

"What?" Vasilije took a step closer, and his confused gaze went from Luka to his father.

There was a wordless exchange between the two older Markovics. Dimitrije's expression softened with the realization Luka knew what had really happened the night of the storm so many years ago.

"Your mother threatened to go to the authorities. There wasn't anything I could do."

Luka's shoulders pulled back. "Not anything you could do? How about not screwing the whore in your own bed? You *wanted* to get caught."

"Someone explain right now," Vasilije demanded. "What'd you mean—"

"You're goddamn right, I wanted to get caught!" Dimitrije roared. "She needed to feel the same way I did when I found out she'd been fucking someone else."

As Dimitrije became angrier, Luka seemed to grow calmer. His expression was erased, and faded into the emotionless mask. His disguise for hiding emotion. "You mean David," he said, his tone flat, "your brother's bodyguard. I guess you were allowed to fuck whoever you wanted, but not her?"

Dimitrije's jaw fell open. "How—"

"You think I couldn't hear you two shouting at each other?" Luka's focus went to his younger brother. "She said she was leaving him for good. So Dad called Uncle Goran and told him she was going to the cops."

Vasilije may not have been as smart as his older brother, but he wasn't stupid, either. His head snapped toward his father. We watched hatred develop slowly, layer by layer.

"You . . . had her killed?"

Heartbreak was a visible reaction in Vasilije. His hands clenched into fists at his sides and his spine snapped straight, like enduring an enormous pain.

"She wasn't loyal." Dimitrije puffed up his chest, as if offended he had to explain himself. "After David told me what they'd done, I couldn't trust her anymore."

"Except David was lying," Luka said. "Did you ever consider she was screaming the truth at you?"

"You don't know what you're talking about."

The air in the room had gone frigid, and Luka's icy tone matched. "I know a lot more than you. David's confession was coerced. He'd done it on your brother's orders."

"What? I'm not going to listen to this bullshit." Dimitrije waved a dismissive hand, but it was clear Luka had planted the seeds of doubt in his father.

"Yeah, you are." The distinct sound of metal clicking drew all of our attention. Vasilije had drawn a gun, and held it trained on his father.

Luka looked unfazed. The room had gone so cold, I expected my breath to be visible. Was this part of his plan? He hadn't been able to pull the trigger on his father, but he suspected Vasilije would. Anarchy raced in the youngest Markovic's eyes.

"Goran never liked our mother," Luka said quietly. "He was convinced she'd turn on the family when she found out how Dad couldn't keep it in his pants, so he orchestrated the whole thing. After, he bragged about it to his sons." He cast a final look at his father and his voice was damning. "You had her killed for something she *didn't even do*. So, which one of you was disloyal?"

"Jesus," Vasilije whispered.

Color drained from his father's face. His hesitant gaze turned to his youngest son. "Vasilije—"

The gun went off, and the side of Dimitrije's head exploded in a bloody burst.

Chapter
TWENTY-EIGHT

DIMITRIJE'S BODY SLUMPED to the floor with a tremendous crash.

Luka nearly fell when I wilted against him. *Holy God.* Vasilije had just murdered his father in front of Luka and me. Would we be next? Luka must have had a similar thought because instantly he was moving, positioning himself between me and the threat of his brother.

"Fuck. He killed her. He took her away from us!" Vasilije's breath came and went in sharp bursts, and his voice shook. "Why, Luka? Why didn't you tell me?"

I couldn't see beyond Luka since I cowered behind his back, but I could tell his arms were out, raised in surrender. "Because I thought I could do it. I tried and tried, but . . . I didn't want you to have to. It was supposed to be my responsibility."

"Fuck," Vasilije repeated.

There was a long, heavy pause.

Rustling announced the gun had been put away, and Luka's arms lowered. I gripped onto the broad shoulders before me, wanting to pull him to the stairs. I wasn't sure I could stay in this basement another second, but I wouldn't leave him either. Instead, he lifted his arm over my head and dropped it around my shoulders, tucking me in beside him and bringing me into Vasilije's view.

Who pitched forward, placed his hands on his knees, and looked like he might be sick. He was struggling with what he'd just done. "You should have told me."

"I know," Luka said to him on a low voice.

"What the fuck am I gonna do?" He was worried about how Goran was going to react.

"I'll take care of it. Ivan got the jump on Dad and killed him, and you had to finish Ivan off." Luka's tone was strong and direct. "If what he said is true and the Russians are escalating, Goran's going to need all the help he can get. This is your time now. You're not finishing your degree. The role you've always wanted in this family is yours."

"What? You're just going to hand that over?"

"Yes. You know I don't want it."

Vasilije sighed. "And what do you want?"

"Out."

My hands squeezed tighter. It was what Luka and I both wanted.

"Protect us until Addison graduates, and then we're gone. Forever."

Vasilije appeared to consider the statement carefully, evaluating the downside to this offer. Was there one? I held my breath. He looked reluctant to give his *perfect* brother anything he wanted, but this was a win-win. Luka wouldn't challenge Vasilije for the position he was desperate for, and Luka and I could flee.

Luka's voice was soft and yet firm. "I don't want this life for Addison. She's already paid too much, and I can't live without her."

My heart thudded along, twisting at hearing him say it out loud. Did he know I felt the same?

"You're *my* brother." Vasilije's statement was tinged with disappointment.

"And I'll always be."

Vasilije's gaze scanned over the two bodies, staring at them with finality. As if the decision he'd make right now about our future could never be undone. I was going to suffocate from the tension. The waiting was agony.

"After she graduates," Vasilije agreed.

A weight lifted from my chest, just enough so I could find new air. It contained a trace of hope and freedom.

"But," Vasilije added, "I'll need your help until then." He gestured toward the floor. "Starting with them."

π

Goran Markovic was eating a late breakfast when we appeared unannounced at his house. He listened with cold indifference as Luka recounted the story of the basement. It was perfectly crafted fiction we'd gone over with Vasilije a half dozen times before arriving here.

I said nothing during it, but my shell-shocked look, which wasn't an act, helped sell Luka's performance.

You'd think Goran would be upset about his brother's death, but no. It wasn't family that was the most important to the Markovics—it was the *family business.*

"I'm going to need you," Goran said to Luka. "Things are changing."

"It's all-out war with the Russians," Luka said. "I don't want any part of it."

Goran scowled. "Put the family above your selfish wants."

"You're not going to want me, either. I hesitated, Vasilije didn't. I don't have the taste for it." Luka took a deep breath. "He's

318

young, but he wants this."

His uncle pushed his plate away and sat back, giving Luka a critical look. "And what about you?"

Luka's hand curled around mine. "This war? They killed my father. They already used Addison once, I'm not going to let that happen again." My heartrate skyrocketed as he closed in on asking for what we were desperate for. "I'll go with her when she goes to school. Get her far away from here."

"Wait just a minute—"

"I'll still be able to handle your finances. I can do that from anywhere."

Goran's expression was callous and his voice rose with each word. "You're going to run like a fucking coward? You're choosing this girl over your own family?"

There wasn't a shred of hesitation. "Yes."

Real emotion finally appeared on his uncle's face. He looked confused, and angry, and perhaps even a little hurt. How would he react to this?

There was a gun hidden in Luka's jacket. Goran's security guard hadn't searched him, and even if he had, it was doubtful he'd have taken it. Luka was family. He was supposed to be loyal, and the gun would be viewed as protection. But if Goran wouldn't let us go, would Luka have to use it? And *could* he?

I prayed we wouldn't have to find out.

"I guess that's the kind of man you are." A sneer flitted across Goran's face. "Quits when things get tough. You're nothing like your father."

Luka tightened his grip on my hand. Was it an attempt to stay quiet, or was he thrilled with Goran's comment he wasn't like

Dimitrije?

"Fine," Goran said, when Luka remained quiet. "Get the hell out of my sight."

I'd never been happier to follow a Markovic order.

π

It was hot for May and I worried I was going to sweat before the ceremony started. The black cap and gown for graduation were thick and heavy, and layered on top of the white eyelet dress Luka had picked out for me. Since I was graduating with a science degree, the hood draped over my neck was gold, casting a sallow glow onto my face.

I ran my fingers down the length of my honor cords. Two cords, instead of the three I'd wanted. The perfect *summa cum laude* had fallen just out of my reach.

When I finished getting ready, I descended the stairs, my gown swishing, and went to the office where I knew Luka was waiting.

I'd spent most of my life working toward this moment, expecting my family to be ready to celebrate with me. Instead, it'd be with this man who had changed my life both for the better and the worse. But I loved him, and he loved me, and I had to believe that was enough.

His head lifted when I appeared in the doorway and his shoulders rose as if he'd taken a deep breath. Luka didn't say anything, but he didn't need to. A smile spread slowly across his lips, widening until it enveloped his entire expression. It sucked the air from my lungs. He was devastating when he smiled, and it'd been so infrequent during the tense six weeks since we'd left

Goran's house.

The smile subsided as he stood from the desk. "I know what you're doing." His gaze fell to my fingers still tinkering with the cords. "Stop it. All the shit you went through this year—" He stiffened. "Graduating *magna cum laude* is impressive for anyone. I didn't graduate *magna cum laude*."

The way he'd begrudgingly admitted it, made me want to smile, but it was hard. I missed my family.

"Don't worry," Luka added. "I have a third string to hang around your neck."

I froze. "What?"

He picked up his suit jacket from the back of the chair and slipped a hand inside the interior pocket. And then there was a long, blue velvet box in his hand. My throat closed up as he extended it to me.

I took it and opened the necklace box with a soft click. Dangling from the delicate silver chain were three shining circles, each with a number engraved inside. It took me a moment to recognize the meaning. Not pi, but dates.

My family's birth dates.

"Congratulations," Luka said, his voice hushed. "They were already, but I'm sure they would have been very proud of you today."

I clasped a shaky hand over my mouth, overcome and unsure what to say. The necklace was elegant and beautiful, and tears sprang into my eyes. He took the box from me, freed the necklace, and motioned he'd put it on me if I wanted him to.

I nodded, making my tassel sway, still unable to speak.

He did the clasp and the necklace clinked quietly as it settled on my neck. I wasn't overly emotional, but this . . . it got to me.

Wearing these simple numbers around my neck made my family a part of the day.

"Thank you," I said, breaking a little inside.

Concern streaked across his face. "Don't cry." He'd probably meant for it to sound like an order, but his voice faltered. "I asked Vasilije to take pictures."

I drew in a cleansing breath, forcing the tears to drain back as his hands slipped behind my head, tilting me up to meet his gaze.

"Tomorrow," he said on a low voice, his lips a breath away from mine, "we start new."

Because we were leaving Chicago first thing in the morning and making the eleven-hour drive to Maryland. His mouth claimed mine, filling me with heat and love.

When the kiss ended, he pulled back. "Repeat it," he whispered.

I gave a soft smile. "Tomorrow we start new."

Luka looked pleased as he led me out into the living room where morning sunlight streamed through the windows, chasing away all the shadows.

FOUR MONTHS LATER

"Addison."

I lifted my head, snapping back into focus. "I'm awake."

Morning light filtered through the blinds of our bedroom. Luka's eyebrow climbed and he glared at me from between my legs. "I enjoy what I'm doing, but it's better when you're not asleep." His lips grazed me, teasing my clit, and drew a sigh from me. Damn, what he could do with his mouth.

I smiled, bashful. "I'm sorry. Please, continue."

He blinked, and annoyance flared. It made me grin widely. Luka wasn't a fan of me telling him what to do, especially when it came to the bedroom, but sometimes it was fun to get a rise out of him. In the blink of an eye, I was flipped over onto my stomach on the bed, and his hand crashed down against my ass. The warm sting washed over me, and I bit my lip to hold back the moan.

"Awake now?" he growled. "Or do you need more?"

My voice choked with excitement. "More."

We didn't get as much time to play once I'd started school. I was spending sixty hours a week studying, and he'd found a job at an accounting firm in Baltimore that was just as demanding, plus he had his obligations to Goran. But at least our cozy two-bedroom apartment was walking distance from the campus, and we had our weekends together.

His second spanking was right at the edge of what I could

handle, and my skin burned and ached in the aftermath. This time the moan slipped from my lips and I lifted up on my knees and elbows, readying for more. For whatever he'd give me.

"So fucking perfect," he whispered, shifting on the bed to kneel beside me. His praise was practically purred, and hearing him happy turned me on more than anything else.

He rained down the blows against me, leaving my skin inflamed, and then he moved behind and pressed himself deep inside. I arched my back, stretching into his hand that coursed up my spine, loving the feeling when he possessed me.

We'd left Chicago and the Markovics behind. Luka had acclimated to his life without a family better than I had, but held onto his hard edge, and I was grateful. It was what had forced me to fall in love with him, and I was glad the morning in the basement hadn't stolen him from me.

Vasilije had only called twice since we'd moved. Once to check in, and once to explain that an uneasy truce had been struck with the Russians. It was fragile, and Vasilije wasn't sure how long it would last, but it allowed Luka to breathe easier. He didn't want that dangerous life for his brother, but he wasn't going to stand in the way, either.

I began to count the moments between us in his rare but beautiful smiles. I'd gotten one when I'd asked him to pull over during our drive to Maryland, wanting my hands and mouth on him. And another the morning of my first day of classes at Johns Hopkins. We'd stood in the bathroom, preparing for the day at our own sinks, and his gaze had found mine in the mirror.

It was all so normal, and exactly the life he wanted. The life *we* wanted. We'd had to go through hell to get there, but we'd done it.

Together.

I came in a spectacular rush, collapsing forward onto the mattress, and braced myself as Luka began to move for himself. His body slid over and into mine, reaffirming our connection with each thrust until he lost himself as well.

His hot chest pressed against my back, and he breathed heavily in my ear. I turned my head to the side so I could look at him.

"Sometimes I love you so much," he whispered, "it hurts."

"It's the same for me." I kissed him gently. "And I wouldn't have it any other way."

A smile broke on his face, and it was absolutely stunning.

THE END

THANK YOU

As always, to my amazing husband. I'm so glad you still love me even though you didn't love this book. There just wasn't enough hot threesome action here, I get it. (Book 5, I promise!) Thank you for continuing to encourage me to follow my dreams, and for making sure the kids are wearing matching shoes.

To my wonderful editor, Lori Whitwam. I'm going to inflict my books on you for as long as you'll let me!

To my FABULOUS beta readers: Joscelyn Freeman Fussell, Andrea Lefkowitz, Rebecca Nebel, Danielle Salinger, Jennifer Santa Ana, and Nikki Terrill. Thank you for enduring the brutal scene that has been removed, for your extremely helpful notes, and for our group conversations on FB that are always hilarious.

To my sexy publicist Heather Roberts. Thank you for everything you do!

And most importantly, to my incredible readers. Thank you so much for your support! It means the world to me.

THREE *simple* RULES

BOOK ONE

I would do anything for my dream job. Now I have to.

In order to save my skin at the office, I'm forced to sell it at an exclusive and illegal blindfold club. He paid thousands of dollars for one night to own me, but when my blindfold comes off, I want more. More nights, more rules, and more from this unavailable and uncompromising man.

Rule number one, no questions. Rule number two, no lies. But, rule number three? That's the hardest one to obey.

THREE *hard* LESSONS

BOOK TWO

I am the woman men pay thousands of dollars to sleep with. I do what I love and what I'm so very good at.

Then he walks in and drops $30,000. He wants to talk. And kiss. And take me home.

In a single night, this man turns everything upside-down and has me breaking every rule I've lived by to keep men at a distance. I'm about to learn some lessons the hard way.

Don't tease him. Don't give him boundaries. And don't think you get a choice in who you love.

THREE *little* MISTAKES

BOOK THREE

I sell sex, sin, and pleasure, but it isn't just my business, it's my entire life. I get off on the power of controlling it all.

She's the one woman I can't have.

She threatens everything, and yet I can't stay away. There's a beautiful, sexual creature inside this timid girl that's desperate to claw its way out. I'm going to set it free, even if it brings my empire tumbling down.

I have to believe she'll be worth all the little mistakes I've made.

THREE *dirty* SECRETS

BOOK FOUR

No man can own me. I negotiate sex for money at an illicit blindfold club, but my body is not for sale. I don't submit and I don't surrender.

Until I meet him. This beautiful artist's tattoo now covers the scar of the worst mistake of my life.

Being with him could expose everything I've been hiding, and although there's so much at stake, I can't stop myself. The battle for control between us is too hot, too powerful to resist.

With all my dirty secrets, what's going to happen when he forces me to come clean?

IF YOU ENJOYED THE BOOK

Thank you so much for taking the time to read my first attempt at dark romance. If you enjoyed it, would you be so kind as to let other readers know via an Amazon review or on Goodreads? Just a few words can help an author tremendously, and are *always* appreciated!

WANT TO TALK WITH OTHER FANS OF NIKKI'S BOOKS?

Join the private Facebook group! This isn't a street team and you won't be asked to do anything. The group is a fun spot to hangout, discuss books (Nikki's or other hot reads), and share pics of man candy. It's called Nikki's Naughty Nymphs.

WHAT'S NEXT?

I am working on book five in the Blindfold Club series (Kyle's book) and hope to publish it in the fall of 2016. Vasilije may get his own book in the future, but at this time I'm not ready to commit to it.

ABOUT NIKKI

Nikki Sloane fell into graphic design after her careers as a waitress, a screenwriter, and a ballroom dance instructor fell through. For eight years she worked for a design firm in that extremely tall, black, and tiered building in Chicago that went through an unfortunate name change during her time there. She is a Romance Writers of America RITA© Finalist, married with two sons, writes both romantic suspense and dirty books, and couldn't be any happier.

Find her on the web: www.NikkiSloane.com

Contact her on Twitter: @AuthorNSloane

Send her an email: authornikkisloane@gmail.com

CPSIA information can be obtained
at www.ICGtesting.com
Printed in the USA
BVHW031144220222
629783BV00003B/25

9 780692 734742